W9-COW-302

CABIN FEVER

Also by Elizabeth Jolley

Cabin Fever

Elizabeth Jolley

Harper Perennial
A Division of HarperCollins*Publishers*

A portion of this novel appeared in *The New Yorker* ("Hedges," 1990).

A hardcover edition of this book was published in 1990 in Australia by Viking Australia. It is here reprinted by arrangement with Viking Australia.

CABIN FEVER. Copyright © 1990 by Elizabeth Jolley. All rights reserved. Printed in the United States of America. No part of this book may be used or reproduced in any manner whatsoever without written permission except in the case of brief quotations embodied in critical articles and reviews. For information address HarperCollins Publishers, 10 East 53rd Street, New York, NY 10022.

First HarperPerennial edition published 1991.

LIBRARY OF CONGRESS CATALOG CARD NUMBER 90-55966

ISBN 0-06-092151-X

91 92 93 94 95 HC 10 9 8 7 6 5 4 3 2 1

For Leonard Jolley

Nowhere either with more
quiet or more freedom from trouble
does a man retire than into his
own soul.

William Penn

Acknowledgments

I would like to express my thanks to the Curtin University of Technology for the continuing privilege of being with students and colleagues in the School of Communication and Cultural Studies and for the provision of a room in which to write. I would like, in particular, to thank Don Watts (now of Bond University Queensland), Peter Reeves, Brian Dibble and Don Grant. In addition, I would like to thank John Maloney, Don Yeats and Ross Bennett.

A special thanks is offered to Nancy McKenzie who, for a great many years, has typed my manuscripts. She is endlessly patient.

Shirt Sleeves

I am still here on the twenty-fourth floor and when I sit in front of my mirror I can see, in the mirror, someone on the twenty-fourth floor across the street. He is sitting upright at a table and is in his shirt sleeves. I have no idea who he is.

'I should never have given you the book about Elisabeth Ney.'
   'Whyever...She was a sculptor and an artist...She...'
   'She had a baby in that book without being married.'
   'Oh! Really!'
   'It must have given you ideas...'
   'Don't, do not be so utterly stupid. How can you be so stupid!'
   'Keep your voice down. You don't want the others to hear you speaking to your mother like that.'

CABIN FEVER

Once when I am sitting with Magda in her white and gold upstairs sitting room I tell her that I hope I won't get wrinkles and frowns all over my face.

'But Darling Child!' Magda exclaims then, she is crouching in the hearth turning over little heaps of underclothes to air them (she always says what a cold person she is). 'But Darling Child!' she says, 'that's where character and experience are, in the lines and the frowns and the wrinkles. Your sweet round face is deliciously soft and smooth at present, you must try to preserve it for ever. But even *you* will have experience one day and you must expect it to alter your appearance. Just look at Daddy, seven deep wrinkles on his forehead and two of the deepest frowns, ulcer frowns we call them, each side of the bridge of his nose. Those are for his nine actresses, Darling. Mummy has never caused him a wrinkle or a frown, d'you see? Look at him next time you are in theatre. You mop him, don't you Darling, with the iced water while he's operating. Well, you count his frowns for yourself, you can't say he's not handsome. He simply, quite simply, is experienced.'

How can I look at Lemmington Frazier as closely as that when he's all gowned up and I'm trying to dab at that angry red space between his cap and his mask with the iced swabs during the long and precise surgery. It's all I can do to try to stop water drops from falling on to his special spectacles and to take extra care not to let unsterile water drip down into the patient's wound.

It seems to me then that Magda is offering me experience. Several times she seems to be offering. And, because I love Dr Metcalf and want to be near him all the time I take what Magda seems to give.

I love Magda too. And then, in a rush of feeling, I tell Magda, 'I can't live without you, Magda.'

'Darling Child!' Magda hugs me and kisses me, and she seems to purr when she talks. 'You don't have to live without me.' Her perfume envelops me. It seems to me then that her perfume is richly purple. But of course I know that perfume does not have a strong colour, I mean it's never purple.

MAGDA'S VISIT

I know now what Magda means that day when she comes unexpectedly to visit me at the Hilda Street Nursing Home. Her visit at the end of a long afternoon, on the day Helena is born, is unexpected and I have to try to take off Dr Metcalf's watch, remove it from my wrist, under the bedclothes.

But I think she has already seen the watch and knows at once that it is his. She does not mention the watch at all. And she gives no indication that she has minded seeing it.

When Sister Peters says at the door that there is a Mrs Metcalf to see me I am not able to think for a minute who this can be. I am not expecting anyone to come.

I know now, when I think of what Magda says then, above love in its purest and freshest, its most innocent and powerful form, I know now what she means then. The idea she says then, is of love existing between two people so that the only thing that matters is that they can be near each other. She tells me that the love I had was not dragged down, mutilated is the word she uses. Your love, she says, was not mutilated by anything, by money, ambition, property – 'you know, Darling, divisions of property, mortgages on land and on houses, and no relatives intervening. It was,' she says, 'or rather, it is a love of the free-est sort and is a blessing.' While she is saying this her eyes and my eyes are full of tears.

'Furthermore,' Magda says, a few minutes later, 'your love is completely untroubled by not knowing too much about the person you love and that is something you cannot expect to have for long.'

Magda's visit, of course, makes me think about Gertrude. When I think of Gertrude now and how she, in her own honest way of thinking, tried earlier to draw me away from the fascination and the excitement of my new, in her words, wild and extravagant, friends. I also remember (I can never forget) how she, as she put it, tried then to go along with me, to humour me as if allowing me a full taste of the Metcalfs as if to tire me with them – when I am at her Place helping her with the fowls and then continuing this, when I am back at the hospital, in her letters;

I am afraid you will think I am interfering with your affairs. Can I explain that I want to avoid for you what I consider to be the Pit Fall...It is strange how we each suffer or have to grope a way in this life we might have had so easily...

And then when for some long time taken up with Dr Metcalf or Magda, or both of them, I do not go out to Gertrude's Place either on my bicycle or by bus I wait in the queue in the hall of the Nurses' Home for letters half hoping for and half afraid of having a letter from her. I have been writing to her and so must expect replies;

I should have written earlier in the week but expected you as your mother said you would be coming and would fetch the eggs...I am very sorry you had the cold. I hope it's better. I am interested and a little amused where in your letter you write you wouldn't mind having a baby. Of course it's best to take out a license to have a baby really as unless anybody is really well to do and has a lot of money its very difficult on ones own to pay for everything and have no one to rely on to help along. Also an Unlicensed Baby is against Public Opinion still the most powerful deterrent there is. But I don't see that its wicked except as things are it has a stigma on its name...

When at last I do go, Gertrude is busy with the incubator in the bedroom which is never used as a bedroom. There is a billiard table in there and a harmonium where she plays hymns sometimes.

'Little chicks,' she says, 'hundreds of 'em all falling around over each other and under each other like lots of hands playing duets on the piano. You can have 'em all if you like to stay, to come in on the poultry with me. I'll make a nice room. I'll make this room nice for you.' She pauses. 'We can paste pictures, bright fashion pictures,' she says, 'out of a magazine on the walls. Put up a border of wall paper too like we've done in the kitchen. That's nice. And you could sleep late, late as you like, till dinner time if you wanted. Or get up with the sun and run free in the field, up to the spinney, down the hill, wherever you want...'

But I am invited again, I tell her then, to a party. Dr Metcalf and his wife Magda are having a party and they want me to come so I shall not be staying.

'I'll be going back to the hospital in the afternoon,' I explain, 'and on to their house in the evening.'

Later Gertrude tells me, after some weeks when I go again to her Place, that perhaps it would be a good idea if these Metcalfs could be persuaded to withdraw themselves from my life. Could my father visit them she wants to know, could he intervene on my behalf explaining that he does not quite understand the matter but that he wants perfect happiness for his daughter. Gertrude says too that she can quite understand how my mother might be about to make things worse by trying to dish up different menfolk I ought to be able to attract. She says if my father is not able to go to visit these Metcalfs she is willing to go. She can put her bicycle on the train, she says, and she will take them some eggs and a couple of dressed fowls in a bag and persuade them not to invite me any more. What times are their parties she wants to know. She will go to the next one instead of me. She is not afraid to go inside their grand house...

I am afraid to even think of Gertrude in her black laced-up boots, her felt hat and her heavy coat over the overall she never takes off, stepping into the splendour and lavishness of one of Magda's parties. I want to stop her from having this idea, to protect her from the fun they would make from her appearance, the ridicule which, though meant in a hilarious joking way, would hurt her and harm her. Their laughter, their exchanged looks and raised eyebrows and their small but extravagant gestures would completely submerge anything she would try to say. They would never see that they should not invite me unless they did not want to. They would not understand her on purpose. The way Gertrude is thinking is not their way.

The last time I see Gertrude to speak to I am quite unable to tell her how things are with me. After all the times of going to her Place, of looking forward to being where the soft green grass is right up to her door, of arriving to find her sitting at this door with her sardine tin of oil and the matches for singeing the boiling fowls after plucking, and the newspaper beside her with the coarse salt she uses to give her capable hand a better grip on the slippery entrails – after all this time I am not able to say to Gertrude that I wanted Dr Metcalf more than anyone else and he wanted me. How can I tell her that I know already how things are with me and that I shall have no one to rely on, no one to help along...

★

CABIN FEVER

Playful spinsters and exuberant lesbians give birth and special seminars are held to discuss the phenomenon of these people wanting to keep their babies. Special committees are set up for discussions about the new infections which accompany new ways of living which are called alternative life styles. Years are earmarked for specific causes, the year of the child, the year of the aged, the year of the disabled – the year of the disabled produced some incredibly heavy swing doors...

How's business? people ask me. What do you mean? I ask. How many croaked? Any deaths? they want to know. How many, for example, died today?

No, I explain, they don't come for death, they come for living. They come for advice for living. The clinic is simply a place for...

How quaint! Do they pay? They want to know who pays and how much.

Everyone pays.

Everyone? Oh, you mean the government and the taxpayer. Specially the taxpayer, crippling, let me tell you my last income tax...

No I wasn't thinking along those lines, I tell them. What *is* your work? people ask me. What is it exactly that you do? they ask. They ask me and I have no clear way to answering. I see people, I explain. People come to see me. Consulting it is called. Appointments are made for consultation. What about? they ask. What do people consult you about? they ask.

I tell them that people want to ask about things which worry them. Like what? they ask. What sort of things and do they have to take their clothes off? they want to know.

Everything. People are worried about everything. All kinds of things worry people. I think I am safe in saying everything. And no, they do not have to take off their clothes, as a rule.

I am a shabby person. I understand, if I look back, that I have treated kind people with an unforgivable shabbiness. For my work a ruthless self-examination is needed for, without understanding something of myself, how can I understand anyone else.

Every day I am seeing people living from day to day, from one precarious day to the next, from one despairing week to the next, without any vision of any kind of future. It does not take me long to understand this because during my own small celebrations of passing moments I have seen the world and my own life, at a particular time in that life, from one narrowed day to the next, from cramped week to cramped week, at ground and hedge-root level, unable to see anything beyond the immediate.

Memories are not always in sequence, not in chronological sequence. Sometimes an incident is revived in the memory. Sometimes incidents and places and people occupying hours, days, weeks and years are experienced in less than a quarter of a second in this miraculous possession, the memory. The revival is not in any particular order and one recalled picture, attaching itself to another, is not recognizably connected to that other in spite of it being brought to the surface in the wake of the first recollection.

It is during an evening passing unnoticed into nightfall that I am, as if late at night, feeling my way once more up and down and along the bookshelves in my mother's house searching for an unrecognizable name or initial on a discoloured fly leaf. And then all at once I am remembering Dr Metcalf, naked and handsome and shameless, leaning back in the cushions of a basket chair, facing the small westward window, high up, his whole body bronzed in the colours of the setting sun. Why should I think now, all these years later on, of his arms stretched out towards me? And why, after all this time, recall his smile contained in his whole body, even in the palms of his hands?

It seems now as if the urchin style, the razor cut, has some remembered significance as does the slow walking in the long wet withered grass of the autumn. It is as if both can be thought capable of bringing about essential change.

Remembered people appear and disappear disconcertingly in the tiniest nutshells of memory. Order is reversed. The longing for some particular way of living or for some particular person or place or possession can come back with a sharpness unparalleled by anything happening and experienced during the present time. Furthermore, understanding the loneliness and despair of knowing it is not possible to bring back a wished for person, and knowing that one person can never replace another, is understanding that this is what bereavement is. Bereavement has become a clichéd word but to feel bereaved and to know it when there is no one to turn to is to experience the kind of despair for which the only remedy is to lie on the warm earth *dissolving the long hours in tears.*

To be beside a little lake with wind-chopped waves in a deserted suburban park and to experience a bottomless depth of loneliness can sometimes lead to an unexpected order in the mind which, at the time, seems to have nothing in it but grief and disorder. And this too can contribute to essential change through the making of a deliberate decision.

SUGAR

Last year on New Year's Day I spilled the sugar, twice. Not a great deal, but even a little sugar spilled seems unlucky, especially if spilled twice on one day. This year on New Year's Day I am here in this ugly overheated hotel, a few days earlier than I need to be for the conference. I have come earlier because I actually thought I would enjoy the freedom of wandering, as if with leisure, through art galleries, exhibitions and museums. I thought that I might go to a concert, a play, the opera. The wish to see colours as I had once seen them with their magic names – cobalt blue, ultramarine, vermillion and yellow-ochre in my paintbox at school, and to see cloth painted in such a way that one might feel it, between the fingers, as cloth and not paint on board or canvas, can only be achieved by searching slowly through a gallery and not by brushing past masterpieces like an impatient housewife who has half an hour to spare, or as a bored delegate between papers at a conference.

SQUIRRELS

I thought too I would like to see Central Park again. The little grey squirrels there, I remember, reminded me once of rats. They do not sleep, hibernate, during the winter as squirrels in other places do. I suppose here they have no tree pantries full of stored nuts. It is below zero in Central Park. The air is still and cold and the bare branches of the winter trees are in brittle patterns against the curiously light sky. The park is frozen into a silence which the noise of New York cannot fill. In spite of my hopes for leisure I have not been out to any of the cultural entertainment as intended.

PRUNES

At about this time the prune plums back home will be intensely blue hanging secretly in the deepest green foliage; an enticing and surprising mixture of blue and green. The bloom on these small vividly coloured plums gives the impression of a delicate mist hovering about the trees.

MAGDA

Perhaps I will try and remember everything I can about Magda. I thought at one time that I could not live without Magda and yet, at the same time, she was dreadfully in my way.

Magda says I saved her life. It is like this. She is brought into the Casualty Dept one night during an air raid. Her nightie has slipped off her shoulders, her hair is all over the place and she is crying. She says she is dying, suffocating. It is asthma, an attack of asthma. While I am waiting for the RMO to come and, because I am the only nurse on duty, I feel I must help her. Not knowing what I should do I bring in an oxygen cylinder. As soon as Magda sees the big cylinder on its little wheels, its handsome dial and the mask attached she is better and she starts at once to say I have saved her life and I must, simply must come to her house on my next day off. I feel awkward and embarrassed when the RMO finally comes. I try to hitch the ribbons of Magda's nightie back over her shoulders...

'Since when, Nurse,' the Night Superintendent says to me later, 'since when has an empty oxygen cylinder been the treatment for asthma?' Just then even though the All Clear has hardly finished sounding there is another air-raid warning and I have to go at once to check the black-out curtains on the stairs.

Magda as it turns out is the Chief Surgeon's daughter. His only daughter. His name is Mr Lemmington Frazier. At the hospital they say she is spoiled, very wealthy and pretending to be studying medicine. Her mother, Mrs Lemmington Frazier, takes a Red Cross trolley round the soldiers' wards. The trolley is piled up with books and chocolate and home-made face flannels and a sort of green jam. She gives to both the officers and the men. Sometimes the jam is red.

Magda is married to Dr Jonathon Metcalf. She calls him Jonty.

Everyone says it is a fortunate marriage for him because of Lemmington Frazier's very high reputation and position in the hospital. I discover quite quickly what his reputation really is among the other nurses.

Spilling sugar in this hotel room reminds me that on New Year's day, last year, I spilled the sugar twice. The sugar on the blue napkins, a fine scattering like snow on a miniature mountain, recalls the dark-blue sugar bags in which I kept the sugar secretly hoarded immediately after the war when sugar was scarce and rationed still.

'The sugar,' I said then, 'a whole fortnight's sugar.' And I added it straight away to my growing sugar weight. But that is a long time ago and before that time there is a time when small jars of sugar, jam and butter are carried everywhere in little coloured string bags.

The nurses all have string bags for their rations. It is Trent who replies to the question, when we are all sprawled, Trent, Ferguson, Lois and me across Trent's bed; what is the most important thing in the world and Trent says sex but not with any of you lot. Of course not I say. And we all get up then and put our aprons and caps straight.

Every year, faithfully over the years, at the beginning of October a letter comes from Betsy who was at school. This Betsy left school early and so was there only for two years of secondary school. She was not a boarder but came, red nosed across the fields, from a farm.

The letter is always the same, about her being in time for the Christmas mail and the number of cards and letters she received the previous year and how she has to answer them. She writes on several small sheets of note paper, schoolgirl's note paper still, closely written on both sides of the page in a hand which time and experience have not changed. It is clear that she still lives, but alone now, in the farmhouse. And it is clear that she loves her own handwriting. Her letters are descriptions of the repairs to the farmhouse, half the dining room replastered, new gutters on the south side, a new carpet in the sitting room because of the rising damp – in spite of fires all the year round. Six windows painted, two front doors, a garden door and the gate painted. And outside the dahlias are lifted, the onion bed prepared, the vegetable garden tidied and all the borders and flower beds still to do...

It is a warm Sunday in March when we are invited to Drinkwaters farm to tea. Helen Ferguson, Bulge and me. In our Sunday dresses and overcoats we set off to walk to the farm which is on the edge of the next village. Helen Ferguson thinks if we walk fast enough we could leave Bulge behind and she, not knowing the way, would be lost and we would go to tea without her. We can say Muriel couldn't come Helen Ferguson says as we walk as fast as we can, the mud clinging to our shoes, taking a forbidden field path. Helen Ferguson calls Bulge Muriel because it is her real name. I, privately, call her Bulge because she bulges. In my secret game of comparisons Bulge is far worse than I am in every respect, her hair, her stockings, her spectacles and her shape.

Bulge, who says at the stile, that we should really keep to the road, persists in following us. Her face is red and she has stepped too deep in the mud. It is all up her stocking to the knee. 'Cow pats and all,' Helen Ferguson can't stop laughing. We can hear her calling to us to wait for her. She's crying. Helen Ferguson laughs till she nearly bursts. 'I'll burst,' she says.

We are always hungry at school and at a small shop, in the village, Helen Ferguson tries to exchange some stamps for jelly crystals. The shop woman is annoyed saying don't we know it's Sunday and she is closed and, even if open, she wouldn't have jelly crystals for us.

Bulge arrives at the farm all muddy and crying just when we are about to sit down to a table heaped with home-made bread and scones and butter, two kinds of home-made jam and a chocolate cake, Helen Ferguson having told Betsy Drinkwater's mother that we would have to have tea straight away as we have to get back to school before dark. Mrs Drinkwater helps Bulge to clean her shoes and she comes to the table and eats her tea without looking across at us.

Betsy Drinkwater, in her soft country accent, one which we mock every day at school, asks Helen to take a photograph. Betsy says she had this box camera for Christmas and has never had an opportunity to use it...

I don't, as a rule, ever look at this photograph now but whenever I do a curious sense of shame comes over me. We are standing, for the picture, in the trellised archway at the front door of the farmhouse. Betsy in the middle with Helen Ferguson on one side and me on the other, both of us replete. We are draped, hanging by the arms, round Betsy's thick shoulders. Our dark serge Sunday dresses, with their white Quaker collars, are too tight and, because of our positions of exaggerated affection, the hems in front are lifted up unevenly. We look as if we are very fond of her. Bulge is not in the photograph because Helen Ferguson told her to take the picture.

It is my pretended affection which makes me ashamed now and which makes me shrink from receiving the Christmas letter. Perhaps it is the remembered boarding-school cruelty inflicted on the innocent victim. It is too the remembered tea table, the empty plates with jam-smeared knives and the tea cups spilled into their saucers which we left that day for Mrs Drinkwater and Betsy to come back to when they were done with the milking and when the hens had been shut up for the night.

On the Monday, in English class, Bulge writes a description of the Sunday walk to Drinkwaters farm. She gets top marks and her piece is chosen to be read out to the class. As I listen I begin to understand that, while I was hurrying to get away from Bulge, to lose her in the mud and to get to the farm without her, I never saw the long-legged lambs running across the grass to their mothers. I never noticed the clear water from the swollen stream spreading and sparkling over the grassy banks. I did not see, either, that the fresh green leaves on the hawthorn, the catkins and the pussy willows were beginning to show, and I must have gone round the curve of the hill, down over the wall of loose stones and past the sheep fold without seeing any of it, and without seeing a newborn lamb struggling to its feet by itself. In her piece Bulge does not say that she ran alone, crying, as she tried to keep up when we hurried on without her. She does not write that we laughed when she fell in the mud. Instead she fills the classroom with the coming spring, the warm March sunshine, the Sunday which was the birth day of the lamb.

Helen Ferguson's essay gets good marks too. Not for the actual writing which, we are told, is full of cliché and spelling mistakes, but for the nobility of the sentiments. Helen Ferguson has written a description of how she helped Mrs Drinkwater clear the table, wash up and dry all the plates and cups and saucers after the wonderful tea we had enjoyed, and how it had given her pleasure to show her gratitude for the kind invitation by helping with this task.

I have always in my secret game of comparisons tried to sit in class like Helen Ferguson sits, one foot a little in front of the other and, with a thoughtful expression, sucking the rounded end of my new pen. In spite of despising Bulge, in spite of how she looks, I begin to try to emulate her.

The first night in this room I am disturbed, soon after midnight, by the sound of running water, overhead and down inside the wall cavity close to where I am lying.

It sounds, at first, as if a bath might be overflowing. There is a lot of water, a flood. If the flowing water forces a hole in my wall the room will soon be full of water. The windows do not open so there is no way out for the water. The door, I understand at once, opens inwards. It would not open against the pressure of the water as it deepens in my room. Water is a very powerful element.

It is very hot in the room, incredibly hot. It occurs to me that because of the heat the water might be boiling. An even more unpleasant thought is that, instead of water, it might be steam.

I think about other people. Are there any other people near? And can they hear this water running? And are they disturbed too? I try to think of the design of the hotel, but, as with the streets seen from high up, I have no sense of direction from here. I have no idea, for example, where this room is in relation to the rest of the building except that it is at the end of a long passage on the twenty-fourth floor. If this is the top floor then there can be no bath above to overflow. I had the feeling earlier that there are rooms on either side of this one but, on reflection, I remember that both the doors out there are service doors of some sort being rough wooden doors without numbers and without key holes. An uncomfortable memory.

The ritual for falling asleep is different for every individual but the position for not falling asleep is the same. To lie with the arms folded behind the head is an indication and a warning. Some time elapses before the realization that this is the final retreat, that sleep is not possible. Sleep has retreated.

On this first night I remember reading somewhere that in order to be able to sleep in a strange room it is necessary to clear the mind; 'to empty yourself for sleep'.

The sound of the running water is persistent, as if it will never stop. I feel the wall above my bed. The wall is warm.

The indecision, one of my faults, is the worst attack I have ever experienced. The sought after isolation in a hotel room is frightening, especially the apparent isolation high up above the strange city with nothing on either side and the water pouring across the ceiling and down inside the hollows of the walls. I am undecided about dialling 9 for the front desk.

THE FRONT DESK

It is an old building a gentle voice soothes and no it is not an overflow from a locked-up bathroom but is simply the heating system which, regrettably, is old fashioned and noisy.

The sound of the water running stops almost at once.

BLACK CLOTHES

While I am travelling my customary good humour disappears. I am unable to bear, after quite a short time, the small jolts of travelling. Small things like having my seat changed in an aircraft, as if it really matters. All the seats are going towards the same destination I kept reminding myself yesterday.

I dislike the crowds. I waste energy wondering which sort of crowd is worse, the crowd travelling or the crowd still at the airport. I try to tell myself that these people in the crowd are really the people for whom I am working. The object of my journey is to further my studies and research in the finding of beneficial methods and treatments for the ailments which attack, at some time or other, these people. Mostly the people in a crowd are not thinking of medical attention or of the possibilities of surgery at some time in their lives. For the most part, though most of them will require some sort of treatment at some time or other, they seem unconcerned.

Perhaps my black clothes are partly the cause of uneasiness. The fellow travellers are all in holiday clothes and are laden with brightly coloured plastic bags stuffed with shopping, French perfume in grubby hand-worn packaging, wine glasses with gold edges and stems, boxes of chocolate-covered nuts and enormous bottles of whisky.

My black brief case and black clothes are out of place in the busy airport thronged as it is with families on their way to and from relatives at this time of the year. I have forgotten that people do, in fact, go to places for a holiday. Places which, for me, are simply unavoidable stops during a long journey. Suddenly my life seems confined and narrow in the presence of the pleasure seekers.

Perhaps one of the unexpected aspects of travelling is not wanting to be in the places where I am expected to be. And, on arrival, being impatient to go on to the next place only to discover a repetition of that same impatience.

Parts of the plane are sprayed with anti-freeze. We arrive in a light falling of snow and recollections of ice on pavements and snow freezing on top of ice packing on roads and footpaths. The cold is intense.

Being unable to leave my hotel room is my own wish to remain in the room. I will rest one more day and then make my way into the conference rooms, listen to the papers and deliver my own. The conference is my reason for travelling, after all. How can I work for people, I ask myself, if I seem, like now, to dislike them?

Sometimes life seems to be all worry and suffering and at other times it has dignity. A certain age, work, and a kind of detachment seem to create this dignity. During the years I have been writing less and less in a diary because I began to feel that this writing extended anxiety and unhappiness. Dr Johnson never wrote his history of melancholy because he feared it would disturb him too much.

Whether things are written down or not they dwell somewhere within and surface unbidden at any time.

THE NURSES

'You know Woods. Sister Woods on Men's PS. Well this morning Woods smacked a junior across the face for cutting the crusts off some bread and butter she was giving to a post-operative haemorrhoids, wiped the floor with her saying didn't she realize what happened to bread and butter, crusts and all, before it got to the rectum. And before thingamajig, forget her name, could say she'd done it because he'd had all his teeth out as well Woods swiped her one and because *her* teeth are the kind that stick out, no not Woods – silly! thingamajig, I'll get her name in a minute, it's on the tip of my tongue, Thomas? No, Thompson that's it, well, because Thompson's teeth protrude rather, the smack on her face made her bite her lip and cheek and you should have seen the blood. Blood everywhere. All over Woods as well. When Thompson did manage to explain Woods reported her straight away to Matron's office for being cheeky.'

'Oh that's rich, cheeky, get it? *Cheeky.*'

'No, don't get it.'

'Well, forget it.'

We are all up in the room I share with Lois. We are high up on the eighth floor. From the window you can see the streets and buildings of the city, you can see the railway line and the canal. The water in the canal seems to shine all night. Water does seem to stay light all night. The best part about this view is that you can see the trees in the park and, beyond all this, you can see across to the fields and the country outside the city. We are here, as we often are, revising for a test. Nursing is like this. One test or exam after another. We are having some currant buns with butter. Lois spreads the buns with her nursing scissors and, when we have finished eating, she remembers she did a taxi driver's feet with them this afternoon.

Lois is short with a round face and a round forehead. She has blue eyes wide apart and a little mouth. We have been sharing a room for some time. She smokes.

Trent is big and makes us laugh with her impersonations. Trent is the kind of nurse we all declare we would like to have looking after us if we should be ill. This is the highest compliment one nurse can pay another.

Ferguson was at boarding school with me. We started training together at the beginning of the war. We used to share rooms but Lois and I, being fond of each other, asked to change rooms. I am afraid Ferguson might have been hurt by this. She has never seemed to lack friends. Having plenty of sex appeal, she says, helps.

McDougal, who shares with Ferguson, is with us on this occasion. I often feel sorry for McDougal.

Since my friendship with Dr Metcalf and his wife Magda began, Lois and Ferguson seem somewhat put out. And now since things have changed greatly for me with the sudden death of Dr Metcalf when he went to the war, to do war service when the war was really over, I am aware of Lois observing me closely. She seems at times a little spiteful and quite often displays a triumphant look as if she is enjoying all that has happened to me. Things never used to be like this between Lois and me. Quite the reverse, there was something mysterious, exciting and special between us at first. The kind of thing – when you go into a room full of people, for example, the big dining room here at the hospital, and you look quickly all round to see if the person you want to be near is there and, seeing her, you cross quickly hoping that there is an empty chair at her table – that kind of thing. Or seeing something in a shop which would please her you go in and buy it even if it takes up all the money you have. I once bought the prettiest nightdress for Lois and she gave it to her mother. Her mother, I thought then, was the ugliest woman I had ever seen. But Lois said, at the time, that her mother had never had nice things. But all this about Lois and me is changed.

I try to re-enter the pages of my *General Text Book of Nursing* wholeheartedly, to learn and to revise, to take my mind off the more sorrowful and worrying things in my life. For a time gossip helps. I mean, when hearing things about Sister Woods and Sister Purvis it is possible to forget other thoughts for a time, but inevitably these other thoughts come back heavier each time than before.

'I can't stand the way Purvis stands over me when I'm poaching an egg.'

'Can't stand poaching eggs, full stop.'

'Can't stand old Purvis, I mean, talk about a battle axe.'

'Yep. A battle axe all right. That's because of her D.U.'

'A D.U.?'

'Yep. Haven't you ever heard of a disappointed uterus? Said to be the cause.'

'Cause of what?'

'Battle axes, silly.'

'I'm not so sure about the D.U. Did you know she hasn't any sex organs?'

'Go on!'

'How does anyone know a thing like that? I mean, it's a bit private isn't it? I mean, it's a bit much, don't you think?'

'Purvis has got them all right. You can hear them rattling when she's mad at someone.'

'Like when you've ruined a poached egg. I don't think patients should have their own shell eggs. Takes up too much time mornings. What's wrong with the hospital scrambled egg? Good honest dried egg!'

'Everything. Just about everything I'd say. It's rubber.'

'Well, about Purvis. Lemmington Frazier, right in the middle of a rectal exploration last week, stopped half way and said, "Miss

Purvis," he didn't, you notice, say Sister Purvis, "Miss Purvis" he said, "this vaseline's about as sterile as you are." And then he looked at Purv. over his mask, you know how he does, and said, "Perhaps I'm crediting you where no credit's due." I mean what could be plainer!'

'I don't get it.'

'Forget it. But about Purvis and Woods. You know how their wards, Men's Private Surgical and Women's PM, share a ward kitchen well, last night Fanny Woods was throwing saucepan lids at Fanny Purvis and *she was* in her own half of the kitchen. Definitely she was on her own side of the kitchen. Woods threw the lids right across the kitchen. You never heard anything like it. Talk about battle axes in combat.'

'Whyever?'

'Well, Woods likes everything rinsed in cold water, every cup, plate, spoon, what have you, all put in cold water straight after being cleared from the trays. And Purvis says that's the wardsmaid's job not the nurses'.'

'And, I suppose Woods insists on the nurses, on both sides, rinsing things?'

'Yep. They were having this argument and then Woods says does Purvis realize that *her wardsmaid* is stuffing her bag with toilet rolls and spam meant for the American officers who are still here. Every night, she says, Purvis's wardsmaid goes off with this fat bag full of stuff. That's when they start throwing things. We don't dare go in there because of the noise. And Woods comes rushing out crying and Purvis has an asthma attack after blowing her boiler like that. Blue in the face she was.'

'That's right the RMO had to be sent for. He put Purvis on parsley tea.'

'I thought parsley tea was for abortions.'

'No stupid, it's raspberry leaves brings on an abortion.'

'Yes. Raspberry leaves. There's a few people in this hospital could do with a dose of raspberry tea.' Lois looks across at me with lowered eyelids. 'Except it might be too late. I mean if it's too far gone the old raspberry tea can't do anything.'

'Describe Leiter's Coils and how to reduce temperature,' Trent says with her finger in the pages of the *General Text Book of Nursing*.

'Better look it up. Look up cupping too and the tepid bath, is it four sponges used or six?'

'Heavens, all these water treatments! However much you cover the bed with rubber sheets – everything gets soaked. And really what difference, four or six sponges!'

'Well you don't have to say that in the exam. And anyway there's no water in cupping and it really works. Purvis swears by it and Woods won't hear of it.'

'I mean, shall we ever get to do cupping?'

'Yep. I've just said Purvis does it all the time for pneumonia, swears by it. She's an old witch with the Bier's suction cups and the meths. She flames the cups with burning blotting paper. You've never seen anything like it! Little torn off bits of blotting paper dipped in spirit, she uses the forceps of course though I have seen her use her bare fingers...'

'No feeling.'

'Yep. No feeling. She uses the forceps when lighting the bits of blotting paper, drops the bits, one in each cup, and then, when almost burned away in the cups, quickly puts them on the patient's back or chest. Woods won't have a bar of this treatment but there's no need to say that in an exam. Don't forget the vaseline – to mention it in the exam, I mean.'

'We'd better look up Trendelenburg's and Sim's positions,' Ferguson says. 'I get them mixed up.'

How can Ferguson mix up these two when Sim's is left lateral and semi-prone and in Trendelenburg's the patient is on her back, head lower than her pelvis, legs flexed at the knees...

'You use straps, fastenings, in Trendelenburgs,' someone says.

I can't help thinking about the money Ferguson owes me. I'm going to need all the money I can get hold of from now on. No more State Express 333 for Lois. I am watching her smoke from the last packet I can give her. And definitely no more lending to Ferguson. If only there was some way I could get back what she owes me. I can't help wondering if Purvis and Woods, when they were young, lent or owed money. People, it seems, either lend it or they borrow it.

★

FORTUNE TELLER

The special thing about being on night duty in the diet kitchen, if there can be, at present, anything special about this, is the surprisingly sweet fresh air where the inside of the hospital flows from its subterranean depths to meet the outside world. Sometimes, at dawn, I go through the half-lighted basements of the hospital kitchens and come out to the ramp where the empty milk churns are taken away. I stand there devouring the cool air of the new morning. Sometimes I help myself to a bowl of fresh milk from one of the new churns delivered during the night.

From this ramp it is possible to hear the city clocks chiming through the dull roar which is the regular, unchanging breathing of the city. A thin trickle of sad tired people leave the hospital at about this time of day. They are relatives unknown and unthought about, having spent anonymous nights in various corners of the hospital, waiting to be called to a bedside where they will not be recognized. At dawn they leave in search of that life in the shabby world which has to go on in spite of the knowledge that someone who has been there for them is not there any more.

This ramp, this is the meeting place where all the weariness and the contamination and the madness of suffering of both worlds, the inside of the hospital and the outside, come together. In this pure spaciousness of the fresh air I have to understand, every morning, that I am one of the ones, who, without having had a silent bed to sit by, has to go on in the world.

The night nurses have dinner in the Maids' Dining Room. We have dinner first thing in the morning when we come off duty; mince and cabbage and boiled potatoes followed, as a rule, by rhubarb and custard. Sometimes there is a steamed currant pudding and custard. Sometimes the meat is cold meat with beetroot. Breakfast, with the bouncing scrambled egg, is in the evening. So that we have some time out of doors we are not expected to be in bed till twelve noon. The rooms are checked every day at twelve. Sometimes the maid, Hilda, does this. She is easily fooled by pillows heaped under bedclothes.

Lois wants to look at the fair. A travelling circus.

'But there'll be nothing doing at this time of day,' Ferguson says. We go all the same. Lois, Ferguson, Trent and I walk on the damp sweet-smelling grass between the tents and the caravans and the cages of animals. A few people, like us, are strolling about peering at the private lives of the animals and the circus people. The grass has been trodden down heavily the night before. This seems to enhance its fragrance this morning, as if being crushed it is now all the sweeter, as if adversity can bring about something pleasant. I almost speak of this to the others and then I don't. I simply hope that this idea has some truth in it for me.

'Cross my palm, dearie,' the fortune teller is sitting on a stool outside her booth. She has on a red and black shawl and is decorated lavishly, as if she slept in them, with rings on her fingers and ears. Her long black hair is loose. She is brushing it.

'Cross my palm with silver, dearie,' she calls across to us.

'Anyone got any money?' Lois is looking at my purse.

'She wants silver,' Trent says.

'Oh come on,' Lois says, 'you've got a shilling there, you've got two.' She pokes a finger in my purse.

'Who's going?' I look at the others.

'It's your money, Wright,' Trent says.

The sweet grass is intoxicating. I can feel the damp when I sit down by the fortune teller. She studies my hand tracing the lines with a black-edged finger nail. The others stand near, listening.

'You've a long life, dearie,' the fortune teller says. She makes me clench my fist and she counts the creases below my little finger.

'You'll have three children, dearie, easy births. You'll be a mother before you're a wife, dearie. Romance is to be yours. Romance will come your way. There's a tall dark handsome stranger in your life...' She stops suddenly and goes on brushing her hair.

'Short and sweet,' Trent says as we move on between the tethered ponies. 'That's all you get for a bob, obviously. Could be that she's off duty, like us, too.'

'Mother before wife. Hm Hm,' Lois lights her last cigarette and surrounds herself with a cloud of smoke. 'Now what can she mean by that, I wonder? I just wonder.' I can see Lois narrowing her eyes as she looks at me through the settling smoke.

'Come on,' Trent says, 'let's get back, the post should be in by now.'

At the hospital, in the Nurses' Home, we queue for letters. There is a parcel for me from my mother. Records direct from the shop in town. The excitement of this is pleasant and a reminder of other surprise parcels in other days when it was possible to be entirely excited about something and to have nothing worrying at the back of the mind.

I hope, as I take the parcel and sign for it, that it might contain the Mozart piano concerto which has an octave leap in the first movement, piano notes an octave apart, not once but several times granting the satisfaction which a realization of the expected gives. This is how staff nurse Ramsden would speak of the octave leap. And in the second movement there is a tender reasoning in the music. Efficacious, this is not a word I use but I feel certain that Ramsden would apply it to the second movement of this piano concerto. Efficacious, the word is more than suitable for her voice.

Back up in the room which I share with Lois we try the records.

The gramophone is in the wardrobe with a towel over it to muffle the noise. I am disturbed by the music, disappointed, not liking it at all. I have never listened to anything like it before.

'God!' Lois says, 'Golly! What a row. Turn it off for God's sake!' I try one of the others. It is just as awful. 'It's Bach,' I tell Lois, 'unaccompanied cello, and the other is a string quartet by Beethoven. It should be nice, it's Beethoven.'

'If you say so,' Lois says. 'Me, it's not my cup of tea.'

'You might not like this music at first,' my mother, without seeing my face, has sensed my lack of enthusiasm which I try to hide during my telephone call of thanks. 'It is a sophisticated music. You will like it very much later on,' she says, 'only listen and wait. You must learn to wait. There is time,' she says, 'for all things but you have to wait till the right time. Listen and wait now.' She tells me to bring my ration book if I am coming home, later on, for a holiday when I have finished night duty. 'The butcher,' she says, 'has some nicehipponstek, but will need ration book.' I tell her that I won't be coming home, that I am not due for any holiday. How can I go home from now on.

'Be sure to bring ration book when you come,' my mother says.

Lois is having her bath so I get undressed and into bed as quickly as I can. The blending of discord and deep sorrow, deepening with each note in the opening of the Beethoven string quartet and the grave unaccompanied cello of Bach seem to have enclosed me inside a wall of heavy solemn thoughts. It is the first time I have heard a cello by itself for more than just a few notes. One piece of music will not replace another wished for piece. It is the same with people.

The deep bowls of milk I scoop from the churns first thing every morning are rich and creamy. This fresh milk should be beneficial for small delicate bones and for the muscles of a tiny heart.

RATION BOOK

Beatrice, Baba. Baba I must talk to you. You and I, Beatrice –
Baba, must have a little talk. Twice today, Beatrice, you have
kicked me. Beautiful Beatrice, the giver of blessings. You, Baba,
seemed never to be growing and now, all at once, you have grown
and you move. Will you be a pretty little girl, Baba, with fair hair
and brown eyes?

Now, the first thing that I must do is to get my ration book.
Yes, Baba, Ration Book. You, Baba, you do not know anything
about things like ration books yet. Ration Book is not for you
to worry about. I have to worry. How to get Ration Book is the
next thing.

Dr Metcalf, I know you always told me to call you Jonathon
especially when you kissed me you said to call you Jonathon or
Jonty like Magda. How could I call you Jonty when that was
Magda's name for you? Dr Metcalf, I must tell you that our baby
moves. If only you could be here to put your hand on me and
feel Beatrice kick, thump thump, here in my side. From the outside
you can see her move, actually from the outside. *Actually see her
moving.*

But the ration book. I must get it. I can't leave here without it.

'Where's your ration book?' My mother's first question, always.
'Why didn't you post your ration book?' Her voice indignant with
her question on the telephone on different occasions. 'You know
very well that Mr Shaw likes to have the ration books. He needs

them, particularly he needs them for the bacon. And the butcher too, he must have the meat coupons. Have you still got meat coupons?' My mother, intimidated by food office officials and by the grocer and butcher, is always angry about ration books.

The women who work at the food office all wear head scarves. They keep their hair in metal curlers all day and cover them with these head scarves. When I get my ration book I shall have to go to the food office to get my green ration book which I can have because of being pregnant. The women, in their head scarves, sitting on the other side of the trestle tables, will keep me standing so long while they put their head scarves together to study my identity card and the hieroglyphic on the top right-hand corner which, I understand, means 'assumed name'. It will not be their business to discuss my change of name, my assumed name which I have taken because I am pregnant and not married. But they will discuss and they will look at me with a hard-eyed curiosity; and they will keep me waiting. Twice during ward report little Nurse Roberts fainted. Here in the diet kitchen I do not have to stand at report. If I have to stand a long time in the food office I am sure to feel faint and they will help me to one of their horrible little chairs and bring me rusty water in a cup.

You, Dr Metcalf, you never had to worry about food rationing. You never had to know anything about the long lines of people waiting outside shops and at the bus stops. For Magda food rationing has never and does not now exist. She never has to queue for anything. The last time I saw Magda she was still hoping that the news of your death, Dr Metcalf, was not true. I still have the same hope but because there are things pressing which I have to do I have to think about these things.

'Why are you so late?' my mother always asks. She is peevish with keeping a plate of dinner warm over a saucepan. She keeps my father's dinner warm like this, too, for when he comes in white-faced and tired from school.

'Why are you so late?' The question persists.

'The bus queue...' I explain, 'so many people...'

'You must not always stand aside,' she says, the irritation

growing in her voice. She is anxious about me. 'You must get the ration book and go to the food office for the green book,' she says. 'And then, always, you must go to the heads of the queue, right to the tip, and hold up your green book, so, and when all can see it you will be first on the bus. Rosa,' my mother adds, 'Rosa is having twins as you know and her mother-in-law, Frau Meissner, takes always Rosa's book and is every time first on the bus.' I start to correct my mother.

'No s on head for queue and tip is not...' I am afraid she might make mistakes in front of the neighbours. It suddenly seems too difficult to explain that 'always' and 'every time' are not in the right places in her sentences.

Rosa and her family are among the first people to escape, with my mother's help, from Europe.

I am obsessed, Baba, with Ration Book. I cannot leave without it. I need it to get the green ration book for you Baba. You will benefit greatly...

It is part of my work at night in the diet kitchen to go round to all the wards to collect request forms for ration books belonging to patients who are being discharged. I usually do this in that quiet time of the night when I have finished dusting and tidying Matron's office. She keeps a little tin of dark polish and a soft cloth in one of the drawers in her desk. Dusting Matron's office is a privilege entrusted only to a few nurses she tells me when I am moved by her well-sharpened pencil to night duty in the diet kitchen.

'The diet kitchen,' Matron says then while her pencil hovers and pauses above the coloured squares on her big map of the nurses' experience and movement charts, 'The diet kitchen is not a place of punishment. It is a valuable part of your training.' And working there on my own, she tells me is an excellent way of having a much needed rest from patients and other staff. She tells me there is no need to cry and that I must have plenty of fresh air every morning before going to bed. When she speaks to me she talks of me as 'one of her nurses'. It is thinking about being considered by her as belonging to her which makes the tears keep coming. I had never thought that she might have thought of me as hers. She takes the opportunity then of explaining something I already know, that the doctors' corridor is out of bounds (her words) for the nursing staff. I have been seen there occasionally apparently.

'No doubt you will have had your own reasons,' Matron goes on and she says she will not question them. She says that the rule is made to 'protect those of our profession who are weaker'. It is then that she tells me she has made up her mind that I am to be a gold medallist. 'It will be hard work,' she says, 'very hard work but I know that you can do it.'

'You, Baba, you come from there, from the doctors' corridor. No one knows this at all. But it is only fair that you should know it. That part of the hospital was bombed and is being rebuilt, Baba. It will never be the same there and you will never see it.'

But the ration books. The office where I have to go for the patients' ration books is also the place where my ration book is. It is in the same subterranean corridor as the diet kitchen and the ordinary kitchens. The radium therapy ward is down there too and a surgical ward for soldiers, officers, mostly convalescent patients who are allowed out during the day.

There is a certain place along this corridor where staff nurse Ramsden and I met one night, each going in opposite directions. It is then that Ramsden, very shyly, gives me a little book of hand-written poems. Some of them are her own and some are poems which she has chosen. At the time, she says she feels she has no right to give me the poems but will I have them all the same. As we are both in a hurry she says not to look at them then.

Ramsden must be having nights off as staff nurse Burrows is in the office on the Lower Ground Men's Surgical. I see her there when I am on the way to the ration-book office.

As soon as I manage to get my ration book there are the other things I must do. I may do all this in one day and in that case shall not see Ramsden again. Often I have walked along the corridor and back simply in the hope of meeting her or of seeing her sitting in the office of the ward bent over the reports she is writing.

I think that, because of the shy and tender expression in Ramsden's eyes, she really likes to see me. It might be because of her being so much older than I am, and more senior, that she does not tell me that she likes to see me. Of course I would not be able to tell her what I am about to do as soon as I can get my ration book. I am ashamed that, in spite of all the suffering inside this big hospital, all I can think about is my ration book and what I have to do... Also, I do not like staff nurse Burrows because she is not Ramsden... I am sorry about this too.

Time has been going very slowly and yet it goes on in an inevitable way. My life seems to spread over an Age, an Eternity. I feel old. My life seems to be a never-ending time of having no one to talk to, of going for lonely walks in the mornings, early, before going to bed. I walk by the Metcalfs' house. I never see anyone coming out or going in. The curtains are always drawn. I think about Magda and wonder what she is doing, who she is with and what she would guess if she knew about my baby. Yes, you Baba. Dr Metcalf's baby and mine. In a curious sort of way, Baba, it is as if you are the Metcalfs' baby. Magda's and Dr Metcalf's.

Every night in the diet kitchen I am tired before I start work. Every night I do the same things. I cut and weigh small pieces of bread and wash lettuce leaves and boil beetroots. I make up the trays and label them with names and illnesses, diabetes, kidney disease – kidney failure mainly. I stew prunes and beat up dried egg powder. I try not to breathe in the smell of the

Vitamin B extract. I work alone. My body aches behind the buttons of my uniform. I think of little Nurse Roberts. As well as fainting all over the place she couldn't stand the smell of the dried egg. It was said she threw up just looking at the packet. I suppose she will have her baby by now. They say, at meal times, that you, Dr Metcalf, are the father of Nurse Roberts' baby.

The smell of the dried egg and dehydrated potato powder makes me feel sick still. When I slice tomatoes I have to turn my head away.

Trent says, one day at breakfast, that though the war is supposed to be over, if a war ever really ends, she says, the dried egg will go on for ever. When she says this she is chasing some scrambled egg as it bounces across her plate and we all laugh. Inside I am not laughing at all really. I am lonely. Alone beyond all words even though we all go together then, Trent, Ferguson, Lois and me to queue for our jam ration. We all have to take a clean jam jar with a well-fitting lid and the Home Sister ladles the warm red jam from a zinc bath into each jar as we file past. She has the bath high up on a table which has been covered with a clean sheet.

When I go home to my mother's house for my nights off I go there by the Back Lane, from the bus, instead of along the street where the neighbours might see me. Mostly I go at dusk and this has not been difficult because the evenings are still getting dark early. How will I go there in the long light evenings of summer? How can I nurse my baby on the bus and then carry her on my arm to my mother's house? This was something I always wanted to do. It was something I imagined doing, something nice to do at some time in the future. I never thought then of it being like this. I mean, I never thought of making the journey with my baby secretly and without the pride of taking her home to be admired.

I never go to Gertrude's Place now.

Sometimes my father is waiting for me at the bus stop. Even in the rain he waits and we walk home together. He comes to the station when it is time for me to go back to the hospital. He tells me, on my last visit there, that they would like me to come home. He tells me that if it would be easier for me they will sell the house and move. 'Buy another house – somewhere else and move,' he says. I think of the walls of books in the house and of all the other things there, undisturbed, for years. They know all the people living near by. My mother is sustained by the people she knows. I tell my father it is not necessary for them to move. I tell him I have other plans. 'Thank you all the same,' I tell him. He takes my hand and shyly kisses the space above the back of my hand.

We walk together up and down the deserted platform. I look along the empty rails to see if the train is coming and I try to think what are those plans of mine. It would be easier to be going to bed upstairs in the back bedroom at home and to have my father bring me the strange half cup of tea he always makes, with the tea leaves floating and with too much sugar, in the mornings.

'I don't want to go,' I want to tell my father. I want to tell him that the diet kitchen is an awful place, that I don't feel well there, and that it is dark and lonely and that I shall be cutting up and weighing and arranging little bits of tasteless food all night.

'Always the same little pieces of bread and the same lettuce leaves for patients for whom there are no medicines and no cure.' I can't help saying this.

'It is God's work,' my father consoles. And, as if forgetting that I shall be obliged to leave the hospital soon, he says, 'Every day new discoveries are made and if these patients can be helped with diets while the scientists, with their research, are providing new drugs then that is a good thing.' As he talks his voice is full of hope. 'Take school dinners,' he says. 'All schools are now providing dinners...' The train comes and our talk has to end. I lean out of the window to wave to him. He has walked, almost running, alongside as far as he can to the end of the platform.

35

He has not forgotten. I see him standing white-faced with one arm raised. He gets smaller and smaller and I can see him till, at last, the train moves round into the great curve. He has not forgotten at all.

There will always be school dinners now. I hear my father saying this often. He says children at school must have enough to eat. 'Plenty of food and plenty of sleep.' Those are the words he says. Sometimes he talks about the school dinners to strangers in shops. Perhaps on New Year's Day when he wishes people he does not know a happy new year and shakes hands with them.

Before the war my father arranges school dinners himself. He employs two women and pays them himself to come to school and to cook and serve the dinners. The children do not have to pay for them. He wants me to come with my mother to the school to see his dinners.

'Is like a dinner for a dog,' my mother says peering into one of the enormous saucepans. 'The smell!' My father is proud of the dinners and introduces us to the two women who are standing, their large arms bare, ready to serve as the children file past. My father is accustomed to eating a pile of bread with his own meals. He stands by one of the desks and cuts thick slices of bread and gives a piece to each child so that the gravy can be soaked up and not wasted.

'He gets up earlier and earlier,' my mother complains to me later. 'He goes on his bicycle to the markets to buy the meat and the vegetables,' she lowers her voice. 'People also,' she says, 'give him meat coupons and carrots. He is peeling himself.' Because I can hear her tears in her voice I hesitate to correct her.

Baba? You there? Baba, you are very quiet and still. I am on my way at last to that dreary office on the lower ground floor. It is not far from the diet kitchen past the Radium Therapy, the Pharmacy and the Officers' Surgical. I don't need to tell you,

Baba, because you have been everywhere with me for quite some time now. Though I have made a point of keeping away from Lower Ground Radium. Might be a dangerous place for you, Baba. As I was telling you I am on my way to get the ration books for the wards and to try to get my own ration book so that I can get the green one, Baba, for you. So keep calm Beatrice Baba, in there. Have a little rest and do not take any notice if I seem nervous or upset. I have thought of a way to get Ration Book. And, Beatrice Baba, I might as well tell you now that if I am successful in a minute, it will not be long before we leave the hospital. We shall be going to a place where I shall be housekeeper, 'a mother's help'. Don't laugh Baba! Do you laugh in there? Go to sleep!

'You'll need a signed slip,' this woman says, 'signed by Matron.' The woman's only a clerk, for Heavens Sake. Who does she think she is! Really, Baba, if you could *see* her.

'Yes. Yes. I know. I've got it. The slip. It's up in my room on the night nurses' corridor. I forgot to bring it down.'

'Signed by Matron, is it?'

'Yes. Yes! I'll come right back down with it. I'll be down with it before you go off duty. But I'd better get these round to the wards first.'

'There's twenty-five. Sign for them here.' She pushes a ledger towards me.

'Sure!' I say. 'Heavens! You *have* been busy cutting out coupons. You must be bored to death.' I examine the stack of ration books. Naturally mine is not among them.

'Just sign please.'

These official administrators! Baba, I can't say this aloud but she is the most boring person I have ever seen. No style. Absolutely no style. I suppose she doesn't need any, sleeping all day and guarding ration books and cutting them up all night. If you could see her hair, Baba. Unwashed string. And her jumper is a hand-knitted hideous shapeless thing covered with yellow and purple blobs.

'You must be bored to death,' I try once more. Must keep her talking, thinking about something else while she looks out my book.

'I am,' she yawns.

'I'm on holiday,' I say.

'I'm so pleased for you,' she says without a hint of pleasure.

'When will you get your holiday?' I'm having to actually *chat*. This woman kills me. The awful thing is that I find myself longing for boredom like hers. Safe solid boredom instead of what I have to get done. In my head I'm telling her to hurry. *Hurry up do! Find my ration book, only hurry before you change your mind or before someone else comes in here. Quick quick find my ration book!*

'This war!' I sigh, 'I know it's over and all that but they say the shortages and the ration books will go on for a long time. You know,' I lower my voice and lean towards her, 'this war's had a terrible effect on my mother. She hoards bags of buns, those iced buns with currants, under her bed. Can you imagine!'

The clerk looks up at me. 'She never!'

'Yep, she does. You have no idea.' Ideas spring into my mind. 'Mention the word "ration book",' I say, 'in her hearing and she bolts off to queue wherever there's a queue. Sometimes she goes in carpet slippers, really old ones. And the mess under her bed. Rats, do you see? Awful!' I'm peering at the ration books in her hands. 'Er, that looks like it might be mine,' I say.

'You got your identity card on you?' she snaps.

'Sure!' I say feeling my uniform pocket. 'It's in here somewhere. It's in my little Bible here.'

She takes the little white Testament.

'There's nothing in here,' she says.

'I must have left it upstairs,' I say. 'I'll bring it down later.'

'Oh never mind! Your name's in here, in the Bible. It's a neat little book,' she says. 'I'm getting my holiday in about nine weeks time,' she offers.

'I'll bet you're counting the days,' I say. 'Jolly nice!' I sit on the edge of her desk to show how relaxed I am. A cramp seizes the back of my thigh.

I can hardly take the ration book without snatching it. It is a long time since I held the book in my hands. I look at it without really seeing it. I hold it as if clamped with my fingers to the top of the twenty-five for the patients.

'Don't mix them up,' the clerk yawns once more. 'They're in order, starting on Lower Ground and going up, makes it easier and quicker for you.'

'Oh ta,' I say, 'ta very much, thank you very much, ta! I'll be right back down.'

'Tonight will do,' she says, yawning straight at me. 'It'll save you coming back. Bring the slip tonight.' She starts to tidy her desk. 'I'm getting off early this morning, a bit early,' she says.

'Good idea!' I say. 'I'll come tonight.' I try to whistle as I go along the corridor but my mouth is too dry.

'Nurse!' I hear her voice calling me back along the corridor. I can hardly bear to turn round. She can't have my ration book back now. I go back. She has actually left her desk and is out in the corridor.

'You left your Testament,' she is holding out the little white Bible. I manage to smile.

'Oh,' I say, 'you keep it. I'd like you to have it. I've got another.'

'Thank you,' she says, 'thank you very much.'

Upstairs the night nurses' corridor is quiet. My room is just as I left it. McDougal, who now shares with me, is in the Nurses' Sick Bay. It is thought that she has diphtheria. She is being barrier nursed. We have all had throat swabs taken. Mine is negative.

I wish I could show you the ugly Ration Book, Baba. I suppose you don't have open eyes yet. You won't have finger nails, Baba, till eight months. Baba, stay till you are full term and then you will have everything. Be a good baby and don't you worry about anything.

This is going to be quite a day for us. As well as Ration Book

I have my trunk up here in my room. This used to be my trunk for school, it's called a cabin trunk. For ship journeys I suppose, Baba. I got it up in here just now, first thing this morning, without seeing anyone except the maid, Hilda, and she took no notice of me except to say did I know that the mice had got into McDougal's box of mince pies and she's taken the box away.

'Atta girl Hilda,' I say to her, 'atta girl!' It seems to me I am saying words I would never use as a rule. Perhaps I have heard Trent say 'atta girl' when she is being funny. Today is no ordinary day. The mince pies, Baba, for heaven's sake, they've been around since Christmas.

I did not go to the night nurses' meal this morning and that is how I am able to bring my trunk up here without seeing anyone. To get your trunk, Baba, you are really supposed to put in a requisition slip the night before, signed by Matron of course, explaining that you have been told to change your room. And the trunk appears later in your room. Well I want my trunk now so I ask the night porter to unlock the trunk room with his skeleton key.

'That'll be a kiss Christmas,' the porter says. He jingles his keys.

'Sure!' I tell him. 'I'll keep you to that.'

The trunk room, Baba, is a very restful clean place. All the trunks and cases and boxes are arranged in alphabetical order on wooden racks. The floor always looks swept. I have a look first to see what Ramsden's trunk is like. I can see at once it is made of something expensive like pig skin. It has brass-bound corners and a sturdy bright lock. Ramsden has certainly travelled, all over Europe it seems. I peer at the partly torn off coloured labels. All sorts of colours and all sorts of places and hotels. Exotic. Amsterdam, Brussels, Frankfurt, Paris, Rome... Ramsden, in her travelling, would have been sure to go on a steamer on the Rhine. She would have seen the miracle of the confluence – the apparently inexplicable appearance of the brown water of the river Main meeting and flowing with the blue waters of the Rhine. An unbelievable division – actually in the water...

'This one yours?' the night porter has my trunk by the door.

He jingles his keys. He has to be off, he says, his wife, who works during the day, will be waiting...

'Oh sure!' I tell him, 'thank you.' And I drag the trunk into the lift easily.

I feel strange, for one thing I have started saying 'sure' to everybody like a character in an American film. It would be easier, I think, to live a life in a film.

Hilda leaves a milk pudding every day in the night nurses' pantry at the end of the corridor. Because of you, Baba, and because I have missed the night nurses' meal time, I go off quickly to the pantry and spoon up nearly the whole dishful. The pudding is meant for all the nurses should they need something more to eat after going out and before going to bed. Not bad, Baba, the pudding not bad at all, a sort of loose blancmange, white and smooth and sweet.

'Atta girl! Hilda,' I say to the vanishing shape of the maid as she goes along the passage to the top of the stairs. Hilda was once Matron's personal maid and is retired but kept on in the hospital to have somewhere to live. She looks after the night nurses' corridor. Some other elderly maids and nurses are kept on in the sewing room, Baba, where sheets are mended and uniforms are made – that sort of thing. Sometimes I think it would be nice to just sit in the sewing room unpicking (they would give me the unpicking to do) and, just sitting, unpicking, untroubled – and bored with my companions. I really do just want to be thoroughly bored, Baba.

Baba, you and I cannot be bored. Ration Book and Trunk all at once up here in my room...

Our headmaster at school always said he knew which boys and girls would hand in their *Golden Treasury of the Bible* (two vols.) on leaving school and which boys and girls would keep them as a spiritual guide for the rest of their lives. I put the two grey nondescript books, Part I a fat book of the Old Testament and Part II, slim, the New Testament, in the bottom of the trunk with

The General Text Book of Nursing and the *Golden Treasury of Songs and Lyrics Book Fifth.* Shoes must go at the bottom too and flat, on the bottom, my Beethoven Piano Concerto, The Emperor. Some of my pressed wildflowers have come unstuck. It is a long time since I have looked at them. I put them back between the pages of the exercise book as quickly as I can. I seem to see, clearly, shining long fingers pulling stalks and holding bunches. I remember the sweet wet grass near the school where we searched for flowers. Saxafrage, campion, vetch, ragged robin, star of Bethlehem, wild strawberry and sorrel. I must hurry. The flowers, the colours are still fresh, I can't help looking at all of them in turn, buttercup, King cup, cowslip, coltsfoot, wood anemone, shepherd's purse, lady's slipper, jack in the pulpit and bryony.

Whenever I think of my father, like now, I hope he is thinking about school dinners. I have all his letters. I put his letters in the trunk carefully. They have underlined quotations in them.

Wherefore I perceive that there is nothing better, than that a man should rejoice in his own works; for that is his portion: for who shall bring him to see what shall be after him?

Ecclesiastes 3 v 22. He includes the chapter and verse because he always hopes I will look up the passage and read for myself.

My white blouse, my white blouse, which I keep for when I am invited somewhere, has to be folded neatly and my good pair of stockings, always clean and in readiness I put in beside the blouse. Then there is the little book of poems written out for me by Ramsden. For some reason I read the second verse of a poem and am surprised that though I liked the first verse very much;

The feathers of the willow
Are half of them grown yellow

I never read on to,

The thistle now is older
His stalk begins to moulder

and realize I have never really known the poem until now, and I feel sad in a quiet sort of way. I never read any of the poems to the end but only took the lines with the images I wanted.

Baba? Beatrice Baba? Will I sit reading poems while I nurse you in my arms? I remember my mother saying once that, before she had any baby, she imagined that she would sit by the window holding her baby and reading a novel. She said she understood later that the idea was not realistic and that it had come to her from something Goethe wrote.

Ramsden will have liked the poems she copied out in the little book.

They have no song, the sedges dry
And still they sing
It is within my breast they sing
As I pass by.

As I read I am overwhelmed with a wish to hear Ramsden's voice once more. I would like to ask her to read 'The Song in the Songless' but she will be either asleep or possibly away still on her nights off.

The trouble with packing, Baba, is that even though it is necessary to hurry I keep opening books and reading bits here and there. It says here in my *General Text Book of Nursing* that a woman is said to be pregnant when she has conceived. You will take, Baba, ten lunar months or 280 days to grow. To calculate the date of your birth, Baba, you can be expected to be born nine calendar months and five days from the last day of my last menstrual period. This reckoning is correct, it says here, within two or three weeks. The only trouble is, Baba, which you probably know as well as I do, that I have forgotten when that last date was. All I know is that it is rather a long time ago. It says here too that *every married woman should be advised either*

*to consult her own doctor or to attend one of the many excellent
antenatal clinics provided, as soon as she knows she is pregnant.*

Obviously, Baba, this applies to unmarried women as well.
It is a bit awkward this being unmarried but it is clear to me that
as soon as possible we must go to a doctor.

When I have finished packing this trunk, Baba, your life and
my life, up to the present time, will be contained inside it.

My trunk looks small in the deserted space of the front hall. It
is not often that the hall is empty of people. Someone is in the
phone box and someone is waiting outside, too preoccupied with
the impatience of waiting. I have to go up to the next floor where
there is a phone for staff nurses and sisters. I must hurry. I must
get my taxi before the nurses pass to and fro in the front hall on
their way either to or from the dining room. The night nurses
will not have been called yet. I want to miss Trent and Ferguson
and Lois. I do not want to see them just now.

I have to wait for this phone too. I wish really that I could be
going home and not to a strange house. The awful truth is that
I like to see my mother and my father but after about half an hour
I want to go away again. I am quite unable to explain why this
is. Of course I never say anything about it. I feel strangled in the
back bedroom at home and more alone than ever, especially when
I sit there looking across the back gardens of the other houses
and watch two people, a man and wife, working side by side, in
their own garden.

My taxi will come soon. I am promised the first available.

On the way downstairs I pass staff nurse Ramsden's door. I
hear some music from her room, something which has the
strength and the stillness of mountains and mountain lakes.
Music with a tender serenity about it. I think I know the music,
something by Sibelius, I think. Parts of this music were played
at school by the school orchestra, every one playing at their own
pace, not keeping together and not in tune. Ramsden must be
getting up already though it is not time yet for the night nurses

to get up. I have not been to bed all day and, though I shall be able to sleep tonight, it will be in an unfamiliar room and an unfamiliar bed.

I stop outside Ramsden's door and listen to the music. I long to tap on her door and to go in and hear her voice once more, to see her, to tell her, really, to tell her everything. But people cannot do things like that. I would like to hear her say 'come in' in her rich well-bred voice. She must be in there because there would be no music if she was not there.

I would like to go right in there and tell her *Ramsden*, I would say, *I have to say 'goodbye' I'm leaving* and then I would be able to tell her everything, even that Dr Metcalf said I was to call him Jonathon – especially to call him Jonathon when we were loving each other... Of course I can't knock and go in to her room. I can't tell her anything. People, well-bred people and I want to be well bred, don't burden each other with their dreams and their mistakes.

It is not like Ramsden to listen to Sibelius though I think she would describe the music as having a haunting quality of loneliness. She might use words like 'a mellow work of poetry'. People say things like this about music but when Ramsden speaks you can tell that she really means what she says. Ramsden could say, for example, that this music has strength and ardour.

It is not like Ramsden to listen to Sibelius, if it is Sibelius. Perhaps she is listening with someone, staff nurse Pusey-Hall. They do go to concerts together. Of course I cannot possibly go in there while Sibelius is being played. It *is* the Andante from something by Sibelius. One of them, Ramsden or Pusey-Hall, might come out suddenly and find me just outside the door. And then there's my taxi on its way and my trunk down there in the front hall...

'Well here's a shock!' I say excitedly as Lois, Ferguson and Trent come up the stairs from the dining room and into the front hall. 'Here I am,' I say to them, 'being moved all of a sudden.' The three of them stand staring at me. Trent has taken off her cap and her hair is loose. They all have their string bags with their jars of butter and sugar and jam.

'Where on earth could you be moved to?' Lois narrows her eyes as she does when she is smoking though naturally she is not smoking at this moment. 'Where on earth!' she says.

'The Accident hospital,' I say. 'Apparently, The Queens, the Accident hospital, is terribly short staffed and Matron's lending some of her night nurses.' Ferguson looks at me in disbelief. Lois lights a cigarette and surrounds herself in her customary cloud of smoke.

'Sounds like your cab,' Trent says. I am relieved to hear the horn.

'I'll give you a hand with your trunk,' Trent says.

I feel hungry, terribly hungry in this taxi. I even think I could eat that awful tripe which cooks slowly all night in the diet kitchen.

In my mind I consider the contents of my trunk safely in the luggage part of the taxi. I have not forgotten anything, my exercise books with the pressed wildflowers, the saxifrage, the meadow sweet and the bryony from school, all my books including my *General Text Book of Nursing* (1942) and the huge book of Embroidery I chose so stupidly from Ramsden's shelves when she once shyly offered to me to choose a book, any one of her books which I would like to have for myself. I have no idea why I chose a book full of embroidery designs and diagrams of needles in the act of making stitches, when I could have had poems, Rilke, for example, the Orpheus poems. In English of course.

I am lucky to have this taxi. With all the shortages, they are called the immediate postwar shortages, it is practically impossible to get taxis. I suppose it is some kind of providence which is helping me just now. I mean, what was it other than providence, which made me, when I ordered the car, say it was for Doctor Wright and that it was urgent. A childbirth, I said. Well you will be a childbirth, Baba, later on.

I really do feel terribly hungry. I have the ration book. The next thing will be the Food Office and the women there. I know what it is like at the Food Office and I have seen the queue there, right out on to the pavement...

But first the house at Clifton Way and I hope that there is something to eat there.

...Abbot Abrahams Ackerman Allwood...

...Arrington and Attwood. Nurses Baker Barrington Beam Beamish Beckett Birch Bowman D Bowman E Broadhurst Brown Burchall...When Sister Bean calls the register and gets to my name I shall not be there to answer. She will call twice and no one will reply, no one will reply for me.

It is only a short ride to the house in Clifton Way. I hope they will offer me something to eat. I am hungry.

CABIN FEVER

THE BREAKFAST BAR

Tomorrow, tomorrow I tell myself, tomorrow I shall, without hesitation, go down to the place where breakfasts are served. At street level there is an L-shaped restaurant, a breakfast bar, where people on the pavement can peer through plate glass at other people sitting among stacks of pancakes, flying fried eggs and bowls of steaming porridge, butter soaked and overflowing. Between the customers, like small traffic islands on the counters, are the cups and saucers over which a hot jug hovers pouring, without splashing, the life-giving coffee. There is a special door for this breakfast bar. Hotel residents need not enter by the street door where there is always a queue of silent hungry people waiting, pausing impatiently on their way to their work.

Yesterday I said that the next day I would go down for breakfast. I remind myself now that all kinds of people are down there having breakfast. Women with intelligent eyes and Viennese accents, on museum or gallery research, speaking English slowly. Elderly men and women, married and living together for years, watery faced and red veined, knowing each other's preferences, speaking to each other without needing to, one addressing the waitress, unasked, on behalf of the other. Over all this hangs the fragrance of hair spray and bacon.

ROOM SERVICE

Because I am tired. Tired and travel shocked, too tired to dress and make my way along to the lift and down the twenty-four floors, I'll dial for room service and have a pot of coffee and some croissants sent up, balanced shoulder high on the palm of the waiter's hand, the heavy tray, silver at the edges, drenched in white linen, bringing with it an unbelievable atmosphere, a sense of offering and of cherishing carried, from the place where it has been carefully prepared, all the way up to my bedside. And here it will be placed, set carefully on the space cleared temporarily as my notes and papers are moved with reverence across the smooth covers of the bed.

I shall lie back on the pillows and breathe in the fragrance of the coffee and of the croissants, their crisp golden warmth, hidden folded in the white table napkin. I shall handle the cutlery, heavy with good quality, and feel with my lips the china rim of the cup. Seen from the consolation of this masterpiece my notes are noble.

THE NOISE

For some hours there has been and still is an incredible noise immediately outside my door. Someone is drilling and hammering and trying to push a cable or an electric wire of some sort through a small space somewhere above my head and in the cavity of the wall behind my head. I have never in my whole life heard any noise quite like this noise. It is a wild and dangerous noise, a noise of discord suggesting pain and trouble, disorder and sorrow.

BROKEN GLASS

Someone out there has broken some glass. It is being swept up.

The broken glass is being swept up in that methodical way in which broken glass is gathered carefully, with the slow sweeps of a small worn-out brush into a metal dustpan. Some larger pieces, I can hear quite well, are being picked up and dropped into the pan. Perhaps there are two people out there crouching over the breakage. Probably it was a light fitting of some sort. I remember now, when I think of the long passage, there are opaque white bowls fitted over the lights. If I do think about these bowls at all, with any kind of seriousness, it would be to suppose that they are made of plastic... Clearly, it is broken glass very close immediately outside my door. There is a murmur of subdued anger, a low growling in a gravelly American accent; one of them, crouching there, must have cut himself.

Shirt Sleeves

I am still here on the twenty-fourth floor and when I sit in front of my mirror I can see, in the mirror, someone on the twenty-fourth floor across the street. He is sitting upright at a table and is in his shirt sleeves. I have no idea who he is.

Cabin Fever

There is no way of controlling the heat in this room. At times I find the heat overpowering. The heat induces dreams bordering on nightmare. Delirium in which harm is done;

> ... *Willst, feiner Knabe, du mit mir gehn?*

> *Will you come with me, my pretty boy?*
> *My father, my father, and don't you see there*
> *The Erlking's daughters with long flowing hair? –*
> *My son, my son, I do see them sway:*
> *It is the old willows that look so grey. –*

51

Mein Vater, mein Vater, jetzt fasst er mich an!
Erlkönig hat mir ein Leids getan! –

My father, my father, I feel his cold arm,
The Erlking has done me some terrible harm . . .

This must be what is meant by Cabin Fever. I heard the expression recently never having heard it before. *Reise Fieber*, I know this, is something *before* a journey.

But the Cabin Fever. This is how I hear about Cabin Fever. Two people are on a holiday snowed up in the mountains, at the foot of a mountain. As the time passes the young man loses all inclination to go out. He sits huddled near the stove in the small hut looking out occasionally at the snow-covered landscape. You've got cabin fever his companion tells him. You must come out walking at once. So the two of them put on their ear muffs and their warmest clothing and go out. At an ice-covered stream they pause wondering whether to cross on the ice. The man asks his companion if it is safe to cross on the ice and his companion says yes it is safe because there are no beaver tracks in the snow. Beavers swish their tails under the ice and the movement of their powerful tails wears away the under surface of the ice making it perilously thin – though this is not evident from above. No tracks to be seen, this ice is safe. But the ice does give way and, at once, they are both soaked up to their chests in freezing cold water. This is how I know about Cabin Fever.

The heating in this hotel room is too powerful. The heat is unbearable and there seems to be no way of turning it off. The windows do not open. I'm suffocating.

I lie with my arms folded under my head, a position which demonstrates a resignation to sleeplessness. Perhaps the position of Islam, a word which means to resign oneself, to surrender oneself completely . . . to . . .

It is too warm for either reading or writing. The indecision which accompanies me in every situation, for a time, keeps suffocation at a small distance.

The heat is suddenly worse. There will be no one at the front desk, down there, between two and three in the morning but I dial the front desk all the same.

The voice from the front desk is a remarkable voice, gentle, well mannered, soothing. *There is someone down there.* Immediately the room is cooler. Perhaps there is a switch actually in the office, something, some method of stopping the assiduous stoking of the gigantic boilers.

Perhaps if I had known more about thin ice, about the metaphor of the strength of the beavers' tails, more about what is hidden immediately beneath the skin, hidden behind the voice of excited enthusiasm or the melting gaze which seems to be, at the time, love – I could have known and understood earlier about things which can not be known purely from the surface, from the outside appearance.

CLOSELY
WATCHED HEDGES

'That you Daddy Doctor? Din-dins ready.'

'Hallo! Mummy Doctor. Just coming. Must wash puddies first. Coming in a minute. Hm! Smells good your din-dins. Grub grub wonderful grub...'

The doctors are proud of their downstairs cloakroom opening off the hall just inside the front door. Daddy Doctor whistles, when he comes out, a sort of proud little tune.

The doctors explain that they met over a crucible. Their surname being Wellington they explain too that they are happy that they have a pair of Wellingtons. Mummy Doctor says that she always believed she could not live without a bicycle and a pair of Wellingtons.

The doctors ride their bicycles to the university every day when the weather is fine. When wet they catch a tram. They seem pleased to tell me things.

Mummy Doctor says she always thought Wellingtons were called gum boots.

'It depends,' Daddy Doctor says, 'on where you went to school. These, this little pair, are Wellingtons. And, you do have a bicycle.'

'Yes of course,' Mummy Doctor agrees.

The little girls drink their milk, their solemn eyes regarding us over the rims of their Beatrix Potter mugs.

'Daddy Doctor? More puddy?'

'Daddy Doctor has had more than enough puddy. What about Mummy Doctor? Mummy Doctor have more puddy?'

'Well perhaps one teensie spoonful.'

The Mummy Doctor one offers to share the last of the apple charlotte, she has made, with me. 'Dried apple rings,' she explains. It is my first meal with the doctors. I shake my head.

'No, thank you. I really cannot eat any more.'

The mummy one drips cod-liver oil on the living-room carpet and, whenever she cuts bread for toast, she makes crumbs in the knife and fork drawer.

I don't know where anything goes in the kitchen and I pick up a plate and put it down in another place. I feel big in my woollen smock, the only thing I can wear now. Under this smock my skirt gapes, expanded on an elastic with a safety pin. My socks are darned solid.

I have been here for two meals now. I have helped with the washing up and fastened the little girls' shoes, little button shoes to wear in the house only.

The mummy one explains that her sister will be coming to stay for her long weekend break soon. She explains too, when we are upstairs, that the daddy one likes to be called upstairs at bathing time.

'Daddy Doctor! Bath time!'

'Coming Angie. Coming Barbie. A and B. Angle, Bangle I'm coming up to the bath! Roar!'

Daddy Doctor comes up the small staircase, two steps at a time. He is laughing, he smiles at me as I try, in the small space in the bathroom, to not be in the way.

They are doing their utmost to make me feel welcome in their house.

They call each other Daddy Doctor and Mummy Doctor and

the little girls are Angela and Barbara. Angie and Barbie. A and B. Sometimes Angle and Bangle. They are twins, four years old. They are very kind to me, the two doctors, and they trust me with their pretty little girls who like to change their frocks and have their smooth hair brushed several times a day. They are well behaved.

The trouble is, the only trouble is that I am lonely. I feel alone all the time even when I'm busy like now out shopping with Mummy Doctor and the twin pushchair which has a big waterproof shopping bag fastened to it. I can't explain to myself what it is like to be on the edge of someone else's shopping. I am trying to be enthusiastic and pleased. Being on the edge of the shopping, walking by the pushchair on the grass-edged footpath, is the same thing really as living in their house, being on the edge of the family.

Two doctors in one house, the Ph.D. sort. Every morning they go off to the university to lecture and demonstrate; maths, equations, physics (hers) rocks, earth, boulders and minerals (his). Sometimes, like today, Mummy Doctor takes an afternoon off to teach me the shopping. And, another afternoon she came home early and we all went to the doctors and sat together in the waiting room. The little girls whispered to each other, their blonde heads shining in the rather dark room. When I came out from my antenatal appointment the doctor came out of his surgery with me and chucked them both under their dimpled little chins. He is their uncle.

As I walk by Mummy Doctor I stare at the beaten earth of the footpath and I stare at the garden gates looking closely into the hedges as we pass. I'm not looking for birds' nests, I'm looking into the dark evergreen foliage and at the dusty thin branches and twigs and at the glossy thick leaves and the prickles of the holly. As we pass I say the names of the houses to myself, Chez Nous St Cloud Prenton Sans Souci The Pines Holly House Barclay and Newton, names chosen and painted on to the gates or on little varnished boards screwed to the gates. Closely watching the hedges I am closed in by them and do not look too much at Mummy Doctor and her two little girls.

Watching the hedge closely it is as if I am about to be a part of the hedge or about to step away through it. A consolation perhaps to pay minute attention to something alongside the walk, as I might at one time have consoled myself at the river shack belonging to Dr Metcalf and Magda, when I so much wanted and needed to be there with Dr Metcalf by himself.

Mummy Doctor is not at all smartly dressed. She wears an old bluish coat and a round hat over her hair which is scraped into an unbecoming bun. I am wearing my school overcoat which is keeping up with my mother's expectations of good quality and lasting for years. The little girls have velvet collars on theirs.

The gardens in Clifton Way will be pretty with crocuses and daffodils later on Mummy Doctor tells me. I, meanwhile, am longing for my baby to come so that I can stop being a mother's help – for a while at least. It is much harder than I thought it would be. I can't think how I could ever have thought it would be a good way to live. Having to get away from the hospital somehow made me look, I see now, towards being somewhere else. I have a little room at the top of the stairs. The room is all right. There is a bed and a chair and a cupboard and the window looks out over the gardens. Just now the winter trees are bare, the branches making patterns, which daily become more familiar, on the pink-edged clouds of a perpetually grey sky. I am in the house all day with the two little girls while Mummy Doctor and Daddy Doctor are away at their university. I have telephone numbers for both of them. Tomorrow Daddy Doctor is going to come home at lunch time and I am to make a treacle pudding because it is his favourite pudding.

Mummy Doctor reminds me to wash my socks when we get home because, she says, feet stay warmer in washed socks. My feet are cold all the time.

We use my green ration book to go to the front of the queue and I collect the extra oranges we can have and the eggs. I carry the oranges in a string bag and try to be agreeable and pleasant but we are now in the streets where I used to walk sometimes with

Dr Metcalf, quite near the hospital. I thought that taking work and living near familiar places, places where I had been with him, would make it easier but it doesn't. I try to enjoy the sensation of the fresh cold air on my face but feel I want to cry. We have come to the corner where I ran to Dr Metcalf once when he had his back to me and I surprised him. I remember how pleased he was to see me that afternoon and we went off alone together for a long bus ride. It was summer then.

Being in this street where I once was able to see him and meet him is not what I thought it would be. Being here and knowing that I can never see him again is made the more painful by this knowledge. The street, busy with people and without him, is empty. I try to listen to Mummy Doctor and to pay attention to the chatter from the pushchair during the slow and incredibly boring progress of the shopping expedition. On one side is a coffee shop where Dr Metcalf and I had some coffee once. It was a terrible coffee, he said then, but it made us laugh. Mummy Doctor does not even notice this shop. Why should she? She has made up her mind to ask the butcher for something extra. She asks me if I like corned beef, perhaps. I try to remember what corned beef is.

Mummy Doctor and Daddy Doctor argue, for fun only, about who shall have the last drop of coffee at breakfast. Every morning there are two hand-painted saucers on the table. One is for real butter, a small square of real butter, and one for margarine. There is always a bigger square of margarine. Both the doctors are careful not to help themselves to the butter. Their knives avoid the butter saucer and, taking a tiny scrape of margarine, they spread it thinly on the crooked slices of toast. Both doctors talk and crunch their toast shamelessly. And, with quick upward movements of the chin, both catch any crumbs which might begin to fall. I spread margarine thinly on my toast too and the butter saucer is returned, after the meal, to the slate shelf in the small pantry.

Putting the butter and margarine out on the table at the same time is a way of not eating the butter. At the hospital we had to queue once a week for our rations. We all carried little screw top jars, one for butter, one for sugar and one for jam, in a string bag. We never went anywhere without these string bags. Often we ate up a whole week's butter ration at one go and then ate the strong-smelling yellow margarine provided on the dining-room tables.

The untouched butter saucer makes the funny stories, the amusing anecdotes, at meal times, simply stupid. The little girls, at breakfast, often have a piece of fried bread each and they do not have butter then either.

During our meals which are, as they say *en famille* (but in this small house where else could I have meals?) they remind them-selves of exotic foods they were accustomed to before the horrid war, before rationing. Daddy Doctor cuts his toast into little squares and moves little heaps about on his plate and remembers a particularly large and juicy steak which had two fried eggs and mushrooms on top of it. Even in their wildest imaginings of rich and plentiful meals they are not able to describe anything which could match Magda's pantry and her ability to disregard completely food shortages. And then Mummy Doctor asks Daddy Doctor does he remember Mrs Whitey and Daddy Doctor says of course he does. They both begin to laugh.

'That Mr Hilter!' he says in a squeaky voice with a cockney accent. He folds his arms. 'That Mr Hilter, if he puts my name on a bomb I'll get it. You get the one with your name on it. See? That Mr Hilter! I'll get 'im first.' Daddy Doctor laughs some more.

'Mrs Whitey,' Mummy Doctor, laughing, explains, 'used to come once a week to do the floors. She couldn't say Hitler. Mr Hilter, she kept saying Mr Hilter. That Mr Hilter!'

I have been here for three days and now while I am awake in the night it seems to me I have been here for ever and simply have no chance of getting away. If my baby would come now I'd be able to leave at once to go away to the nursing home. My baby can't be born yet, it isn't time. This evening I burn the potatoes and both the doctors keep on saying how much they prefer to have bread in their gravy instead of potatoes. The meal is only potatoes and gravy in any case, bread and gravy. I can see too, all through the meal, that they are trying to think up amusing little anecdotes to tell in well-bred voices. Even with all this I do not want to stay here.

I am cold in this little room at night. It is worse in this place, worse than anything I have ever known. I can't help hearing the doctors talking in low voices in bed, in their room. The Mummy one says the twins seem subdued, unnaturally subdued, she says. Are they sickening for something, she wonders. Perhaps, she argues, she should not have accepted the position in the department after all. Perhaps it was not the right thing to do. The Daddy one consoles saying that the children are fine, they are just a bit shy with a new person, it will soon pass, he says, the shyness. I can hear him telling her to enjoy the university and I can hear them turning over in bed towards each other.

Someone else's household is not the same thing as the one you come from, not at all. And working in a house looking after the children of the family is not at all the same as working in a hospital. For one thing there is no one here to work with and to talk to.

The little girls have piano lessons. A shabby old man comes to teach them. He has pencilled in on the lines and spaces 'F.A.C.E. "face"', he says. And 'Eat Good Bread Dear Father. E. G. B. D. F.' All the notes in the music books are labelled in pencil. He takes off his long black overcoat and his black hat when he comes and I make cocoa for him. Mummy Doctor says I am to give him something to eat. She makes a sort of ginger bread using hardly any sugar and no butter and no real eggs. She says to give him some of that and to have some myself. I can smell the dried egg inside the ginger. I still can't eat dried egg. This is a part of being pregnant. Nurse Roberts, at the hospital, was the same. They said just looking at the packet made her throw up all over the place. Trent said the dried egg would be with us long after the war was over, it would be with us for ever. They said Dr Metcalf was the father of Nurse Roberts' baby. Roberts, they said, stayed too long at the hospital. She showed dreadfully. I mean everyone *knew*. At least I got away before I was really *showing*. At least, even if Trent and Ferguson and Lois guessed, they didn't really *know*.

The little girls take turns to sit on the old man's knee to play their notes. He guides their small rosy hands and lifts their delicate wrists with his splayed and yellow fingers.

Suddenly it seems that I am bigger. I feel clumsy and slow when I move, but the little girls never run away when we go along the street for a walk. They walk with dainty little steps and hold my hands, one on either side, with their furry little gloves which are attached to an elastic passing through their sleeves and across inside under their coats. This, I can see, prevents the gloves from being dropped and lost. I shall do this for my baby when the time comes.

The closely watched hedges are all along this street and the next and the next. The leaves are dark green and glossy sometimes shining wet and, at other times, marked with the dust. Looking closely at the hedges I can see places where the grass of a lawn shows or, beyond the lawn, the lighted windows of a front room or the stained glass of a front door. The hedges are old. They are the evergreens, the laurel, the privet, the rhododendron and the holly.

On the afternoon of the first music lesson I could see that, after I had made the old man's cocoa, I could have some time to myself. Now, in this cold bed I can recall the bleak moments of something I began to understand. I thought that during the music lesson

I would have some time to myself and I looked forward to a kind of freedom. I thought I would write something, a letter to someone. I listened while the old man, the music master, played something himself for the little girls to dance to. He played from Schubert, *Rosamunde*. He thumped on the piano and I could hear the little girls laughing and dancing, thump thump, round and round in the small sitting room. Upstairs in my cold bedroom I sat with my pen and my writing pad and suddenly there wasn't anyone I could write to.

Rosamunde, my mother despising the people in the house next door (when I was a child) said every night that the only music those next-door people could play and listen to was *Rosamunde*, and only a part of the overture at that. She described it as an infectious music because people all liked it, a music which people, who knew nothing about music, could safely learn the piano arrangement and appear to be musical. 'On cheap piano,' she said, 'and, worse, on pianola!'

These people next door made a tiny lawn on the slag which was the earth of our gardens. Carrots and sunflowers grew on this waste from the coal mine and sometimes a coarse tufty sort of grass. The neighbour people tried to *actually cut* their tiny lawn. Every night *Rosamunde*, a part of the overture, could be heard from their piano. And my mother despised their choice.

While I sat in this cold little bedroom remembering my mother I wished for her. Now, in bed here, it seems to have been a silly wish but, because I am cold and not asleep, I do wish, all at once, to be in bed in my mother's house.

If my baby could be born tonight, I could go away now. I could go in to the doctors and tell them I am in labour and need a taxi, at once, to the nursing home. But I am not in labour.

At bath time, in the evenings, Daddy Doctor comes upstairs and they all laugh and splash together and Mummy Doctor says they must not be too excited just before beddy-byes and I am not at all sure what I should be doing so I stand there trying to smile and to look like a part of the happiness. I feel clumsy and in the way. I wipe the floor and the next minute it is all wet again which is quite good really because I can wipe it once more and look as if I am doing something.

Now, in the night two things are in my mind. One is the awful remembering of how I felt and do feel, when the thought comes to me, that there is no one for me to write to. I had never imagined this. Especially I took for granted the letters I sent to Gertrude and, perhaps even more as my right, the letters she wrote to me. All our letter writing stopped when I told her I did not want her advice and when she wrote to say she felt she had betrayed my confidence (her words), and I did not reply.

The second thing is that I understand that I am living through each small event of the day to get to the end of each small event. For example, like the bath time, I start off by looking forward to the end of it, to the time when bath time is finished, bath cleaned, floor wiped, bath toys hung up to dry and the little girls neatly in their beds and then I have to realize that this end to which I looked forward is nothing. I came to nothing, nothing at all. And straight away I am looking towards the end of the next thing. Like this evening when Daddy Doctor has to go back to his department for a meeting and Mummy Doctor says as we're going to be on our own we'll be cosy and eat our supper on the floor by the fire.

I can't wait for the end of this supper. It is some little pieces of boiled celery on toast. Mummy Doctor makes it. The celery is a bit burned and has a strong taste but it is not exactly that. It is more Mummy Doctor talking of where we'll put my baby's cradle and how she will make some little cot sheets and pillow cases out of some of my old hospital aprons and, though I long for the end of the evening, I can see too the prospect of my being here for ever in the house after my baby is born. I know that this is the arrangement but I have never considered it as I have to consider it now.

These are the heavy things in my mind.

It is strange too to think that I actually looked forward to Daddy Doctor being out for the evening when it is in fact easier to sit there while the two of them talk to each other. His absence contained, I thought, something I could look forward to like a promise of something nice because he would be out. When I think about my life before Dr Metcalf left for the war (which was in reality over), I was always getting through time and things, working towards the hours when I could be with him. This habit kept up now, when he is not here to be with, is of course a way of living which does not offer me anything except an unbearable emptiness.

I do feel I want to be at home with my mother. I know this is stupid. The very stupidity of the wish is enough to make me start crying. I know that after a very short time in my mother's house I always want to leave, to go on to some other place – somewhere else. Now, of course, there is nowhere else to go on to. I can't sit with Lois and Trent and Ferguson complaining about the food, the patients, the ward sisters or revising for exams.

'Infection takes the line of least resistance . . . '

'The patient is placed with the head lower than the pelvis . . . '

'That's not Sim's position, that's something else. For Sim's you have the semi prone, on the left side, both knees drawn up, the right more flexed than the left . . . Remember?'

'Ah! yes I remember. Now name the varieties of catheter . . . '

I can't laugh now with the others when Trent pretends to bandage a chair with a many tailed bandage. And I can't go to Gertrude's Place. It is easy to remember the field sloping up, deeply green, right up immediately outside her window, sloping up to the sky which always seemed to be low as if to rest on the rim of the soft grass.

And of course I am not able to write to any of them.

★

THE SECOND ANTENATAL VISIT

'Are you, at least, were you a gymnast, a gym teacher?' The doctor asks me on my next antenatal visit. 'Your muscles...'

'No,' I tell him, 'a nurse. I trained as a nurse.' This time I have come alone to my appointment.

'Ah Ha! All that walking, fast walking, back and forth,' he gives a little laugh. 'Walking not running. Nurses can only run for a fire, a haemorrhage and a vomit bowl. Correct?'

I give a small smile and a nod. He says, when he has finished the examination, that everything's fine. He says he's booked a bed for me at St Luke's nursing home. He suggests that I go, one afternoon, to see Sister Peters.

'Gladys will take you,' he says, 'they were at school together.'

'Gladys?'

'Yes. Gladys, my sister-in-law. Three Wellingtons,' he laughs, 'and one little pair.' He says the joke's wearing thin. It's clear that he loves his little nieces. 'The little pair of Wellingtons,' he says. I want to linger in his friendliness. I wish that he could remember me, not from my previous visit, I mean from when I was working at the hospital.

I almost tell him that I remember him. That in an exam once, a practical exam I pushed the monaural stethoscope towards him. Lois and I were in charge of the diagnostic instruments. He was supposed to diagnose a patient from her own description of symptoms and his own observations. The patient was simply pregnant. It was a trick question. A normal condition presenting symptoms. My pushing the monaural stethoscope towards him was the smallest movement, the slightest hint. Mostly, the doctors taking the exam, and being given that particular question, did not recognize the normal state of early pregnancy but diagnosed all kinds of hereditary conditions, tropical diseases and even diabetes and kidney failure.

I almost ask him, while he writes up my card, if he remembers Dr Metcalf. If, by any chance, he knew Dr Metcalf. Dr Metcalf would be older but they may have, at some stage, consulted or worked together.

I am dressed and ready to leave. Of course I can't speak to him about Dr Metcalf. And of course I don't really remember him from a doctors' practical exam. It is just that I wish so much to remember him, to be able to talk to him, a sort of hope and a wish for some kind of conversation of remembering with perhaps something to laugh about.

'A shared practice,' he is saying. 'Next time you will see my colleague Dr McCabe. She is very nice and will look after you well.'

I remember McCabe. Some of the nurses called her the cold fish. They did the supra-pubic catheters themselves, during the night, rather than call her from the residents' corridor.

Dr Heartless, Trent said once and we all agreed. It can be a disadvantage to know the doctors but when training in a large teaching hospital it is inevitable.

I walk back to Clifton Way instead of taking the bus even though I know it says in my *General Text Book of Nursing* (seventh edition 1942) that a pregnant woman who does housework and shopping does not need to take a walk every afternoon. I consider the hedges as I walk, the varying states of the bushes, some well cared for and others neglected. Since I am alone I do not need to study the hedges as carefully as I do as a rule. I notice the places where railings, sacrificed for the war, have been removed and I look into the laurel and the privet, the rhododendrons and the holly, evergreens in a series of repetitive quartets. There is one garden scattered with toys, a doll's pram on its side and three tricycles crashed together on the path. I like this garden and wish that it was my place with the children's toys all over it and a husband coming home in the evening.

When it is time to register my baby, though she will have to have my surname, I shall have her father's name, Dr Jonathon Metcalf, in the place for *father's name* on the birth certificate. Who will see this certificate? I mean, my mother and father will not see it, neither will Lois, Trent or Ferguson. And certainly Magda will never see it. The garden with the wild toys and this thought about the certificate make me reasonably pleased.

Mummy Doctor's sister will be coming soon for her short visit. Saturday is to be considered my free day, though this can be changed if necessary. Sundays I can have some time to myself in the afternoons. Sometimes I sleep the free time away and sometimes I walk out here to the far end of Clifton Way to this little park where there is a small lake. Just now I sit on the bench nearest the water and watch the small choppy waves as they hurry, in the wind, towards the shore. It is not at all sheltered here and the wind is cold.

I sat here, in this little park, once with Dr Metcalf. Once, before I was to go home for my day off. The Red bus passes the end of Clifton Way, mostly anyone who is in the park is waiting for the bus. Dr Metcalf was due at the hospital for Mr Lemmington Frazier's theatre list at nine and I was waiting for the eight-thirty bus. That day Dr Metcalf said that because of me, because of his knowing me, it did not seem, any longer, as if the whole world consisted entirely of haemorrhoids. It was summer then. We laughed here on this bench and watched the ducks and I forgot I was waiting for a bus, and that in a few minutes I would have to leave him. When I remembered suddenly that I had to go on the bus without him, I cried and told him I couldn't go and I begged him to take the day off, to stay with me. Very gently he explained that he had to go to his work and that I must go on the bus. It was summer then but, without my realizing it, the summer was ending.

I began that day, from the bus window, to look into these hedges, closely watching the hedges for as long as they lasted.

It is while I am sitting here frozen on this bench in the little park, on my way back from my appointment with Dr Wellington G.P. that I make a decision. I have been sitting here for some minutes staring at the regular movement of the icy waves on the lake – it is more of a duck pond really. I decide to stop being such a sad and depressed person. It is not good for anything. And all my sorrow, no amount of sorrow can bring anyone, or any times, back. There is the possibility too that Dr McCabe will either be on holiday or ill. She might even be dangerously ill when I start in labour and then I might have Dr Wellington G.P. for my delivery after all.

I walk on alongside the hedges. Dib Dib, this Dib Dib will be with us soon. She is good fun, Mummy Doctor has said so several times. Dib Dib's visit hangs heavily above the house. I can't help wondering what her fun will be like. I think it will be best to go home for my day off this Saturday.

It occurs to me too that I have made some decisions, important decisions, in one afternoon.

✳

FRAU MEISSNER'S
BATHROOM WINDOW

'Your father's at the station. He went early on purpose to meet you.'

'I came on the Red bus.'

'Never mind. He'll wait for one more train and then come home. Frau Meissner is locked out of her house,' my mother explains, 'and Rosa has gone to town with the twins.' Frau Meissner is, as usual, sitting at the kitchen table with a large cup of coffee in front of her. Rosa is mysteriously related to Frau

Meissner who uses the twins' green ration books often, for her own purposes. Frau Meissner is one of the people my mother has tried to help from the time of her forced exile and her arrival as a refugee before the war. She often walks into the pantry and looks at various plates and dishes saying, '*Das schmeckt mir nicht*,' before taking her place at the kitchen table. My mother with an unusual good humour pays no attention to this.

I keep my overcoat on in the warm kitchen. My mother puts a cup of coffee on the table for me. I am not able to take my coat off in front of the visitor because she will see at once how things are with me. The coat is no longer all that much of a disguise, but I keep it on all the same.

'Good morning Frau Meissner,' I say in a cheerful voice. I have come home for my free Saturday. I am keeping to my resolution not to be a depressed sort of person.

'What about your rations?' my mother asked when I telephoned to say I was coming home for the day.

'I shall be able to bring a piece of corned beef,' I told her.

'It doesn't matter,' her voice changed, 'your father fetched some eggs from Gertrude.'

My mother worries dreadfully that she will not be able to provide enough food. She is generous to all kinds of people. She tries to make people friendly by giving gifts of food.

'Frau Meissner is locked out of her house,' my mother explains again. 'The door slammed with her key on the table.'

Frau Meissner spoons up the generous amount of sugar, she has taken, from the bottom of her cup. She leans forward and reminds me that she remembers that when I was a schoolgirl I often climbed, for fun, on to the coal-house roof and then from there climbed up into the house through the bathroom window. Her English is not very good.

'Barserum vindo,' she says. I see the gold fillings in her teeth when she smiles.

'It vos a game wiz you zen,' she says, 'bot could you not do ziss for me now?' she asks.

'No, she cannot.' My mother is bent over the sink showing

displeasure in the rounded back of her flowered overall. Frau Meissner leans closer towards me across the kitchen table.

'Pleess?' She gives another gold-tipped smile. She tells my mother that her coffee was very good.

'Pleess?' she says and gives me an encouraging nod.

'You are not to climb up,' my mother says quickly to me. I can see from her movements my mother is annoyed and agitated and afraid.

I, in my not being a depressed sort of person, say that of course I will climb into Frau Meissner's house and will unlock her front door for her.

'We'll go right away,' I say as if there is no change in me at all from being the kind of person who used to do all kinds of things, like climbing on the roof, to being the person who keeps on her winter coat in an over-heated kitchen in an attempt to hide herself, to keep hidden within herself her secret.

The hedges on the way to Frau Meissner's house are the same as the hedges in the streets round Clifton Way. I look into the hedges as we all three walk by. My mother says she is afraid the coal-house roof will be wet and slippery.

'What if you fall?' her voice is low and angry. 'And what if the window is too small now? You cannot do this thing! We should wait till your father comes home.'

We walk on. Frau Meissner's house is identical with my mother's. I know the coal-house roof and the bathroom window.

I look up at the roof and on up to the small window with some misgivings. The bathroom window seems to be very small and very high up. I cannot take off my coat, that is certain.

I pull the dustbin closer to the wall.

'She should not climb now,' my mother's agitation is evident. But Frau Meissner, her eyes bulging behind her spectacles, eggs me on.

'Warum nicht?' she asks. 'She is, how you say a fine young vimmin. *Sie ist eine Valkyrie.* Wiz her strenz she can do anyting she vants. See her beautiful skin! She is healsy und stronk und yong. She vill get me beck into ziss house.'

I put my whole effort into concentrating on being able to climb up from the dustbin on to the ledge of the coal-house door and up on to the flat roof. And then from there to place my foot on a particular bulging drain pipe and from there to draw myself up to the narrow window, to reach into the window, to open it fully, and from that move to the next move that of pulling myself up and into the narrow space.

When I am half way through the window the bath looks a long way down on the inside and my feet are no longer able to be supported by the pipe outside. I notice the greenish stains in Frau Meissner's bath. I am stuck. It seems I am too big to squeeze through the window. I should have taken off my coat. I try not call out in panic. I make one great twisting effort. It hurts my side and I am afraid but I lean down and am slowly head and hands down into the bath.

'You should not do things like this,' my mother says when we walk the shortest way home afterwards. I am sorry she has been frightened and I look closely into the hedges of the gardens. These are something the same as the hedges in Clifton Way but have more of the familiar about them. These are the hedges containing the secrets of childhood. I am relieved, for once, that I shall be at home for the rest of the day.

'I don't think Frau Meissner guessed,' my mother says. 'Do you?'

'No, I don't think she did.'

'Do you hurt anywhere?' She is anxious. 'Have you hurt yourself? Anywhere?'

'No, I don't think so.'

'I don't think she guessed anything,' my mother says once more.

'No, I don't think so.'

'She is always locking herself out of her own house.' There is a small note of complaint in her voice. 'Your father has to go there so often now to help one way or another. Always something wrong.'

'Yes,' I say. We are alongside the familiar hedges. My mother stops to speak to some neighbours. She holds her scarf, which is over her head, with both hands under her chin. I push my hands in my coat pockets and push the coat out in front. It hardly meets but my hands in the pockets give a casual appearance. At least that is what I hope. I look closely into the hedge and wait for my mother.

MY MOTHER'S HATS

I waited once high up in a window. My head was wrapped in bandages. I waited for my mother.

I waited for my mother to come. From the tall window high up, I could, if I pressed up against the glass look right down to the street. I could see the tram lines gleaming along the wet cobbles. I could watch the trams and I could see the people moving along the pavement in both directions. I searched this movement for my mother's white hat. She had a white hat with a broad, soft brim. She said she would wear the white hat so that I could see her coming. She said that when I saw the white hat in among all the people I would know that she would soon be there. So I waited. Everyone else had gone home. My bandage was low over my eyes.

'What are these stalks of dry grass here for?' I asked the nurse. She said they were not stalks of grass but only the rough edges of the bandage.

'It's a bit frayed,' she said, 'that's all it is. A bit frayed but it's all right.' The nurse disappeared through the door and I was alone at the window. The ward was empty, all the beds and cots were empty and the screens, pushed together, were folded in to a corner. No toys had been left out. I pressed closer to the window. It was a long way down to the street. The winter afternoon was beginning to get dark.

'Your mother's not coming,' another nurse came by, 'you're not going home, you'll have to stay here,' she said.

'I'll see my mother's white hat in a minute,' I told the nurse. The nurse looked out of the window.

'I don't see any white hat,' she said. 'She's not coming, your

73

mother. She must've forgotten you.' The nurse and another nurse laughed then.

'She is coming.' I couldn't say more because of the tears showing in my voice.

The hospital ward was closed because of scarlet fever. My mastoid dressing would have to be done in the out patients.

My mother had other hats. There was another one with a broad soft brim. A navy blue velour. Deepening the shadows round her eyes, it made her face fragile, increasing her delicate paleness. I liked this one very much.

'Why are you so sad?' I asked her once. 'Is it the hat?' She said she was not sad and yes perhaps it was the hat.

There was too a small round hat. Light coloured, a colour as of peaches and the colour wrapped in silk round the hat. A small veil went with this hat. A spotted dark gauze. My mother's eyes seemed to shine in the spider-web net as if they were caught there and pleased, all the same, to be caught. The soft peach of the hat was same peachy lining, smooth and fragrant, of the fox fur when that golden vixen lay asleep and yet not asleep, alive and yet not alive, on my mother's gently sloping shoulders before a concert.

'Your mother has such pretty arms,' my father said. The glass eyes of the fox were yellow, overflowing with tears which did not fall.

The white hat was the hat I was looking for. The people moved in both directions down there on the crowded pavement. A tram went screeching round the bend at the top of the hill and another tram came with a similar cry from the other side of the hill. Some horses pulled a brewer's dray up the hill. And suddenly there was my mother beside me, laughing. She had a new hat. A hat of fur encircling her head low just above her eyes. Her eyes were clear and bright and tender and laughing at the same time.

'Why do you cry so?' Her arms held me close.

'I thought you were not coming. I looked and I thought you were not coming.'

'Don't cry! Of course I was coming.'

Her cheek was cold and soft and smooth. I breathed in her scent and pressed my face to the soft smoothness and melted into it. I stayed against the softness of her cheek as if I could stay there for ever. As if I need never move away.

'Don't cry. See. I've brought a present.'

'But it's not my birthday.'

'It's a present for coming out of hospital. Hold it. Guess what it is. You can open it in the taxi.'

'Aren't your legs cold?' My mother has finished talking to the neighbours.

'Yes.'

'I suppose you can't wear a suspender belt now.'

'No.'

'Your socks look dreadful.'

'Yes, I know.'

In the hedge near the collapsing gate post there is a little piece of pink wool, thin like darning wool, caught in the green leaves. I have seen it before. I look out for it every time I come home. Because it is there and, because it is always there, I feel certain it means something which I have thought all along, that my baby is a girl. Beate, Beatrice, Baba, Baby.

For some reason my mother keeps the ugly scarf on her head in the house. It is a war-time habit this head scarf. Even though the actual war is over, in many ways it is still as if there is a war. As if the war will never really come to an end.

MY MOTHER'S BATHROOM

The evening after I have climbed up into Frau Meissner's bathroom window, my mother, back in her own house does not take off her coat and her head scarf. She rushes into the rooms and opens all the windows, in spite of the cold, saying that the air in the house is not good. And she begins, at once, to do some cooking, chopping noisily and frying and breaking eggs, real ones from her bucket of water glass, into a basin.

While I am upstairs washing my hair I hear her angry voice, subdued but quite clear, complaining.

'Just treating the house like an hotel. Coming in and then straight away hair washing, just as if house is hotel.' There is apparently another trouble too, a visitor has sent a parcel with a toilet roll in it.

'And I am always so careful about bathroom.' My mother's hurt anger is accompanied by crashings on the stove. 'It is not now the war time. Bathroom had toilet roll.'

It always takes time for my mother's mood to change. My father, not knowing the disturbance of Frau Meissner's command, tries to explain that the war caused people to send parcels with toilet rolls in them, that the war caused people to feel that they should be good neighbours. I hear his voice talking like a boulder in the middle of the flying utensils. It is sad, he is saying, that people only become good neighbours when there is a disaster to be shared.

'Insults!' my mother says, but my father persists saying that he had been shocked during the Great War because people, in the streets, had been so excited in anticipation of bloodshed. He had never expected, he says, that people would look forward to killing. His deep voice talks on, consoling.

I stay upstairs trying to rub my hair dry in the cold bedroom. For some reason I remember the way in which my mother had thrown some red sausages, once, across the kitchen table saying that, even if there was a war, she did not require visitors to the house to bring their own food. The guest, blinking behind thick spectacles, gathered up her unwanted gift in silence and, in a touchingly clumsy way, tried to stuff the sausages, not wrapped up, into her handbag.

'Come down,' my father calls upstairs. 'There's a nice fire downstairs.' When I go down my mother puts a hot plate of bacon and two fried eggs on the table in front of me.

'You must eat,' she says, 'before you go back.'

The wearing of the head scarf in the house makes me think she is about to go out again but she sits on her side of the table knitting furiously.

'I am always so careful about bathroom,' she says, not slackening her knitting speed.

'Soap too!' she says. 'How could she do this thing!' She pushes the tablet of soap across the table.

'It's not bad,' I say, 'the soap's not bad, it's violet. Who sent the parcel?'

'Recha,' my mother says, 'she was here last week to tea. We helped her years ago. Remember? When she was refugee?' A tear runs down my mother's cheek.

'Perhaps that day you didn't have any in the bathroom, perhaps it was a sort of hint?' I remember Recha very well. She mistook the lending of a dress for a gift.

'No, not so. Everything was in bathroom. I am always so careful about bathroom.'

I almost correct my mother; 'it is not usual, in English, to leave out the definitive article . . .' so that she will not make this mistake in front of neighbours, but I think better of it. She is upset and I am, after all, terribly hungry.

CABIN FEVER

A PAUSE

The poet Shelley compared the mind in creation to a glowing coal. How can I best describe my own state of mind during this pause on the twenty-fourth floor of a hotel in New York? This pause, this not going out of the hotel, as I had intended, is much the same as sitting in a suburban train within reach of a woman who looked like Ramsden *might* look after all the years which have gone by – and then, repeatedly, not speaking to her. To come to the end of a journey, several times, without asking the intended question intensifies the pause till it becomes a scar.

When I think now of my mother I think of the idea I have often had. Not a new idea, I am sure many other people have thought about it. This idea is to write down all the things I remember about my mother. One thing, of course, leads to another.

It often seems to me now that earlier, at the time of my mother's hats, when women wore hats to please themselves, to please other women and to please men, there were little pauses and spaces of mystery and respect between men and women. There was the exchanging of the small graceful nod, there was the lifting and replacing of a man's hat and the slight bringing together of the heels to accompany the hint of a bow. These small, hardly perceptible actions created a tiny pause between two people. In the exchanging of the greeting the broad soft brim of a hat could obscure, for a fraction of a second, the expression in a woman's eyes. There was, too, the bending over and the acceptance of a woman's lifted-up hand in order that the space immediately above the back of the offered hand could be kissed.

Long before the ugly head scarf, worn during the war and afterwards, there were the hats. The white hat, the navy blue velour and the little round hat wrapped in the peachy silk. The hats belonged to gallant attitudes of devotion. The quiet unobtrusive actions of greeting suggested the deeper feelings which might be contained, unobserved, in the conventional and the acceptable. The little pauses were a part of the artistic methods of manners and of love. These were picturesque and, with restraint, passionate and had often a beauty and a power, a grandeur even.

My mother, during the war, often listened, without making a secret of it, to Schubert Lieder on her records. Whenever she saw photographs or pictures of Churchill on newsboards or on the front of the *Radio Times* she tore them up. I always hoped she would not do this outside the newsagent's when I was with her.

Later, much later, at the time of his death, she sat with a neighbour in front of the neighbour's television set and wept all through his funeral.

'I was deeply moved,' she wrote in a long letter to me. A letter in which she described the funeral in great detail.

CLOSELY
WATCHED HEDGES

DIB DIB AND DUB DUB

'Oh but surely, Dub Dub, Beethoven's violin concerto is old hat nowadays. Surely no one *discovers* Beethoven now. After all, we discovered him years ago. Remember our gyrations to the old wind-up gramophone!' Seriously they are talking about music. Dib Dib's toast-crumbed knife plunges across to the square of hitherto untouched butter on its little painted saucer.

They, the sisters, call each other Dib Dib and Dub Dub. They have used these names since they were small children and they are quite shameless with the names. In the street, in shops and on buses and trains.

'Angle? Bangle? Love Auntie Dib Dib?'

'Of course they do. They *adore* you. You must know that.'

'And you, Dub Dub, you know I absolutely adore them.'

'It's Dib Dib's long weekend hols,' Mummy Doctor explains to me. The house is full of pet-names which, of course, I do not use. I mean, how can I?

Dib Dib is house mistress at a boarding school for girls. She will come again during her long holiday when I have to go to the nursing home to have my baby. This way, Mummy Doctor has already explained, she will be able to keep her post in the university department. Dib Dib will be coming back when she is needed and there is nothing for me to worry about.

Dib Dib, for this visit, is to sleep on the couch downstairs in the doctors' tiny study. They have cleared all their books and papers off the couch on to the floor. When I am away she will be able to have my room.

Dib Dib is good fun, the doctors tell me.

I watch from my cold bedroom, at the edge of the window, early, when they are all out in the garden with their skipping ropes, their feet pounding the fragile frosted grass in time to the horsey-mouthed counting and chanting of skipping rhymes;

I am a girl guide dressed in blue
These are the things that I can do

and:

My mother said
I never should
Play with the gypsies in the wood.

They are all out of breath in the cold morning air. The little girls have bells on the handles of their ropes.

The sisters do not look alike. Dib Dib, though much younger than Mummy Doctor, is much bigger. Very tall, with enormous thighs, she gives an impression of huge-ness. When I look at her it seems as if I am seeing her without clothes on. She is big in that way. I think of her in the Trendelenburg's position.

The two doctors are short, shorter than I am and, in the presence of the visitor, seem even smaller. The little girls are small partly, of course, because of being twins.

Dib Dib has an appetite. In the kitchen she pops things into her mouth during preparation and has often eaten most of the meal before it reaches the table.

Boarding school, they explain to me, makes you hungry. I do not tell them I know this and that, in any case, I am hungry in their house. Dib Dib attacks the butter saucer as if without any thought that it might be sacred. The doctors, it is clear, would never actually mention anything about not eating up the butter.

Running on the spot and high knee raising follow the skipping. As I watch them in their physical exercises my bedroom seems removed, for the time being, from them. In a small house it is not easy to ever feel private. I wonder where, in this small house, can two people really have the secret things of their lives, the things which belong with being together. However hard I try I am unable to imagine the two doctors undressing each other, playfully, fondly, unbuckling and unhooking each other, drawing off and slipping out of their clothes, leaving their clothes scattered where they drop them. They must have undressed each other, taking turns to unbutton something and pull something off, at some time. At least once, they must have.

I did see Daddy Doctor, once, tugging at a jumper, pulling it up over Mummy Doctor's head inside out, the neck of it being too small and it was caught on her ears which are quite big. But that is not the same thing. They had come in from a walk soaked in sudden rain. He was helping her because she, in a hurry, was upset inside the jumper. At least I thought she was upset but she showed no signs of being upset afterwards and went to fill the kettle as if nothing had happened. Neither of them laughed. When I think about it I don't think either of them said anything. They each have thick sensible dressing gowns which they put on for the two steps in one direction to the little girls' bedroom and for the two steps in the other direction for the journey from their bedroom to the bathroom. Dib Dib comes up from the study downstairs in her Burberry raincoat. It was not worth packing a dressing gown for two days. Her muscles seem to have the faint odour reminding of the school sports pavilion, a mixture of linseed oil and human sweat. It is not hard for me, in my mind, to put her up in Trendelenburg's, for examination only so that she does not have the benefit of an anaesthetic.

'J'ai une petite few pensees extrorodinaire,' Dib Dib confides in her sister while biting heartily into an enormous slice of breakfast toast. 'Dub.Dub, I mean, en français, *Doub Doub.*' She washes down the toast with a long drink of the concentrated orange juice which is meant for the little girls and for me because of my baby. '*Doub Doub,*' she says, 'avez vous considered les dangereusements de TB? Je mean vous bringez an autre dans la famille?' The school French is pathetic. I look down at my plate.

'Alors! Non, Dib Dib. Elle est straight d'ospital so we feel considerably au secours, savez? Staff TB Testé vouz comprenez? A l'ospital they would know, n'est ce pas?'

To add to this way of trying to talk so that I shall not understand Dib Dib turns to me and tells me that what I need is a three-mile walk after breakfast and she will supervise it if I can be spared for half an hour. She raises an eyebrow in the direction of the doctors as if to ask their permission.

I don't think that I can walk three miles in half an hour I tell them. Not now. I feel the tears coming to my eyes so I leave the table and go to the kitchen and start on the washing up.

I walk slowly, closely watching the hedges, the laurel, the privet, the rhododendron and the holly, the evergreens. Dib Dib is alongside. We are on our way back. I watch the hedges, mainly the places low down near the earth, trying to think of something other than this walk. There is a cold wind which makes my face ache. My real tears can mix secretly with the tears made by the wind. I think the cold has made Dib Dib's face ache too because just before we reached the little park at the far end of Clifton Way, the place where I always pretend to myself that I shall see Dr Metcalf again sometime soon, she said to 'right about turn'.

'I expect I am too slow for you,' I tell her on the way back.

It is my bath night. My turn for the bath. Looking into the hedges I long for my hot bath and then the warmth in bed afterwards. Out here by the hedges my bedroom is a sanctuary with a number of hours to go through before I can get to it.

The doctors share their baths. This is supposed to be a secret and private thing – as if two people could share a bath in this kind of house, even with whispering all the time and hardly moving in the water, and not be heard. The shared bath means that they can have two baths a week. It is not really an economy. One bath a week between them would be a real economy. They did not have their bath last night because Dib Dib, with the cunning bred in boarding schools for girls of good families, was up in the bathroom first and the water could be heard gushing for a long time filling the deepest of deep baths. Steam even appeared under the door. Something I saw at the hospital once when Trent said she would take cold baths in the mornings since the rest of us were doing it; but never in this house have I seen steam actually coming out from under the bathroom door.

'I don't suppose the thought occurred to her. I mean she didn't think...'

'Yes, she did. She laughed on the landing. She called out and laughed and said, "The wise virgin got here first".'

I heard the low voices of the doctors, indignant and consoling, and the sound of their bed as they turned towards each other in chilled resignation.

In the afternoon Daddy Doctor says he will take Angie and Barbie to see the rocks in his department so that Dib and Dub can play at being sisters together.

Mummy Doctor suggests I have a couple of hours to myself. 'A nice rest with a book,' she smiles at me. I tell her, 'Thank you,' and go upstairs.

Really I do not need to be here at all today but, in the arrangements, this Sunday is not my day off. Stupid really to have to be here. Two hours is not long enough for me to go anywhere. I mean, it takes too long to go to my mother's house and back.

The grey sky presses down on the winter trees. It seems that spring will never come, that my baby will never be born. I put on my light and get one of my books from my trunk. It is an art book, Monet with reproductions of paintings; *Au Bord de l'Eau* and *Camille sur la Plage de Trouville* and others.

On June 28 1870 Monet married Camille-Leonie Doncieux.
That summer was spent at the seaside resort of Trouville. Monet
commemorated afternoons on the beach with a series of small
paintings...

It is too idyllic for me to read. The word 'married' swims in
my tears. I long for such afternoons.

The afternoons at Magda's were nice. Sunny and warm. I think
of Magda, like the time she was baking and making a mess trying
to make a pastry for Quiche Lorraine. A luxury, because of the
butter and the chopped up bacon and the mushrooms. An onion
pie would be easy she said then, plenty of onions. The flour was
all up her arms and round her on the kitchen floor.

'So sorry Mrs P Darling,' she kept on saying, and Mrs P was
sour and did not reply. Magda made more mess because the
crosser Mrs P was the harder she worked. Magda often made
a terrible mess on purpose.

That afternoon, that was before Dr Metcalf had ever kissed
me, that afternoon Magda said she liked best the bit in the Hardy
novel, she couldn't remember which, when they are baking apple
pies.

'Practically out of doors, my deah, in a shed. So of course the
flour on the floor didn't bother anyone a scrap.' And then she went
on to remember a Chekhov story in which the air is laden with
the sweet smell of cherry jam, the jam being boiled in a copper
out of doors. 'Heavenly,' she said, 'to make jam like that.'

Why can't I be with people like them. Why did it all have to
change. Why can't I still be with Magda and Dr Metcalf.

I can hear music from downstairs. They must be playing some
records in the study. I open my door and go half way downstairs
to try to hear.

'It's Albéniz. Tango,' Dib Dib is saying. 'I love it.'

'An expressive counterpoint,' Mummy Doctor starts to say.

'Oh Dub Dub! Always so mathematical. Why can't you be more
romantic. Listen! Wonderful melodic music. Can't you feel the
ductile movement...' Dib Dib's voice changes suddenly and she
sounds as if she is crying. It is a kind of howl. She has burst into

tears in the middle of the tango.

'Oh Dub Dub,' she sobs, 'it takes two to tango. I know it's a cliché, but it's really true, that statement. What's wrong with me? Am I really so hideous?'

I go down three more stairs. The gramophone has been stopped.

'Why can't I be married with a nice husband and children and a house – like yours,' Dib Dib says between her sobs. 'I'm so sick of being house mistress. I hate boarding school. I really do.'

As I move quickly back upstairs I hear the low beginnings of Mummy Doctor's voice as she starts to comfort Dib Dib.

Back in my room I lie on my bed and stare at the darkening afternoon. There is a soft tap tapping at my door and Mummy Doctor's voice is asking me if I will make a pot of tea please and bring it to the study.

Weekends, the doctors wear shabby clothes. It is a sort of point of honour with them to wear crumpled ancient corduroy and Harris tweed patched with leather at the elbows. Mummy Doctor has a big jumper darned all over with the wrong colours, I mean the darning wool is not the same as the wool of the jumper. They stay in these clothes all weekend.

Because I am worried about my bath I ask, in my politest voice, half rising in my chair, to be excused from supper and am upstairs lying in my rightful share of the hot water while they are probably still hovering over the mathematics of sharing a hard-boiled egg, since I have said I do not want any, equally between three people instead of four.

As it is clear that I never help myself to the butter and, it is clear too, that they will never confront Dib Dib with any form of reproach about her taking such a lot, I feel quite safe to go downstairs very quietly, after they have all gone to bed, and eat a thick slice of bread spread with butter as thick as the bread itself. I help myself to a second slice and take it and the concentrated orange juice back upstairs to bed.

Who is to know whether Dib Dib, with her boarding school habits, did not have a midnight feast? Neither of the doctors will raise the subject with her. They will know it is a sort of boarding-school thing to do. They are far too concerned with their attempts at being well-bred, buttoned up, Trent would say, to ever mention the butter which was on the saucer. And as for the orange juice I have only taken my baby's share and have not touched the bottle belonging to the twins.

It is difficult to know real names from which the pet names are made. Dub Dub is nothing like Mummy Doctor's first name which is Gladys. I can only think it must have been some sort of game once upon a time, a make believe between them. But when I see them and hear them together I am unable to see any possibility of make believe.

Trendelenburg's position would be acceptable for both of them. Tilted so that the head is lower than the pelvis, with the ankles fixed to the lower flap of the operating table and the knee joints flexed exactly over the hinges. That way there is no danger of either of them falling into the anaesthetist's lap; but of course, if it is for examination only, then there will be no anaesthetist. This Dib Dib and this Dub Dub! If I ever do see Dr Metcalf again. I mean suppose, just supposing it is possible and I meet him in the little park at the end of Clifton Way, past all the closely watched hedges, the laurel, the privet, the rhododendrons and the holly, and if I do talk about Dib Dib and Dub Dub he will not begin to understand what I am talking about.

Already I am in a different world.

CABIN FEVER

The constant sound of motor horns and sirens, fire, ambulance and police is a kind of music in this city. This symphony of rising and falling noise and the endless voices on the television must be for a great many people what a mountain stream was for Wordsworth. Back home I have, instead of the screaming crescendo and the dying fall, the doves. They sidle to and fro, back and forth, along the edge of the roof above my window, endlessly scraping and tapping and rustling along the tremulous gutters. If there are doves or pigeons above the windows of this room I am not able to hear them.

Half asleep, wrapped in concrete and an indestructable nylon carpet it is hard to recall, because of the similarities in the present day hotels, which hotel, which town, which city, which country.

This hotel with an ancient hot-water pipe, unhidden and undisguised, passing across the ceiling and making its perilous descent just inside the bathroom door has retained its characteristics from an earlier time. The lamps have unreliable switches and the chairs are made of cane. Dust laden in the crevices they have faded chintz-covered cushions. The writing table is made of cane too. There is a shabbiness and a continuation of recognizable hotel towels, linen, furnishings and ornaments which have not yet been replaced by nylons, plastic and imitation marble.

Twenty-four floors down to street level, down on the opposite corner of the intersection there is someone living on the footpath. Gathered partly into a cardboard box and, partly surrounded by bags stuffed with rags and possessions, the person living there sits close into the space where part of the wall is at right angles to the rest of the building. Every few minutes I get up and go to the window to look through the blinds to see if there is any movement down there. Once, I saw the person crawl out, turn round and crawl back into the heap. That was at dawn. Since then the streets and pavements have become crowded with ordinary people on their way, to and fro, busy with all the things they have to do. The TV announces the temperature at below zero and that there will be light falling snow with the danger of snow freezing in places on the roads and on the footpaths. Watching at intervals the life of the pavement person, the movements rather, as it can scarcely be called a life, is becoming an obsession. I am timing my restless visits to the window, it is only four minutes since I last looked out.

There are a great many of these people who live on the streets. It could be that there are, on all the floors of these tall buildings, people inside going to the windows and peering out to look and to watch the people living in their heaps of boxes and plastic bags. Perhaps these people, inside the buildings, are recording too the number of times they get up, harassed, to go over to look down the great distance to the street.

This room is so warm. It is hard to believe that the temperature out of doors is below freezing. I remember once before in this city taking a long bus ride out to an old monastery. It was cold on the bus. The intense cold crept from my feet through the bones of my legs and up my spine. As the bus travelled through dreary streets of apartment houses I found I was actually longing to be inside one of those uncompromising rooms. It seemed then that the pale sunshine, as it lay slanting weakly across the boards of a covered broken window, or where it touched on the dirty curtains of another window, might have put some warmth into the room beyond. There were frozen fenced-in and locked playgrounds and small poverty-stricken shops, open from before six in the morning till late at night. The bus, that day, slowly ate up the streets and spat them out behind.

I have lost count of the hours or days I have spent in my hotel room. Sometimes it seems as if I have just arrived and the porter, having placed my luggage on the rack provided, has explained how the TV is turned on and, taking his tip, has gone. At other times, like today, when the femme de chambre, ignoring my 'Do not Disturb' notice on the door, insists on changing the bed linen. She cleans the bathroom crooning as black mothers croon to their little children. I would like to ask her to stay and sing some more but I busy myself over my papers on the cane table and do not say anything. I make some self-conscious notes in a handwriting much smaller than my real handwriting. I write about things done on purpose and then forgotten about and about other things which are done unintentionally and which, when we think we have left them behind, chase us later. I thought as my pen hovered fussily over the note how it would be possible to live in the setting and through the events of an Ibsen play but as if written by Brecht or Pinter. Music: Gustav Mahler. I laugh aloud at Mahler and wonder why I laugh. The conference is certainly no laughing matter. The conference, it is emphasized, is not directly a confrontation with AIDS though it is clear that several of the papers and much of the discussion will be reasonably close to the most grave and pressing problems in society. In the programme there are titles which indicate the nature of our study. *Symptoms of Panic Disorder. Cupboard Infections. A recent study of Closet Relationships.* Several surveys of Regional Inpatients' Units and the usual new discoveries about Diabetes and the manifestations of Anorexia. My own *Perspectives on Moral Insanity* contains various examples of present-day venereal infections drawn from my Thursday evening clinics.

All aspects of human life are being examined and a wide range of specialists are to be present; psychiatrists, physicians, surgeons, pharmacists, general practitioners, nurses and social workers. I look through the names hoping for the familiar and it seems that there is not one person, not one colleague whose name I know, present at the conference. I read through the lists again, once more, surely there must be someone...

Once more the water runs somewhere in the cavity of the wall and through the exposed pipe in my room. The ugly water pipe is the only familiar thing and is of course, I am able to be reasonable about this, the cause of the memories which haunt. Long ago water pipes like this one lined rooms, passages and corridors and, like this, were the then ignored source of heat and noise.

THE HILDA
STREET WENTWORTH

MY MOTHER'S VISIT

'I should never have given you the book about Elisabeth Ney.'
    'Whyever...She was a sculptor and an artist...She...'
    'She had a baby in that book without being married.'
    'Oh! Really!'
    'It must have given you ideas...'
    'Don't be so utterly stupid! How can you be so stupid!'
    'Keep your voice down. You don't want the others to hear you
speaking to your mother like that.'

It is a cold day with the wind howling outside. I can see the dull
green leaves of the trees shake as the branches toss wildly.
Occasionally there are bright patches of sunshine and the jug of
red tulips on the window sill suddenly seems alive. The light
shines through the red waxy petals. The day seems to be one of
warmth and sunshine changing suddenly to the greyness of rain
lashing in the wind. Smoke is whirled from the chimney pots
opposite. It whirls into space and blossom flies from some trees
in a nearby garden. My mother has come to visit me. She has
brought some lilies of the valley, her favourite flowers, in a small

green vase shaped like a stork.

Helena is in a little wicker cradle half hidden by a screen at the foot of my bed. I almost make a cruel remark that I suppose my mother is trying to pretend that the stork brought Helena. Perhaps the hardest thing is not having any visitors, I mean not having a husband or the baby's father to come. The other women have husbands who are also the fathers of their babies.

'My baby's father is dead,' I tell one of the women when she asks me. After that she does not say anything else. I lie far down under the blanket during the times when visitors are allowed. I try to read. I hope Helena will not go on crying. She has been drawing attention to us both and to the empty chair beside my bed. I have been reading where Virginia Woolf writes of 'the clock which marks the approach of a particular person' knowing that I have no such clock.

Helena cries the whole day, the first day of her life, a heart-broken crying as if she knows straight away some secret awful thing about the world into which she has come.

'Why does she cry so?' My mother's eyes fill with tears. She holds Helena trying to quieten her. I see something about my mother then, something which must have belonged in her life and which I have never seen before. She tells me she has brought a present. I unwrap small pink knitted things. They look like dolls' clothes.

'The clothes are very sweet,' I try to thank my mother. I did not expect her to come. Her journey will have been quite long and complicated. Two buses and a train as well as the walk to and from the buses. I try to thank her for coming.

Suddenly it is quite dark outside and snow flakes are whirling about against the panes of the tall window. I watch the snow. It settles on the green leaves and, melting, slides off the shiny surfaces. It is late for a snow storm. The crocuses and daffodils are in flower in the gardens, my mother says, the front lawn is pretty with them. I feel a fear about the snow instead of the half-remembered childhood delight when someone would cry, 'It's snowing!' A journey is made so difficult when it is snowing. I think how will it be when I have to leave the nursing home with Helena. My mother is saying she is glad I have called my baby Helena. It will be easier for her to spell when she goes to school. She sees that I am looking at the darkened sky and the whirling snow flakes. She looks towards the window too.

'It's not settling,' she says and she says she is sure it will be sunshine again in a few minutes. Before my baby is born I call her Beatrice, *the bestower of Blessings*. I feel her little round head in my side and I keep reading about Dante's love for Beatrice and how, in his poem, he sees Beatrice as being a guide through Paradise.

'No one calls anyone Beatrice nowadays,' my mother says. She explains that Helena means light and that the name is considered to be the symbol of beauty. 'And, in any case,' she says, 'the child must have a Saint name.' She says do I realize that over a hundred churches in England are called after St Helena because of a certain Helena who was made into a saint because, while she was on a pilgrimage, she dug up the True Cross in the Holy Land. 'Imagine,' my mother says, 'her having the good sense to take a spade in her luggage.' My mother says she has always liked the idea of a pilgrimage.

'You certainly made one to come here today,' I say. Helena is actually quiet for a few moments and my mother looks at me again, the tears welling up in her blue eyes.

'No,' I say as if she has spoken. 'I can't come home to you. I don't want you to sell your house and move because of me. I shan't come so don't do anything silly.'

Before she leaves my mother stuffs some pound notes into my purse.

I hold my baby. She is new-born and small and wrinkled with grief. I hold her close to my face and feel her soft skin. She smells clean, of Vinolia soap.

★

Magda's Visit

Magda's visit is a surprise. She seems tall in the doorway. Her arms are full of blue and yellow irises. She comes straight towards me.

'Precious child. Darling child,' she sinks down on the side of my bed and holds me close in her extravagant embrace.

It is then while Magda is strewing her flowers all over the white quilt that I try to take off Dr Metcalf's watch under the bedclothes. I do not want her to see the watch. I do not want her to see anything which might hurt her. But I think she does see though she does not show this.

Dr Metcalf gave me the watch, his watch. I have been wearing it ever since he gave it to me except when I was on duty and had to have it pinned inside the pocket of my uniform dress. He gave it to me up on the resident's corridor on the fourth floor of the hospital. We were just leaving his room, both of us, to go on duty. He said he wanted me to have his watch so that I would always think of him.

'I'll think of you in any case,' I told him then.

'I believe you really will,' he said looking at me closely. His eyes seemed deep and thoughtful. 'I believe you will,' and he kissed me.

'The watch strap,' I told him then, 'has your scent.'

'Has it a scent then? Do I have a scent?' he was laughing. We had to part at once, leaving the corridor separately so that we would not be seen together.

Always I am breathing in the scent of the leather strap trying to catch something of him.

'So. Is this why you stopped coming!' Magda leans over the

cradle. She moves the small fold of sheet with one jewelled finger. 'An angel,' she says softly as if to herself. She is dressed exquisitely in black, very high heels and with something gold at the throat with pearls showing a little below the gold. Her hair shines. Red gold, the colour of a fox.

'I've just come from the hairdresser, Darling,' she explains. 'It's more than half a year now and I'm still trying,' she says. 'And you, Darling Child, why didn't you come to me?'

Suddenly she is sitting close to me and talking about Dr Metcalf in that low intimate voice she has. Jonty, she calls him as she used to. She can't get over his death, she tells me, this unnecessary death and the war practically over when he went. 'That damned war!' she says. She tells me she dreams at night that she is with him at the Army camp near Swindon, that she is about to warn him, to stop him from being crushed by the lorry. 'As if I could ever have saved him,' she weeps silent tears without moving her head. The tears pour down her face.

'Magda, your make-up,' I want to warn, but she searches in her handbag.

'I've got a hanky somewhere here,' she says, 'I'll put my eyes back in a minute.' And then, laughing a bit while she's still crying, she shakes her head and says she's sorry and I feel I'm the one who should be saying something like that but I can't think of the right words.

In her handbag, Magda tells me, she has some seed pearls.

'These are for her,' she nods towards the cradle. 'Please,' she says, 'take them.' She explains they were a present to her from Dr Metcalf's mother. 'In a sense,' she says, 'they are a present from him.' She leans towards me with a kiss and somehow it is as if I am accepting the little necklace and saying thank you. As usual it is Magda who is doing everything. It is then she describes love which can be pure and fresh and unspoiled by all the squalid details of everyday living. 'You may not believe this now,' she says, 'but I actually envy you!'

I want to ask Magda how she knows where I am and how she knows about Helena. I don't need to ask because she tells me the next minute that she saw two of the nurses, girls, she says she knew by sight but did not know their names. She asked them about me, at the hairdressers.

'I guessed the whole hospital would know,' I say and I feel my face and neck all burning hot.

'Oh no, Darling!' Magda laughs. 'Only two of the gels and they were absolutely discreet. I really guessed.'

'Oh Magda!' I say. And she hugs me and kisses me again.

'Tomorrow,' Magda says, 'is the court case. Poor Daddy. But poor Mummy, even more poor Mummy.' She tells me that Marigold Bray, Mr Lemmington Frazier's tenth actress is taking him to court with all kinds of wicked accusations. The case comes up first in the morning.

'I expect the accusations are all true,' Magda says. 'That's the worst of it. Poor Mummy. I'll be there in court with her. Please think of us. Remember? I told you once that one or all of Daddy's *affaires* could ruin him, and Mummy too of course. It's the relatives who are so vindictive.'

I think of gentle Mrs Bray who worked in the public baths and who, on the day that Dr Metcalf left for the Front, consoled me behind the screens in the ward telling me he would be sure to come back. Marigold's real name was Edna and her mother wished she would come and visit.

'I can't imagine Mrs Bray,' I begin. 'She was one of my patients, very quiet and...She had a hernia...'

'Heavens no!' Magda says, 'it's Marigold's husband and his brothers and family. You never saw such a bunch of crooks.'

I have never before considered this kind of possibility that a whole unthought of family could become all at once something sinister. As if knowing my thought Magda says, 'This is the awful part, d'you see Darling, that you find yourself involved without wanting to be, and this goes for Daddy too of course, with the most awful people. The kind of people you could never have imagined existing. How d'you think I'll look in court?' she asks making her face into a smile. 'I mean, I'm dressed in a sober way aren't I, with just enough

elegance don't you think? And not too much expenditure.'
'Oh yes,' I say, 'yes dear Magda you will look...'
'The damned war!' Magda says again. 'And that man Smithers!
Oh why Smithers? Why did Jonty...?' Once more her eyes fill
with tears.
'I'm studying,' she says. 'I'm really trying to study. I'm going
to lectures on Comparative Religions. Next week,' she says, 'it's
Islam.'

I can't eat my dinner after Magda has gone. I keep crying even
though I'm hungry. I do not want Sister Peters to think that I don't
like her meal and I ask her how she makes the gravy so that it
is thick and dark. I try to ask her but I cry instead. Sister Peters,
trying to be kind, asks if I have a picture of Helena's daddy and
I say I haven't. She wants to know if I have a letter or anything
belonging to him that I could look at and I say no I haven't and
I go on crying. How can I tell her that Dr Metcalf is Magda's,
that he belongs to her and she belongs to him? And because she
has just been to see me I can't help crying. How can I tell anyone
this?
Sister Peters moves me into a small room before the evening
visitors come. She says I can have the room to myself. She says
lots of women have a good cry after childbirth and she says I'm
not to worry about anything. She fetches the pudding from the
dinner tray. It is a little steamed ginger pudding with treacle and
custard. It is very nice and I ask her how she makes all the little
puddings like this. She explains that she has a whole lot of cups
without handles and she uses them to make the puddings. While
she talks to me she changes Helena and admires her and says she's
very intelligent with a well-shaped head, long fingers and
aristocratic limbs. It comforts me to hear these things. I feel I want
to tell Sister Peters that Helena is Dr Metcalf's little girl. But of
course I can't. Instead I show her the seed pearls.
Sister Peters admires the little necklace and says that it is
probably an heirloom handed from one generation to the next.

'They were given to my friend,' I explain, 'and she brought them.' We look at the seed pearls together. They nestle, glowing on silk, inside a pretty little box made of beaten gold decorated with tiny blue and pink enamelled flowers. Sister Peters thinks they are forget-me-nots.

Sister Peters says I should have a tablet and go to sleep early. She says she will put Helena's cradle in her own room for the night. She tells me that her husband has just bought two hundred scrubbing brushes.

'He's sitting in the kitchen now,' she says, 'trying to work out a way to sell them and the two hundred buckets he...' She pauses. 'Two hundred buckets,' she says, 'that came with the brushes. They're all flawed,' she says, 'there's something wrong with every one. He's got to find two hundred people who won't notice the flaw...Imagine!' Sister Peters gives me a tablet.

Though it was snowing a bit during the afternoon it is really the spring, seriously the beginning of the summer. The evening is light and is a daylight evening. I think of the loneliness of the long light evenings of summer.

The branches of the sycamore immediately outside the narrow window of this little room are tossing in the wind and the fresh new leaves are shaking towards me and away from me. The leaves seem to have nervous little faces they seem to be talking, passing on messages, just out of my hearing.

Magda looked as if she was on the way somewhere. She is trying to get on with her life. She looked dressed up for going out to some place. If she dressed simply to come to see me then she would be at home now, sad and alone, taking off her nice clothes and putting them away. Perhaps she had a practice dress up ready for the court case tomorrow. Perhaps she is putting on the old dirty dressing gown made of towel material. She wears it when she's ill or sad.

Was it Ferguson or Trent or Lois talking in the hairdressers? How could they explain to Magda what had happened to me since I never told them? Trent would never go to a hairdresser, come to think of it, neither would Lois or Ferguson. We always did each other's hair. And in any case it's practically six months since I ran away from the hospital.

What is it that hurts Magda most? It seems I am not the only one causing her the greatest pain. It is Dr Metcalf for going away when he did not need to go, she says, when the war, which seemed to be never ending, was really coming to an end. Smithers. Smithers, she says, Dr Metcalf, Jonty, Magda says, wanting to be with Smithers. She said once that a person will travel the length and breadth of a country to be with the person they want to be with. Is this, is it this which hurts Magda so much or does she understand it and resign herself? Islam, she used the word, means to resign oneself, to accept, to submit.

Smithers, which one was Smithers? The pale orderly in theatre who looked as if he steamed himself every day in the sterilizer – in with the instruments – or was Smithers the shave orderly? Or was he Lemmington Frazier's rectal orderly? Was he all three? How can I forget certain things, Smithers for example, so quickly? I don't suppose it matters. Except that it was for Smithers, Magda explained once, that Jonty, Dr Metcalf, went away. Smithers, I remember now, wrote poetry. I remember he once asked me to read a poem he had written.

The buckets all have something wrong with them, Sister says, they are flawed. Perhaps they all have a small hole somewhere or perhaps they don't have handles...

I lie in for the customary fourteen days and when I am allowed to get up for the deep hot bath Sister Peters says I can have, my legs are so weak I can hardly stand.

★

THE HILDA STREET WENTWORTH

'The little white collars. I love them.'

'The little white collars?' My mouth is full.

'Yes. You know, the little lint collars you've made.' Sister Peters' mouth is full also. She tells me I am the first person to do her castor-oil bottles like this. She has in the past, she says, had various nursing assistants but not one of them ever cleaned out the medicine cupboard.

I have washed and polished the glass water jugs too and Sister Peters is pleased. She says the medicine cupboard is a treat, quite different now, not swimming in castor oil for one thing and a lot more space now the empties have been thrown out.

There is a lot of castor oil in this place. It is given on white earthenware spoons. The oil floats on orange juice and this makes it easier to swallow. It is given before all the births. Many of the mothers think it makes for an easier birth, Sister Peters says, they don't really understand the orifices in their own bodies. And castor oil is not expensive. Some doctors prescribe it to accompany the normal enema.

'This cheese,' Sister Peters says, 'it's mouse-trap but it's not bad, not bad at all.' She has a rabbit sitting on her lap. We are all, Sister Peters and her husband, Mr Hoob Peters, and me sitting by the kitchen range eating all our cheese ration at one go. Sister Peters fancied a cheese and pickle supper. We have a whole square of cheese each and some new brown bread. I have one more week of my month, paid for by my mother, at the Hilda Street Wentworth nursing home.

'No pickles for you!' Sister Peters says to me, 'they'll turn your milk. Hoob!' she says to Mr Peters, 'she mustn't have pickles.'

'If we had strawberries,' Mr Peters forks the onion off my plate on to his, 'you wouldn't be able to have them either.'

'Bad for your milk.' Sister Peters jumps up then pushing the rabbit off her lap. 'Look at that, will you. Wet me right through.' The rabbit, with her heavy under-carriage, hops towards a corner of the kitchen.

'She's due any minute, I'd say,' Sister Peters nods towards the rabbit and tells Mr Peters he should get on with the hutch. They are going to keep rabbits, like they keep the fowls, Sister Peters explains, to put towards the patients' food. She has to feed the patients well and it is quite a struggle to do this. That is why they are trying to grow the quick summer vegetables.

For the last three days I have been helping in the nursing home, carrying basins of warm water to the lying-in mothers, changing babies, carrying away basins to empty them and preparing the hot baths for the mothers who are now able to get up for a bath. Not only do all the glass jugs on the bedside lockers sparkle but all the brass taps and window fittings in the big old-fashioned bathroom are bright and shining; especially in the late afternoon these taps really glow. I have polished them too. I have fed the fowls twice now for Mr Peters and I told him I would like to weed his vegetables. I feel much stronger. I enjoyed cleaning the medicine cupboard, especially I liked putting the neat little circles of lint on the oily necks of the bottles – something I learned to do at the beginning of my training. The white collars on the dark-blue castor-oil bottles remind me of staff nurse Ramsden. I never actually saw her cutting out these collars but I can picture her doing so, meticulously and in the perfection of a silent concentration. I am reminded of Ramsden too when I mix the deep hot baths for the patients who have had their fourteen days in bed. Ramsden, who could reach unspeakable heights in an intellectual conversation with staff nurse Pusey-Hall, ranging from music theory to deeply religious philosophy, sounded like a poet when she described the bathing of a patient in Obstetrics Ward 4. She said then that the warm soapy water should be deep and that the patient should be encouraged and shown how to give herself a thorough washing of the vagina and surrounding areas. Many women, she said, did not understand how to wash themselves and it was the duty of a good nurse to teach this.

In the sharp fragrance of the medicines and the antiseptic lotions, on the lower shelf, I felt restored and happy and Helena slept peacefully, for once, while I was busy.

I do not want to go back to the house in Clifton Way.

'I don't want to go back to the Wellingtons,' I say suddenly to Sister Peters and Mr Peters. 'Can't I stay here with you and help with the work?' I ask them.

Sister Peters shakes her head.

'There's two reasons,' she says. 'One is simply that I can't afford to pay anyone, and the other is that I was at school with Gladys and she would be upset thinking that I've taken you away from her.'

'There's never more than one reason, one real reason,' Mr Peters interrupts. 'A person can't have two reasons that really matter,' he says, 'and this real reason is that we can't pay. You don't give a damn about the Wellington woman. You never liked her at school, you've said so yourself.'

'All the same, Hoob, she'll think...'

'Bugger what *she* thinks! Vera here might like to sell the buckets and the scrubbing brushes, it's up to her...'

'Oh really, Hoob! Of course she can't. Do have some sense for once. Those buckets and scrubbing brushes, she can't eat them or live in them.'

'I don't mind not being paid, really I don't,' I say. 'Please let me stay here, please. I can't go back there.'

I help Sister Peters take the six babies round to their mothers for the ten o'clock feed before going to sit in the small room, which is almost like a cupboard, to feed Helena. I want to stay here with Helena. I feel I cannot face, in spite of all the kindness, that other house. Mummy Doctor has been to see me several times bringing crayonned pages for Helena from Angie and Barbie and some little clothes, pretty treasures, saved from when the little girls were newly born. And, one time, she brought a surprise parcel, some clothes she made in secret, perhaps sitting up in bed late at night in the quietness of the sleeping household with Daddy Doctor snoring politely on his side of the bed.

Daddy Doctor and Mummy Doctor, the Wellingtons, would never eat cheese the way we have eaten cheese this evening. Mummy Doctor would make a thin cheese sauce to pour over some boiled carrots or onions. Or, she would mash a tablespoon of grated cheese into a saucepan of boiled potatoes. Or, she would cut some cheese in thin slices, almost like paper, and toast it on very thick slices of bread. The cheese would be made to seem endless, the only trouble being that no one would know it was there at all.,

The two doctors graduated together, at the same graduation ceremony. They very nearly didn't. To begin with Daddy Doctor was already a year ahead of Mummy Doctor – at the time of the sharing of the Bunsen Burner. He was demonstrating that day, when the crucible shone white in the intense heat of the blue flame, that a mysterious substance became heavier as it burned in air. Daddy Doctor, for a whole year, marked time with deep breathing and thinking about something else till Mummy Doctor was up to where he was. Of course they were not doctors then and only one of them was a Wellington.

I do not really want to think of them while I am here in this place but I do keep thinking of them like this; Daddy Doctor and Mummy Doctor. The Daddy one putting his mind on something else and, with held breath, waiting till the Mummy one is ready. Their separate pillows, when I was in their house, were always indented neatly where their heads, well ordered, in separate hollows, had been all night.

The Peters' bed is hardly ever made. One of them is nearly always in it, mostly Mr Peters, snatching a nap, as Sister Peters calls it. The babies are often born at night. Sister Peters says the only thing Mr Peters is reliable about is when he says he's going for a sleep. Their bedroom opens off the kitchen. Sister Peters says it's best to be downstairs. She can bring troublesome babies down there at night.

Before I go to bed I go down to the kitchen, quietly, and set the six trays for the patients' breakfasts and I cut a neat plate of bread and butter which I cover with a clean damp cloth. I like the night silence of the Hilda Street Wentworth, everyone asleep for once. Sister Peters says that newborn babies mostly sleep well. It is only when they get home they start bawling their heads off. Back upstairs in my small room I write a letter to Mummy Doctor telling her I am not able to come back and will she please send on my trunk, which is all packed, to this address.

I packed everything (some things had not been unpacked) during the night I started in labour so that Dib Dib, when she came to stay, would have cupboard space for her things.

They are so concerned about health, the two doctors, accusing each other, with affection, of bringing home a cold. They gargle at night with hot salty water if they feel they have been breathed on in a bus by someone who seemed to have a cold.

Dib Dib, in particular, was afraid I might harbour diseases, something mysterious and infectious brought from the hospital.

Night Sister Bean once, during a lung haemorrhage, paused in her ward round to tell me that I should not take such a personal responsibility, that there are times when another responsibility takes over and I must learn to recognize that. She waited beside me at the bedside during the choking rush of blood and watched while I cleaned away the clots and removed, as quickly as possible, all traces of the haemorrhage. Afterwards she got down on her knees and, leaning on the bed, she drew the man's head on to her arm and prayed there beside him. She said to me to follow the prayer in my heart so that I would know it for another time if she was not with me. In between the words of her prayer she muttered to me that it was very important to nod and smile during haemoptysis as if everything was going to plan and was satisfactory. She said too to always remember that there were times when the proximity of a sympathetic nurse was the only remedy.

Night Sister Bean at the time I am thinking of – at that time – had been on night duty for thirty years. She was said to be a witch. They said never let her look directly at a blood transfusion. They said always stand between Sister Bean and the drip. If she looked at the drip, they said it would stop.

Sister Bean said that if a patient lay in bed with his arms folded under his head he was awake. No one, she said then, sleeps with the arms in that position. A person lying like that in bed should be promised a cup of tea. The nurse, she said, should tell him that she is going to make some tea even if she knows the tea and sugar ration tins on the ward are quite empty.

The patient, Sister Bean said, in the relaxation of knowing tea is being made will usually fall asleep in the time it takes to boil a kettle. In the event of a failure, he should be slipped a Mickey Finn.

At the Hilda Street Wentworth the patients all sleep well. If a baby is noisy in the night the cot is pulled away from beside the mother's bed and put in the bathroom or downstairs. A delicate baby enjoys the honour of being at the foot of the Peters' bed. Both the Peters will walk the floor with a fretful baby, all night if they have to, but this does not seem to happen often.

When Dib Dib was worrying about tuberculosis, it somehow did not seem possible for me to explain to her and to the Mummy and Daddy Doctors that, in spite of being close to disease, I do not think I am anything but immortal.

If I post my letter first thing in the morning the doctors and Dib Dib (whose special leave from school is about to end) will receive it in the afternoon post.

When I set the Hilda Street trays I search the sideboard for the best spoons and I choose cups which are not chipped and which have saucers to match. I am pleased with the neat breakfast trays and I roll up the sleeves of the overall Sister Peters has lent me. With an extra high rolling up of the sleeves I feel efficient. I go to answer the front door with Helena tucked under my arm, dangling in her shawl, carelessly, as the midwives carry the babies.

'The head's on the perineum,' I tell Dr McCabe. She, with her black bag, sweeps past me and goes straight upstairs. We have just admitted an emergency, a multipara premature, a seventh child.

'Vera!' Sister Peters calls over the bannister. 'Mrs Thingummy's worried about her rhubarb jam. Tell Hoob, will you, to go round on the bike and turn off the gas. Her back door's open. Same address as before.'

Dr McCabe isn't such a snow storm after all. She actually smiled when I opened the front door. She was not bad at my delivery either, though for the last part I was hysterical and had to be put out or under as they say. That was not McCabe's fault. It was me not able to handle childbirth as I thought I would be able to. The marks of the forceps are disappearing. Sister Peters says this every time she looks at Helena.

Everything is sweet and nice at the Hilda Street Wentworth. The lines of nappies and towels blow in the damp wind. Every day we hope for the sun. Two mothers and their babies will be leaving and two more patients will be coming in. Mrs Rhubarb is resting uneasily after her seventh boy. She cries when I give her a bowl of warm water for a wash. She wished, she says, for a girl.

'What did you get?' She looks up at me, her eyes overflowing with tears.

'A girl,' my voice an apology, sounding vague, as if I'm not really sure what I gave birth to. She understands, though, that I have a girl and weeps afresh.

'People often cry after childbirth,' I console, trying to be wise like Sister Peters.

'I should know,' she says.

'I'm the only one here with a boy,' Mrs Rhubarb says.

'They come in runs,' I say. I've heard Sister Peters say this too. 'All boys and then all girls. Uncanny. Really!'

The new baby gets called Rhubarb Jam by everyone.

It is sunny in the garden and for half an hour, a little gift of time, I thin out and transplant some tiny cabbage plants. My knees make hollows on the warm earth and the doves in Mr Peters' dovecote, a ramshackle affair which Sister Peters declares should be taken down before it collapses, talk to and fro softly; a contented murmuring reminding of the tiny gulping noises when the new babies are feeding all at the same time. This gentle and sustained music is a reminder of the incredible contentedness which accompanies the temporary moments of pleasure while hunger is satisfied and survival for the next few hours is promised.

Because of working in the garden, whenever I have the chance, my legs and arms are already sunburned and I feel stronger every day. Only one thing disturbs my peace and that is that any day now I shall have to receive a reply to the letter I sent to the two doctors. I dread the arrival of the postman and, worse, a visit from Mummy Doctor.

The Hilda Street Wentworth is a large old house which has been partly converted. The previous owners of the nursing home called it St Lukes, a name Sister Peters likes but forgets to use. She likes the notion, she says, of St Luke being the patron saint for physicians and surgeons and the symbol of the wingéd ox is particularly pleasing. She intends always to say 'St Lukes' when she picks up the phone but before she knows it she has said, 'Hilda Street Wentworth.'

The rooms in the house have honey-coloured floor boards and there are trees, fresh with the leaves of early summer, immediately outside the windows of the rooms facing the street. Some patients stay only for the fourteen days of lying in and others stay for the month. Those mothers who are up do most things for themselves and their babies, and they walk out into the garden to sit on the lawn with their babies and their visitors. I still find it unbearable when the husbands are visiting and I have to overhear the little jokes about plucked chickens and force myself to smile.

Sister Russell is here today as there are two patients coming in, probably on their way already. With each new birth two things happen to me. One is that I am overwhelmed every time with the strength and determination of the newly born individual and how each one resembles the one born previously but is, in fact, entirely different. The second thing is that I am unable to stop recalling my own experience. On that day Mummy Doctor made a milk pudding with some rice and jam. And, in order to have enough milk, she rinsed out the empty milk bottles with a tiny drop of water and added the milky water drops to her pudding. I thought it was strange that she should do this so calmly when I was starting up in labour. All that day and all the night I was slowly approaching Helena's birth day. I had the same thought early in the morning about a woman in the garden overlooked by the window in the Hilda Street Wentworth. This woman was hanging out her washing while I was walking up and down the long passage and pausing to look through the window while my pains came and subsided. It seemed, at the time, impossible that anyone could be so peaceful, at *this* time, as Mummy Doctor was with her drips of milky water and this woman, too, with her clothes basket and her hands nimble among the clothes pegs. I watched her going from clothes basket to clothes pegs to clothes line, a gentle rhythm of movement, interrupted only as she gave each garment a shake before hanging it on the line. This extraordinary peace was within calling distance of the confusion of pain and drama about to take place in my own body. It seemed to me then that the most vivid and beautiful thing I had ever seen in my life was a white sheet, folded and pegged, beginning to billow against dark-green foliage. I thought too, on that day, that the sheet was in a place where it was too damp and leafy for it to dry properly.

At the Hilda Street Wentworth we make a rice pudding or a blancmange every day. Sister Peters is never short of milk because, in addition to what she is entitled to have, the milkman comes to her last and leaves half a crate, or sometimes a whole crate of extra bottles. He is glad to off load them.

I work very quickly with the cabbages and splash some water on them. I can hear Helena crying in the kitchen. I have her little cot in there every day now. Trying to keep ahead with the work and trying to squeeze in little extra things like working in the garden I fully understand that I am, all the time, evading the burden which is on my mind. And this is the immediate burden of the doctors and my not going back to them as arranged. I am paid with a cheque every month and I fully understand that this way of being paid requires a month's notice on both sides when it comes to leaving or being asked to leave. If I look beyond the immediate there is the question of where can I go with Helena if Sister Peters refuses to have me stay. I know she would not *refuse* but it really may not be possible for her to manage to keep me. I am, for one thing, taking up the tiny room she likes to keep for use either for emergencies or for special reasons...

I am in the kitchen. Sister Peters and Sister Russell are upstairs. Both the labour rooms are in use and Dr McCabe is on her way. Mr Peters has been putting up some shelving which, he says, he picked up for peanuts. The kitchen is in a mess with tools and dust and plaster everywhere. I have Helena under one arm and I am stirring a big saucepan of soup made from the carcasses of two boiling fowls and some cut-up onions and carrots and potatoes. I cover the saucepan with a tea towel to stop the dust falling into it. Mr Peters' drill is screaming and Helena, who is not yet bathed and fed, is crying when suddenly two stout women in navy blue out-door uniforms wheel their bicycles up to the back door. They come into the kitchen without knocking. One of them explains that no one answered the front door, and the other one says they have come to see me and my baby. Immediately I feel afraid of them. Mr Peters turns off the drill and explains about the shelves. They ignore him and ask me what I am doing and why am I standing at the hot stove holding the baby and will I prepare her bath as they want to see me bath the baby. They will need to see the cot too – *if* she has one. I understand, at once, that they are Health Visitors checking on me. I understand too that Mummy Doctor will have been obliged to tell them where I am.

The two Health Visitors poke about the kitchen and examine everything. They look in at the Peters' bedroom and mutter to each other. I show them Helena's little cot, not too clean this morning, and pushed in behind the kitchen door. With great speed I prepare the small zinc bath which I now use for her. For the last three days I have bathed her in the kitchen in front of the range.

The two visitors sit, knees apart, skirts stretched, on kitchen chairs and watch me bath my baby. They watch me feed her. They each, in turn, pass a hand over her little round head and mutter in low sinister voices about the anterior fontanelle.

'You haven't spoken to your baby at all, not the whole time we've been here,' one of them accuses. 'You used to handling babies? Eh? You had several? Paid for your pleasure with pain eh? Didn't think of that did you? Can't have the one without the other, can you!'

Only this one. I want to tell them. Only this one.

Where's her daddy? they want to know next. Even though they will have all the details.

'He's dead, you say he's dead. We've heard that one before, haven't we?' They nod knowingly, lips in thin lines and chins pressed down and back.

I change Helena to the other breast.

'Oh Ho! That's a quick change. Not much milk, I see, losing your milk eh?'

They want to know why I am still in the private nursing home. Surely I was booked in for the two weeks only, just for the lying in and not the whole expensive month. 'Who's paying?' they want to know. 'Your mother paid, you say. Did she now! Private nursing home!'

'Did she now! That's a very generous mother you have, or is it your Gentleman Friend, is it? Is that who's paying?' They sit square on their chairs looking at me. One of them, as if struck by a thought suddenly, asks if I have my other children here with me.

'You seem very experienced,' she says, 'handling this baby, much too quick and easy with the baby. Can't believe it's a first. Are the others here with you?'

'That's enough!' Mr Peters, in the corner with his tool box, stands up suddenly. 'She's a nurse that's because and why.' His voice is unlike his usual voice.

'Oh Uncle, there you are,' I say, surprised at my own words. 'Uncle I didn't know you were still here in the kitchen. Could you please hold Helena for a few minutes. I must see to the soup.' My legs are shaking and I feel I will cry.

Mr Peters holds out his dirty hands.

'Come to Uncle Hooby,' he says. 'Come along to Uncle Hoob.' He takes Helena and holds her up to his face and then puts her up to his shoulder and pats her back gently.

'Clear up the bath quick, then Vera,' he says to me. 'Her lady-ship, your Anti, will be down soon. Her and Sister Russell and the doctor will be through upstairs soon and they'll be down here looking for a bite of lunch.' He turns to the Health Visitors.

'You two ladies like a bowl of soup?' He jerks his head in the direction of my enormous saucepan. The visitors scrape their chairs on the tiles as they get up; they do not want soup, thank you. They must be on their way. Thank you very much!

Mr Peters jogs Helena on his arm and guides them to the door.

'Call in any time,' he tells them. 'Vera's stopping with us, her folks, for the time being. She'll be here for a while. Just you call in whenever you're passing. Always welcome! Bowl of soup or a cuppa tea. Any time you're passing.'

He closes the door firmly on them and peers through the lace curtain.

'Bitch one and Bitch two, excuse my French,' he says. 'Pity!' he turns from the window. 'Pity!' he says, 'I've missed a sale. Should've flogged 'em a bucket and brush each.' He walks up and down the kitchen still holding Helena. He keeps laughing, little laughs.

'Uncle!' he says. 'Your mother,' he says to Helena's wrinkled face, 'she's a sharp one. Me, uncle! You've no need to worry with a mother like you've got.'

Two things are on my mind. One is the afternoon post. A letter might come from Mummy Doctor in answer to mine. I am afraid to have a letter from her. She might come to see me. Both a letter and a visit, or one or the other, I am afraid of them. I would like not to have the letter or the visit. Simply I would like my trunk to arrive, by carrier, without either of the two doctors.

The second thing on my mind is really a nice thing, at least I am supposed to think of it as nice. Sister Peters tells me that one of the patients, a rich patient, who has her third baby now would like me to go home with her and to be a 'live in' nanny. I can take Helena with me and I will be well paid. They live, Sister Peters says, in a beautiful park near Worcester, the house is a mansion, she says. Sister Peters says it is worth considering because of Helena's future. But, she says, it must be my own choice, what I do. I have a fortnight in which to make up my mind. Lady Poynter, she says, is really nice.

It might be Mummy Doctor and Daddy Doctor all over again. On the other hand it is a big house with extensive grounds, and there are other staff members in the house. For example, Sister Peters explains, I would have a nursery girl working under me. There is a cook too and of course there are maids and there is even a manservant and a chauffeur.

'Imagine the dinner service needed just for the staff!' Sister Peters sighs and breaks a cracked plate in half. 'I've been meaning to do that for ages,' she says. She was tired, she added, of trying to avoid giving that plate to one of the patients.

'Think about the position,' she says to me. It would be easier if Sister Peters would say either that she wants me to go because she can't keep me or that she hopes I'll stay because I'm useful and she can't manage without me.

I keep thinking that the postman has come and I go repeatedly to the front hall to look for letters.

Rhubarb Jam has his own pram at the Hilda Street Wentworth. The eldest boy pushed it round and left it ready for when his mother and the new baby could come home. Mostly the babies do not have their prams here, just sometimes if a mother lives very close. Rhubarb Jam's pram is useful. Sister Peters suggests I put Helena in the pram and go for a little walk. She says to go to the park and back – just half an hour, she says it will do me good. One of the babies won't settle after her feed so Sister Peters puts her in the pram too. Two babies, like dolls in a dolls' pram.

'Bring back some dandelion leaves,' she calls out after me. Walking with the pram with the two babies flat on the mattress, tucked in a piece of flannelette sheet and both of them quiet in the smooth movement is one of the nicest things I have ever done. I never imagined it would be like this to push a pram. It is a high pram with big wheels, a bit shabby, but the shabbiness makes it less conspicuous.

While I walk with the pram I give myself up completely to the soft sound of it on the pavement and to the feeling of the fresh air on my face. Both babies sleep immediately. I wish the pram was mine. I look at the houses and the gardens, at the sky and into the summer green of the trees along Hilda Street. The horse-chestnuts are in flower. I had forgotten the horse-chestnuts with their creamy candles of flowers. Hilda Street is a main road, navy blue and efficient, and the traffic is pouring westward away from the city.

When I pause to cross a side street I hear, in the distance through the faint roar of the city's breathing, the chiming of the clocks. An old woman pauses too and peers into the pram and tells me that I have beautiful children. Twins she supposes and very very young. So I tell her, 'Yes'.

'You will have your hands full,' she says and I tell her 'Yes'. We smile knowingly at each other. She fumbles with her purse and drops two florins into the pram.

'Silver,' she says, 'it's an old custom for a baby boy. You have one of each,' she says, 'I see the pink and the blue. I can't give to one and not the other, can I.' We smile once more, knowingly, at one another.

I am the mother, the mother of twins, a boy and a girl born, it is true, two weeks apart – almost three to be exact, but, here in the pram, twins. Back home music can be heard, something, an arrangement of the wedding march for the piano, by Liszt – piano music can be heard through the open french windows, the maid is making cucumber sandwiches for afternoon tea and my husband, the twins' daddy, will be home from the office. . . Daddy will be home to bath you both tonight. . . Perhaps Daddy will be home early from the operating theatre. . . He will leave his dressers to sew up. . . Not the office, the theatre. . .

In the field at the edge of the park I hastily gather some dande-lion leaves. I take off my cardigan and roll it up with the leaves inside and put the bundle across the foot of the pram.

In the afternoon post there is a letter for me. Sister Peters says, 'There's a letter for you Vera.' She has taken the post up to the patients, mine is on the kitchen table. Sister Peters has made the tea. She pours a cup for me. She says to leave the babies asleep by the back door.

I do not want to open the letter. I know it to be the reply from Mummy Doctor. Slowly I open the envelope. The letter is very short. It is from the Nurses' Insurance Company explaining in the politest phrases that a payment to a nurse in my circumstances can be made only once. With the letter is a cheque for four pounds.

'What's this for?' Sister Peters takes the cheque and holds it between one scrubbed red finger and her red thumb.

'For my food,' I say.

'Aw! Go on with you! You don't owe me anything,' she says. 'It's yours. Put it away for now and pay it into your bank quick before *Uncle Hoob* gets his paws on it.'

Mr Peters is trying to fix one of his new shelves. Sister Peters explains it came away from the wall as soon as the saucepans were put up.

'Everything slid off,' she says. 'I've laughed myself silly. Oh God! I'm that tired!' She tells me to run upstairs with a cup of tea for

Sister Russell before taking the trays with the little tea pots, all filled from the big tea pot, round to the patients.

When I open the rabbit hutch, later on, to feed the rabbit with some of the dandelion leaves, I count six baby rabbits. In all eight births in one day at the Hilda Street Wentworth. A record.

When I think about it, I know I have never actually heard staff nurse Ramsden describe how a nurse should teach a patient how to wash herself, but it is easy for me now when I am thinking about her to put the concept and the words, which are in fact from my *General Text Book of Nursing*, into her richly serious voice, even though I shall never be able, ever again, to hear her speak.

How soon can a rabbit be pregnant again? Sister Peters wants to know.

★

THE PRUNES AND THE PRESENTS

'But you must eat it,' I say. 'Sister Peters has poured her soul into this dessert. Her whole soul.'

'Dear child, of course I'll force myself, if only for your sake.' Lady Poynter's plump fingers curl round the stem of a second little glass of the delicate frothy Apple Snow. I tell her it is one of Sister Peters' special successes, made from stewed dried apple rings and powdered milk.

'It is indeed a triumph,' Lady Poynter says. She goes on to tell me she is grossly overweight, that child bearing has completely ruined her figure. She is definitely going to start dieting as soon as she gets home.

'I'm hoping, we're hoping, that you will be coming home with me,' she says, letting the words slide from the corner of her mouth. 'You'll be a tonic,' she says, 'in our household.' She takes a teaspoonful of the Apple Snow closing her eyes for a moment and then opening them to regard me earnestly; 'All the fragrance of ripe apples,' she says, 'in one delicious mouthful.'

When I look at Lady Poynter's pursed red mouth it seems as if in the experienced adult there can still be a baby feature. A red mouth wanting to suck.

'We do hope, very much that you will decide to come. We shall treasure you and Helena very much. You have no idea how much!'

I thank her and take second helpings to the two other mothers in the room. Nursing and lying-in mothers are always hungry. Food for the nursing-home patients is a constant concern. Private patients, in particular, must have good food, well cooked and nicely served. Whenever we are near the rabbits we feed them.

At the Hilda Street Wentworth the rooms are all named and the names are painted in faded pink and blue or green and yellow over the doors. Some are decorated with flowers and foliage, these painted backgrounds almost disappearing with repeated cleanings. So, on the upstairs corridor there's 'The Rose Garden' and 'The Meadow' each with three mothers and their babies. Sister Peters can have up to six mothers and their babies. I am causing her to have seven. My little room (unnamed) is really required if there is some sort of emergency. Sister Peters says that private nursing-home patients like the rooms to have pretty names and, for some women, the term labour theatre would scare their wits out of them so she has the 'Gooseberry Bush' and the 'Cabbage Patch'. She hardly ever uses the names herself, perhaps only when talking to a new patient or a husband.

It is disconcerting to see babyish details in the features of grown-up women. I pause, laden with trays on the landing at the top of the stairs, and, in the landing mirror, I straighten my own mouth into a grim line. I manage to reach the kitchen without dropping anything.

'Mr Peters not back yet?' Sister Peters, still in her hat and coat, is prising the slats of wood from a small crate, a present from a grateful husband. 'Prunes,' she says, 'that's nice. Very useful.' She takes a glistening wrinkled prune and eats it explaining that she's sorry she's late back. She missed the bus, she says, because of nipping into someone's front garden after some dandelion leaves just as the bus was coming. The order, she says, from the markets will be delivered later.

'Mr Peters,' she says, 'he should be here by now. You didn't give him that money? Did you? You didn't lend him the money?'

'What money?' I am pushing the patients' plates down in the big bowl of soapy water we keep in readiness in the old-fashioned sink.

'The money. The four pounds you got.' Sister Peters is serving a plate of dark gravied stew for me and one for herself. 'You didn't let him have it? He's a fool with money.'

'No,' I tell her, 'I didn't give any money to him. I've still got the four pounds.'

'Never lend him any money,' she says. Her long hungry fingers seek out another prune which she hands to me. 'He's a good man,' she says, 'but a damn fool with money. Well I can't *do anything,*' she adds. 'Sit down and have your lunch. Never lend Mr Peters money. Just remember that.'

We eat in silence, quickly.

'Last time,' Sister Peters says, 'we got a tub of butter and now prunes. With their first we got a whole Danish cheese. Imagine! Patients have their ways of being grateful. And that reminds me, there's some presents for you.'

'For me?'

'Yes, for you, why not. You've done a lot... There's a pair of stockings, pure silk, for you and a dress length and the cost of having it made up is to be covered. That's nice isn't it.' Sister Peters unwraps the material.

'It's very nice,' she says, 'good quality. It'll suit you. It'll be the devil to iron, you'll have to have it just right, not too damp and not too dry. It'll hang well. Keep it for best. I'd keep it for best.'

'Yes,' I say. 'I never imagined presents,' I tell her.

The material is linen, a navy blue background with a pattern of pale green and white flowers. A better quality than anything I have ever possessed.

Sister Peters has saved an Apple Snow for me. She says it's really for Helena. 'It's lovely,' I tell her.

Upstairs, once more, I rush round with six bed-pans and the six little enamel jugs of the dettol and warm water mixture. These jugs, the little douchings are poured with the usual jokes about plucked chickens and being ripped to ribbons. There is no such thing, Lady Poynter declares, as self-conscious embarrassment while lying in.

At last I get to my room. Helena has been crying. I could hear her despair all along the passage. When I pick her up I see her little face is swollen red and puffy with crying. As quickly as I can I sit down, facing the window, to feed her. The traffic is pouring both ways on Hilda Street. Perhaps tomorrow I shall be able to go on the early bus to visit my mother. Perhaps tomorrow I shall know whether or not I ought to take Lady Poynter's offer.

It occurs to me as I rest, holding Helena upright and patting her tiny back, that the presents from the patients could all be for Sister Peters if I was not here.

★

THE SLEEPLESS NIGHT

I do not know what is wrong with my baby. Every time I try to put her back into her cot she cries. I have never had a night like this with her before. I think she might be hungry and I try to feed her and she seems eager and then turns her head away and cries and cries. This crying, I can't stand it.

I am tired. I am afraid her crying will disturb the mothers and babies in the rooms just along the passage from my room. She is only quiet if I walk and rock her in my arms. Every time I think she is asleep and I put her carefully on her little mattress she lies quietly for a minute and then, as soon as I am in bed, she starts crying and crying. I pick her up and shake her.

I stand at my window. It is wide open. I can smell the night sweetness of summer grasses and leaves. Helena, quiet now in my arms, gives a tiny sigh and a shudder passes through her small body. She seems vulnerable as if at any moment she might stop breathing. But worse than this is the thought that I am the only person she has. She is defenceless and helpless and I am ashamed of the anger in my action. She will have felt it and there is not any way of telling her I am sorry.

'Baba,' I say, 'Baba please forgive me.' I mean, can my words mean anything to my baby?

I am alone here, with my child, by the open window of summer.

Hilda Street is a main road, blue-black at dusk, it crosses Wentworth Street. We are on the corner of this crossing. At night the buses slow down for the cross roads. This slowing down and starting up is a kind of lullaby. Sometimes the buses stop for the Hilda Street-Wentworth bus stop. Sometimes lately, when I have been in my room, I have watched the buses with some anxiety in case either the Mummy doctor or the Daddy one should, after receiving the letter I sent, be coming to visit me.

The long light evenings, the horse-chestnut trees, lit up with their flower candles, and the wet tyres rasping on the wet road after a light summer shower have, in the last few days, brought back to me similar evenings. Evenings from last summer.

In spite of everything I am still the same person who raced ahead of Dr Metcalf that special evening, that other summer evening, uphill, breathless and both of us laughing, knowing we were going to be together all night. We found, that night, a cottage where the woman had placed a Bed and Breakfast sign in the window. On purpose we went out for a walk knowing that we could return. It was not like being at the river shack, the Metcalfs' place, where visitors or Magda or Magda's father and his current actress might turn up at any time. With the walk we prolonged the secret long light evening, putting off, on purpose, the night we were to have together.

There was beetroot soaking in vinegar in a glass dish on the table, as well as the other things for breakfast, the next morning. He laughed, Dr Metcalf did, and ate some of it to please the landlady, as he called her. She called him 'sir' and said we should come again. 'Any time,' she said. 'City folk,' she said, 'should come out to the country more, for peace and quiet, to enjoy themselves.'

We set off, laughing still, down hill for the bus. A fox, crossing the path in the wood, stopped and stared before slipping off into the undergrowth. The sadness of parting was upon me before we reached the main road and I begged Dr Metcalf to let me stay with him the rest of the day. 'The river shack,' I said to him then, 'couldn't we just go there?' But he explained that the river shack was not such a secret place. It was, after all, Magda's and, at any time, she could take it into her head to go there. He reasoned about our work and how we should be in time for it. His reasoning, I thought then, is so much the truth and he is right about the reality of what we must do. I believed in him, then, completely.

The evening, without, it seems time passing, has become night. Something disturbs my baby. She cries and then stops crying and a bit later on she cries again.

All at once a memory returns and it is as if I am, late at night, feeling my way, once more, along the bookshelves in my mother's house. The shelves in that house are from the floor to the ceiling. Shelves full of books industriously read by my father and, with equal industry, brushed and dusted by my mother.

Often, at night, I went along the shelves taking down books and, looking inside them, discovered names and dates of previous owners and faded records of Christmas and birthday gifts. These gifts, often given and received by people unknown to me, provided endless speculation. People known only by names or initials on a discoloured fly leaf, the date sometimes too far back to be believable.

This evening, earlier, horribly disturbed by screams from the Cabbage Patch (Sister Peters' name for the little labour room along the passage) I have been reliving at a too short distance the final stages of my own wild pains and hysteria. Crouching by the open window I am taking, with one hand, my own books, one at a time, from my trunk which was delivered quite late after supper and carried upstairs for me by Mr Peters and the carrier. The trunk is here with no message, not one word from either of the two doctors in reply to my letter.

Holding my books, one after the other, reminds me of the times when I pulled books from the shelves at home to see which of them belonged to my mother, having been given to her at some time or other by a particular friend, signed with initials only, each discovery or attempt at discovery exciting the midnight curiosity. I change my position and move Helena to my other arm and continue this search for some trace of my mother in my own small store. Perhaps her messages and quotations chosen especially to be suitable for her gifts to me, these things, in her handwriting, I want to find now. Perhaps in the quietness after the earlier than expected labour and delivery, three doors down the passage, and Sister Russell's late departure followed soon after by Sister Peters' final footsteps going downstairs, in that wonderful silence which follows childbirth, I am making a curious attempt after what seems a long time to, somehow, be near my mother. To bring her close in some way. I can't help wondering what this alarming compulsion, this searching through the books, opening them with an unrealistic eagerness only to put them aside, can mean. I must have been looking at my books for more than an hour. Because there are so few it is a distressing symptom experienced alone and at an unearthly hour.

The Hilda Street Wentworth is quietly asleep. Even Helena, in the aching crook of my arm, is asleep. I am tired and sleep evades the welcome I could give. Often I stood beside a sleepless patient fingering with longing the smooth pillow and the cool sheet amazed that, in such comfort, the man could not fall asleep when, had our places been changed, I would have slept at once.

Perhaps there is a deeply felt wish which I must acknowledge. Perhaps I must recognize the wish to have my mother bend over my baby with all the pleasure and tenderness expressed in the words and gestures of cherishing which I seem to recall clearly as coming to me from her when I was a child. The gestures especially, the soft sound of scented hand cream being smoothed over and between her fingers before she bent down to kiss me, the soft coolness of her cheek felt lightly on my face as I turned to resume the pleasure of approaching sleep after receiving her caress.

Perhaps this time is the one time when the child turns back towards the parent in that curious bond between parent and child in which the child is always moving away.

My mother has seen my baby but only here, with certain restraint, in the room Sister Peters calls the Rose Garden where there were two other mothers and their babies. She has not come a second time.

I would like to take Helena home to my mother where she can, in her own kitchen, unwrap and exclaim, and where she can nurse the small perfect body in front of the kitchen fire and sing in that sweet, suddenly remembered voice which knows the music but is not able to reproduce it.

Why do I remember now, Dr Metcalf, naked and shameless, leaning back in a basket chair beside the small westward window in the cottage, high up, so high up that, though dusk was filling the valley, the last colour of the setting sun made his body golden as he waited for me and, smiling, stretched out his arms to draw me to him?

Why does the next summer have the same fragrance of the summer before?

I will take Helena to visit my mother. We can go on the early bus, the one we always called the workmen's. This decision is not so hard to make. I can be there before the neighbours wake up.

I have two things on my mind. One is that when I wrote to Mummy Doctor I returned her cheque, a month's wages. I scribbled all over the cheque and now I keep seeing, in my mind, the childish scratching of my pen all across her neat mathematician's handwriting.

The other is simply will I, would I, fit into the Poynter household? If only I could know beforehand.

Visit To My Mother's House, The Bus Ride

'I didn't know you wrote poetry.'

'Poetry?'

'Yes you left a poem here, last summer.'

'Oh, did I?'

'Yes I showed it to Gertrude. Remember how ill she was? I showed her the poem. She liked it, said it was nice but she thought the hospital was near the canal, not a river.'

'I took the bus to Worcester. There's a river there.'

'There's no need to cry over Gertrude. She was very fond of you always. She would not want you to be sad and to cry over her.'

'No, I know. I'm not crying. Really, I'm not.'

When I look at the other people on the bus it seems to me that even the most hopeless sort of person knows what to wear. I mean, take Sister Peters and Mummy Doctor, they both look awful when they go out. Mummy Doctor, in particular, has no hesitations. She heaves on her greatcoat over whatever she has put on, a badly fitting skirt and jumper mostly, and considers herself dressed.

This morning I hesitated and changed my mind so often I was almost too late for the workmen's. Mummy Doctor never ponders uneasily on the landing wondering whether to start off downstairs or whether to go back into the bedroom to pull her other skirt out of the wardrobe. It never seems to occur to Mummy Doctor that she looks a mess. She even darns her stockings with wool which doesn't match. Sister Peters, who is always in a hurry, pulls a coat on over her uniform overall. She never hesitates either.

The summer morning is fresh and sweet in the mist when I leave. A cuckoo calls through the mist reminding of the fields at school and the long wet grass where, in soaked shoes, we searched for and gathered wildflowers. I wait under the dripping horse-chestnuts in Hilda Street opposite the nursing home. Helena, wrapped in a shawl, is quite heavy. I feel pleased that I did not put on the new silk stockings, that I have saved them for some future time when I might be invited somewhere. The early bus, the one we always call the workmen's, is almost full when it comes. I find a seat upstairs at the back.

The early morning mist promises a fine day. I can't help wondering about my mother. I suppose old conversations are coming into my mind as I try to prepare myself in advance for the visit. She is hardly likely now to recall the poem she found last year. I remember it starts: 'Keep the Love...' I wrote it for Dr Metcalf but, of course, never gave it to him.

Helena is six weeks old. I've had my six weeks check. Dr McCabe is very quick with an examination, almost as if she is embarrassed. I have been at the Hilda Street Wentworth for just over six weeks. My mother will have things to say about this, that she can't have me staying there without paying and I'll have to try to explain that I'm helping Sister Peters.

'What d'you mean helping, doing all the dirty work which no one wants to do? You with your brains and your training...'

'No. No. I'm bathing the babies and...'

I look out into the mist. The front gardens and the old houses and the trees are still half hidden in the shreds of mist. The bus will turn off soon away from the ancient suburb and go into the heart of the industrial yards, the factories and the iron and steel works. When Helena is bigger I'll be able to sit up here with her on the bus and point out the canal to her and the barges and the horses on the towing path and the place where artificial silk and rayon are made and where buttons come from and the old road, where I used to go with my father, to see the women working in the chain shops. But before all this there's my mother.

'A servant? What do you mean about working? A servant. I do not understand. A servant only.'

'No, not a servant. I'm offered a post as head nanny to...'

'A nursemaid! After all your studying, after all your exams. How can you do this. A nursemaid!'

'It's a good position, I mean – place. It's at Poynter Hall, Lady Poynter is...'

'A *position*! and worse, a *place*! Just like an uneducated cook or a kitchen maid with nothing in her head. *You* doing this?'

'I would have people under me. Head Nanny with a...'

'Already you talk like one. "*People under me.*" It is too much. Head Nanny. How could you! Poynter Hall. Poynter Hall. Where is this Poynter Hall? This Lady Poynter. What is she? Some parvenu with money and vulgar feet and ugly overdressed children. Lady Parvenu with much money and no intelligence or culture. What about your music? I always wanted for you to go to Europe to study music. What about your music?'

'But first there was the war and now there's Helena...'

How shall I be able to discuss with my mother, as Sister Peters suggested I should, my future? It's too difficult either in imagination or in reality.

Daddy Doctor is in the bus. Up front, in the very front of the bus. Whatever can he be doing going so early on the bus, on this bus? He must have been sitting there, in front, all this time. I can only see him from the back but I know his coat, his light summer coat and the hat he wears. I suppose his brief case is down on the floor by his legs. I don't want Daddy Doctor to see me. If I get off the bus at the next stop I might not be able to get on the next one. The buses fill up and further on they only stop to let people off. I can't afford to miss buses. I must be early at my mother's house. Down the Back Lane, early, with my baby and into the kitchen before the neighbours are up.

I am hungry.

'For whom did you write the poem?'

'Who did I write the poem for? Oh, no one really.'

'Poems are always written for someone.'

'This isn't really poetry. Anyway, if you must know, I copied it out of a book.'

Really, I must stop this. My mother is sure to have other things to talk about.

If I get off last when the bus reaches the terminus I'll be able to turn away to the window while Daddy Doctor passes to go down. Wherever can he be going to at this time of day, on a bus going in this direction? We don't go anywhere near the university. I must keep calm.

Helena's eyelashes are resting on her round cheeks. I put my face down close to her face feeling the wool of the shawl and breathing in the baby smell of Vinolia soap. The bus is full. The man next to me is too big for his half of the seat. I look out of the window and see people at the bus stops. We pass them without stopping.

Perhaps Daddy Doctor is going to my mother's house. In his quiet, well-bred way he will sit at her table moving the food she gives him from one side of his plate to the other. He will relate an anecdote, keeping his voice soft and, in a slightly amused way, will suggest to my mother that I go back with him to the doctors' house and the two little girls.

The question is how does Daddy Doctor know that I am going home to my mother's house for the day today. Does Sister Peters tell the two doctors everything? Does she telephone Mummy Doctor? After breakfast, with a cup of coffee in mid-air, in that space between the table and her mouth.

'That you Glad? Got a minute? Yes, she's going with her baby. Yes, with the baby, to her mother's place. Yes, just for the day. No, not train, the early bus, yes the workmen's, yes that's the one. Yes, if he gets that one he'll be sure to meet her. It'll be easy. You'll have her back by evening. The trunk? It's not properly unpacked, just a few books out and some dried flowers, petals and stalks, yes a mess but nothing much. I'll get it back by carrier. Yes tonight, yes carrier. Don't you worry...'

Daddy Doctor is still in his seat at the front. Quite a few people are getting off now that we are passing factory entrances and side roads leading to the iron and steel works. If only he would be getting off at the next stop. He could be going to visit a factory. That's it. He is probably visiting in the capacity of advisor to any one or several of the artificial silk manufacturers. Or, he could be going to meet a group of students. Yes that's it, meeting some students to take them round the iron and steel works or down a mine.

Helena, seeming to like the movement of the bus, sleeps on rolled up in her shawl. My breasts, too full, ache. Of course Sister Peters would not talk to Mummy Doctor about me.

It will be a quiet day at the Hilda Street Wentworth today.

No new patients expected yet and the present ones all able to get up to the toilet and for their hot baths and all able to walk about and do things for themselves and their babies. Sister Peters said it was a good day to choose for the visit, the beds being booked in advance, so if all keep to expected dates everything will be very tranquil there.

'What about your ration book? Have you brought your ration book?'

'I've a piece of corned beef and a pound of prunes, the prunes are a present from a patient...'

'If I had your ration book today I could get some extra cheese. Why did you not think to bring the ration book?'

My mother's first question, for some years, has always been about ration books.

We have gone past the factories and have left the iron and steel works behind. A good many passengers have left the bus and a few people, office-girl sorts are getting on. Daddy Doctor has not moved from his seat.

From the top of the bus there is, for a long way, an exceptionally good view of the canal. It will be nice, when Helena is older, to explain to her what a roan horse is and that the barges are loaded with coal and that people live on the canal barges and decorate them with castles and roses in bright new paint.

I want to enjoy this ride. I have not been on a bus for a long time. It is Helena's first bus ride. Not far from the main road, just about here, there are some fields. The housing estates stretch for some way, new houses built by the council, council houses, and then there are the left-over fields with their tattered hedges. There is a sand quarry out across there too. The quarry is partly overgrown with grass. Just now there will be the long summer grasses and the scarlet poppies. I went there once with Lois, before I knew the Metcalfs. Lois danced on the edge of the quarry, high up. Looking at her from below, seeing her against the sky I thought then, in the excitement of knowing her more, that she was beautiful and that I would always want to do things for her and to give her the things she might want. I mean, I washed her stockings for her and I bought her favourite cigarettes, State Express 333, and sometimes, with pleasurable extravagance, I bought an Art Magazine. We were on bicycles that day coming upon the curious little patches of country which lie between the factories and the rows and rows of small houses. There is a small triangular farm near the quarry. We looked that day through the elderberry and the hawthorn at the cow and the pig and the chickens. There were children there too. We watched them playing in the dirt. At the time I thought they were quaint and had a nice life on their little farm. It is only today, on this bus thinking about them, that I begin to understand that the farmhouse is small and derelict and that they are poor and probably do not have enough to eat. I remember the white and pink hawthorn flowers and how I once decided to store them in my mind for ever so that I could think about them. I have always tried to store prettiness in my mind so that I will not forget it. I realize today that I have not been able to make use of this storage when I needed to.

I have been thinking about this journey for some days, this bus ride when I would be taking my child home to my mother and father for the first time. It is unfair that Daddy Doctor is sitting up there in the front of the bus. It's as if I am not free from the doctors' house. Not at all. Sitting there, like that, he's spoiling the journey.

'I tode 'em as she's been planting out them cabbage plants and that's why there's all dirt on her knees, I tode 'em.'

Late last night. So late it's nearly morning, late last night I am in the kitchen putting the Hilda Street breakfast trays ready and covering the slices of bread and butter I have prepared with a damp cloth when I hear, through their partly open door, the low voice of Mr Peters talking to Sister Peters in bed.

'She's not dirty, I tode 'em. She's been on the ground planting cabbages.' For some reason when he talks in this half voice and half whisper Mr Peters sounds more and more as if he comes from Yorkshire though he's told me several times he was born and bred in the Brickworks near here. 'They make this note, see,' Mr Peters goes on, 'they make this note of her knees, all the same, and when they come back they're going to get on her back about 'er knees. And listen here, Dolly, there's summat else, you can't let 'er go to that place.'

'What place? Hoob, I'm dead tired, it's late.' Sister Peters can't remember. 'What place?' she keeps asking, telling Mr Peters it's late and she needs to sleep. Mr Peters tells her she knows full well the place he's talking about. 'Poynters Park,' he says. 'Lady Poynter. *You know*!' He keeps on about me not going to Lady Poynter's place and that Sister Peters must stop me from going. Sister Peters keeps on with a terrible yawning and tells Mr Peters that she's sorry about my knees, saying she thinks they probably were very dirty. I can tell she's tired and put out because she calls Mr Peters Hubert instead of Hoob and she tells him that she can't possibly tell me what to do with my life. 'I can't stop her going,' she says, 'and that's that!'

'You can if you've a mind to,' Mr Peters says. 'You can do anything if you put your mind to it.' Sister Peters tells him that it's up to me to choose and how can I, a mother with a child, go on managing without money. Mr Peters says there are more important things than money. 'She's nowhere near ready to go anywhere,' Mr Peters raises his voice. 'You know that as well as I do. She ought to have three months and more...' Sister Peters tells him she knows all that but it would be a shame to miss a good chance. There may never be such a chance again. 'Lady Poynter's good fun,' Sister Peters says. 'She gets on well with Lady Poynter. They're always laughing about something.'

'You know as well as I do,' Mr Peters says, 'she'll not be likely to be having afternoon tea with her ladyship. Any woman, and this goes for her ladyship, any woman as refers to her husband as "sir" ought to be let alone and that's my last word.' Sister Peters tells Mr Peters that nothing can be done to stop me from leaving.

'Yes there is,' Mr Peters says. 'Tell her. You tell her you'd appreciate her staying a while longer. She'll stay. She likes it here. I tell you, Dolly, if she goes she'll regret it – you know what it's like in places like that. She's smart as a button but she's not tough. She'll never hold her own in a place like that. She needs looking after. And I'll tell you this, she's right valuable. I might make mistakes over buckets and horses, Dolly, but not with people eh?'

From the darkness in their room the Hodson baby starts crying. Sister Peters has been having him downstairs at night as he's fretful. I can hear Mr Peters getting out of bed, and I wait with one foot carefully on the bottom step of the little staircase which goes straight up from the kitchens to the end of the passage where my room is. When the Hodson crying is at its loudest I go up the creaking steps as quickly as possible. I hear Mr Peters telling Sister Peters that he'll walk Master Hodson for a bit and then make a cup of tea.

'It's all right Dolly,' I hear him, from the top of the stairs, 'he's quietening. Have a nap. I'll brew the tea.'

Daddy Doctor is not spoiling the journey after all. He's getting off the bus just now and it isn't him. How could one man look so like another from the back and then not be that other person? This man as he passes me to go down from the top of the bus is not one bit, front view, like Daddy Doctor. There is no dreaded glance of recognition and no vague smile of the stranger. Nothing. When I see him getting up and coming towards me, I look down into my bag and, as he goes down the stairs, I look up quickly, sideways, through my hair. It is not Daddy Doctor. Absolutely not. Not at all. One person simply cannot be another person. This time, I am able to be pleased with this thought.

In the freedom, the wonderful freedom of thinking about things on this bus now that the person who is not Daddy Doctor has gone, it seems to me that I was afraid of Mummy Doctor somehow taking my baby over along with her little girls, apart from other things to do with being in her house. Another thought is that I have come now, during these last few minutes, to the conclusion that there is no need to discuss (Sister Peters' word) with my mother my going to Poynter Hall. This conclusion comes about because I like being at the Hilda Street Wentworth. The Peters seem to quite like me and find me useful. Unless Sister Peters tells me quite firmly to leave, it goes without saying I'll stay there.

I am pleased to discover something about myself and this is that once more I have been able to come to a point of reasoning and decision.

From the bus terminus it is not far to walk to the Back Lane.

THE SURPRISE OF
THE SUMMER-FULL GARDEN

'Your father mends for other people, he mends every one else but not himself.' My mother tells me she has been standing looking out for me. She stands complaining, the surprise of the summer-full garden, the lupins, the roses and the big red peonies crowding behind her, at the front gate which is, as always, wedged permanently half open on the wet earth. A curving border of pinks leads the way to the front door, the little path is almost hidden. I have forgotten the garden in summer I tell my mother, I have forgotten the garden in summer.

'The pinks are for her.' My mother takes Helena from my aching arms.

'The peonies! Your favourites!' I follow her along the pink-edged path. 'The peonies!' I say.

'Your father is taking cabbages. He puts them on people's

doorsteps, without asking he puts them there. He was going to meet you, he went early on purpose.' With one long finger my mother moves the soft curl of shawl away from Helena's face.

'I came on the workmen's.'

'Yes, yes he intended to be there.'

'Will he go straight on to school then?'

'School, school? Why the school? Today is Saturday.' My mother's long finger caresses the curve of Helena's soft cheek.

'Oh yes, Saturday of course.' I am surprised that I can forget the days, not know what day it is.

The mist has lifted but the grass in the back garden wets our shoes. A cuckoo calls over and over again, muffled by small distance, like the one in Hilda Street. My mother buries her face in Helena's shawl. I look once again at delphiniums, light blue and dark, reaching up into the arms of the little apple trees, into the abundance of the small green unripe apples.

When my mother looks up at me it is as if my baby has inherited these jewels, my mother's blue eyes. My baby looks like my mother.

'She looks like you,' I tell her.

'Your father will say she looks like his mother,' my mother says. 'He has always said this about babies.'

'Only if they are related.'

'No, not always.'

She has picked some pinks. They are in a little jar on the kitchen table. They are for me to take back with me. 'All babies look like someone,' she says after a bit. She sits down with Helena and starts to unwrap her. Once again I am seeing something I have not known about before, in my mother, like the time she came to the Hilda Street Wentworth, the day Helena was born.

'How the child has grown!' she says. 'Did you meet anyone in the Back Lane?'

'No,' I tell her, 'no.'

Helena's eyes are intensely blue. I hoped once for brown eyes like Dr Metcalf's. Helena's resemblance to my mother is striking and cancels any other resemblance.

'She is like you,' my mother says. 'She looks like you when you were a baby.' She has made a little sleeping bag for Helena. It is of a fawn woollen cloth decorated with pink rabbits, embroidered by hand, and she has made soft cloth-covered buttons. Eagerly, like a little girl with a doll, my mother undresses Helena to change her on the kitchen table. I look on, seeing her doing the things I imagined her doing. I take the necessary items out of the bag I have with me but she has it all, in a little basket, baby powder, nappies – everything all prepared. She bends over Helena who lies kicking on the folded blanket. In their smiling at one another it seems, for a moment, as if they are exchanging the blue brilliance of their eyes.

My mother, holding Helena dressed now in the sleeping bag which is a bit too big, wants to take her next door to show her to her neighbour.

'But it's a bit early, isn't it, to go visiting.'

'In a little while,' she says. 'Feed her first and I'll cook an egg for you.'

I can feel my mother's excitement and pleasure mixed with her nervousness. She takes Helena and carries her to the door.

'What will you tell them?' I am eating toast solidly as if I haven't had anything to eat for weeks.

'That she is my grandchild. I shall say to them she is my grandchild.'

I feel ashamed to be eating so many pieces of toast. I have another piece with butter and jam as if satisfying my hunger is my only concern.

My mother returns immediately. They are not up yet, she tells me. It is Saturday, of course they are not getting up early on Saturdays. Mrs Bright was up, in her hair curlers still, my mother explains, and she adds that she was not invited inside.

'All in a mess there,' she says, 'and of course they have seven children!' She supposes they, the family next door, with seven children are not very interested in a baby.

'No, I suppose not,' I say. A curious grief seems to engulf me. I am sorry for my mother, for her almost childlike eagerness to show off Helena, in spite of the shame I have brought, to someone – and for her disappointment.

My mother displays an extraordinary resilience. She suggests we walk carrying Helena up the Back Lane to meet my father.

'We might even walk in the field a little,' she says. 'And later we will bath her and she will sleep and you,' she tells me, 'you must sleep too.'

In her eyes is her disappointment and the reflection of a great hurt. I wish for my father to come now.

Go to sleep. Go to sleep. Go to sleep. My father comes creaking on bent legs along the hall. He crawls flickering across the ceiling crouching double on the wardrobe. Go to sleep he says. Flickering in fire light and candle flame. Flickering and prancing he moves up and down the walls, big and little, little and big, colliding in the corners with himself.

Go to sleep. Go to sleep. My father folding and unfolding comes closer. I'm the engine down the mine, he says. I'm the shaft. I'm the wheels turning and turning down down the mine. I'm the shaft. I'm the steam laundry. I'm a Yorkshire ham, a cheese, a Cheshire cheese, a pork pie. A pork pie that's what I am. I'm a mouse now, he says, I'm a mouse in the iron and steel works. I'm a needle and thread. I'm a cart wheel turning in the road, turning over and over turning and turning. I'm the horse pulling the cart. I'm turning the cart in the roadway. I'm the tired horse, the tired horse. Go to sleep. Go to sleep.

My father's voice is soft and softer. His voice, my father's voice is singing down through the years to me. I'm the tired horse he sings softly, so softly, the tired tired horse. Go to sleep now go to sleep.

It is my father singing to Helena. Not singing he says only groaning. Helena is sleeping. She sleeps, he explains, without him noticing. One minute her eyes wide open wide awake and the next minute fast asleep. I have forgotten the short a in my father's speech. When he says fast asleep she is even more asleep.

I have been asleep here in my mother's house sleeping away my whole life for two hours, for over two hours, while my mother and father have been watching over Helena. I wake weeping and do not know the reason.

Helena sleeps and when she wakes to my mother's face close to hers, she smiles with her mouth, her eyes, her whole face.

It is time to leave to go back to the Hilda Street Wentworth. My father comes to the bus with me. We walk up the Back Lane and he tells me again that they will sell the house and move and that I should come, with Helena, home. I tell him yet again that I do not want them to move and that if they do move I shall not come and live with them.

★

THE SEASONS

THE LITTLE CELEBRATIONS AND THE GROWING SUGAR WEIGHT

There is something I do and that is to make a little celebration, an occasion, a reason out of something quite small. As time goes by these little celebrations become more frequent since they are the way in which Helena and I go out together. I am, in reality, taking her out either in a small pushchair or else walking very slowly. Too slow for me is too fast for her. The walk is to the second corner in Hilda Street where there is an ice-cream shop, or we might go a little further to a funny little shop where broken dolls are mended; these are the things we do for our outings. These are the things I am looking forward to doing while I rush the trays back to the kitchen and slide the plates and cups into the big tin basin of soapy water. And then, while I am wiping them on the worn-out wet cloths which we use for drying up, my impatience to go out increases and I sort, as quickly as possible, the knives and forks and spoons into their compartments, moving my lips as if I am praying and not just checking and counting them.

With a sort of restrained eagerness we go out from the Hilda Street Wentworth to certain known and named corners before we turn back. Sometimes we go to a small park. Usually we bring back from these expeditions dandelion leaves and handfuls of grass for the rabbits. The places we reach before turning back are the witch's house, the garden full of toys, the churchyard and the holly hedge. We are always back at the Hilda Street Wentworth in time to give the mothers their washing bowls and their afternoon tea. About every six weeks or so Sister Peters insists that I take a day off in order to visit my mother. These visits are not always the happiest as my mother insists on weeping over Helena saying her arms and legs are like sticks and that she needs to be looked after properly and why do I refuse to leave her at home with them.

On the bus ride back to the Hilda Street Wentworth I feel afraid and I try to measure Helena's arms and her little thighs with my fingers. She does seem very light in weight and I try to make her eat something from the packets my mother has given me. Helena is always sick on this return bus journey.

I feel afraid that Helena will somehow be taken from me.

I notice the changes in the weather especially between the fine days and the wet days because of the great rush to be out early with the nappies to catch the sun. And then there is the rushing out at the first sign of rain to gather in the partly dry washing. Mr Peters has made some big wooden clothes horses which are propped up permanently as much out of the way as possible. The big things, the sheets and counterpanes, go to the laundry. Laundry is a big item on all the accounts. Cotton wool and cascara are on all the accounts too. Every patient is charged for a whole roll and a whole bottle. No one ever complains about these things and Sister Peters explains to me that it is a method of fighting the overheads, and that patients accept these items.

'Probably they never even read them,' she says. 'Did your mother,' she asks, 'did your mother complain about anything on the accounts?'

'No,' I tell her, 'no she didn't.'

'A very generous lady, your mother,' Sister Peters says.

The summers are encapsulated in the fragrance of boiling jam. Plum jam because Mr Peters goes to the markets late on Saturdays and brings back cheap yellow plums. We pick over the fruit, the three of us together. It won't keep, Sister Peters says, and often at midnight we are at the stove stirring the golden boiling contents of the jam cauldron. A good rolling boil Sister Peters calls it as she tests for setting. She tells me to put the shining clean jars above the stove to warm. We use up the carefully hoarded sugar. Saving out the sugar from all the weekly rations has become for me a sort of hobby, perhaps like stamp collecting or like collecting fishes' eyes in matchboxes. I add to the sugar store a cupful or two whenever I can and I take great pleasure in weighing the dark blue bags. Throughout the year I record the growing sugar weight on a card pinned to the back of the kitchen door. On this door too are the marks I make to show how tall Helena is from the time when she first stands up to take her first steps and then onwards. She is quite a tall little girl. I enjoy recording her growth in this way.

Perhaps the summers in the garden are the best, idyllic and peaceful for short times when I am crouched small and insignificant on the earth, planting out tiny cabbages and cornflower seedlings, beneath the great dome of a summer blue sky lined at times with nests of pure white clouds and resounding with the contented murmurings from the dovecote which, in its repaired state, towers above the busy fowl yard and the increasing number of rabbit hutches. Helena makes mud pies in the dust and runs with both hands outstretched towards Sister Peters whenever she returns in her hat and coat from some bus journey or other. Helena, alert to the familiar sound of the side gate, runs across there at once both to Sister Peters and to Mr Peters. They seem fond of her though often Sister Peters shakes her head saying things like, 'That poor child', and 'What is to become of this poor child?' and 'It's all right now, Vera, but what are you going to do later when she's expensive?' At these times I lie awake at night wondering what I ought to do. Sometimes, as if sensing my uneasiness, Helena wakes up and cries and I go down quietly to the kitchen and make us each a piece of bread and butter, without disturbing the Peters whose bedroom door is never properly latched.

I snatch time for being in the garden. Sometimes, when Sister Peters suggests that I take some time off, I have a whole afternoon in the garden. I have come to need the safety and the privateness of being enclosed within the mellow brick walls; and I look forward, with a sense of comfort, to the coming of the blossom on the big old pear tree and to the yearly transformation of the vegetable garden from the dark rich forked over earth to the neat little rows of summer lettuces and radishes, spring onions and beans.

The pantry shelves, every summer, are like the pages of a book which is being written. Every day something fresh being added to what was there before. In the long light evenings of summer when Helena's face is a white, peevish, half-moon at the edge of the bedroom curtain, I am in the yard, at a makeshift trestle table, with Sister Peters, preparing vegetables and fruit for preserving. Some of these are gifts from grateful patients and some are bargains brought from the markets by Mr Peters who walks with the heavy baskets balanced on the handlebars of his bicycle. Tomatoes, carrots, green beans, plums and black currants. We do the apples and pears later and, still later, the Seville oranges – an unusual yearly present from a previous patient. We make, using as little sugar as possible, a rough-cut marmalade. Sister Peters' own recipe. The evenings are already cold and dark by the time we are slicing the bitter fruit. The Peters, who never spend on a newspaper or a magazine themselves, send me upstairs to 'scout for something to read', papers discarded by the mothers.

141

Mr Peters, in shirt sleeves, with his feet up at the kitchen range reads aloud to us the spicy bits from *The News of the World* and, changing his voice, from the 'anxious blue eyes', problem pages in the magazines. Sister Peters and I work quickly. Drying our hands, we take turns to answer a bell or to pace up and down with a fretful baby.

The Rose Garden which, at one time, must have been a gracious, upstairs drawing room, has a large fireplace. In winter we have a coal fire there and the mothers, who are up, sit round the hearth. Husbands, at visiting time, join the fireside. It is then that I experience again the deep-felt wish to be part of a married couple, to sit by a fire in winter with the man who is my husband. So intense is this wish that I try to avoid seeing the mothers with their husbands, and if I write the word husband on a piece of paper my eyes fill with tears. The word wife is even worse. So much do I long to be someone's wife, with a cupboard full of knitting patterns and scraps of left-over dress material, that it hurts me to hear the word 'wife' spoken. The husbands, with an ennobling sense of chivalry brought on by fatherhood, often help me by fetching coal to make up the fire.

'Watch,' Sister Peters says, out of the side of her mouth, 'to see that they are not too generous with the coal.' So I develop a method of placing a coal ration in a bucket at the top of the stairs. I like the coal fire, the look of it, and, in spite of the extra work, I spend time polishing the grate and the brass fender and the brass top of the fire guard. At night, because of the cold, I wear my old hockey jumper in bed and long woollen stockings left over from school.

Sister Russell and Dr McCabe often have quiet conversations during the second stage of labour. They are capable of discussing some philosophical or literary point while standing, one each side of the patient, holding up the heavy white legs and commenting, during the abstract discussion, on the position on the perineum, of the emerging head.

'I can see the head, doctor,' Sister Russell, says to Dr McCabe. And to the patient, 'a lovely head of hair, dark hair, dear, a lovely head, it won't be long now.'

Usually this is a false declaration suggesting a more advanced stage in the labour. This is in order to encourage the mother, who is now in a panic and beyond any feelings of embarrassment at having both legs raised and pushed back, flexed at the knees, till the knees are on her chest in a home-made stirrups position. She pulls at the knotted sheet on the iron rail of the bedhead and screams, one scream following another, pausing only to give a weak smile and the repeated words of timid apology as one pain fades and before the unbearable force of the next.

'I declare this head of hair,' Sister Russell says, 'this head is a beautiful head, well shaped, dear. Now Push!' She encourages, 'One more push, dear.'

I have heard this often enough to know that the head is not yet visible. Along the passage, too close to the screams, I am holding a small block of wood behind a frozen pipe while Mr Peters hammers the ancient lead, tap tap tap, gently, as he tries to close the crack, to mould the edges of the burst pipe, its ice protruding, together.

'Better go shut them doors,' Mr Peters says as the screaming starts afresh. He has brought up two kettles of boiling water as he has to thaw the bath outlet which has frozen solid during the night. 'Life!' he says, 'it's all pain and noise coming and all pain and noise going. Like teeth,' he says, 'take teeth, nothing but trouble. Trouble when they're coming. Trouble when you got 'em. And trouble, talk about trouble!, when you lose 'em.' He goes on patiently tapping the burst pipe and gradually the sinister ice jewel, the unwanted ornament, is covered delicately with hand-beaten lead.

'There!' Mr Peters stands back from his handiwork. 'You'll have to watch,' he says, 'it'll drip in the thaw. Get one of my buckets, it'll do till we get the plumber.'

★

One bitter day in winter a coloured postcard comes for me. It is from Magda. It is over two years, almost three years since I have seen Magda, since Magda's visit the day Helena was born. The card is written in ordinary ink instead of the flamboyant purple of the earlier letters. It is brief and with the same quality of telling. It is a sudden reminder of another world and the one-time excitement and longing I experienced in receiving her letters and invitations.

For a moment I am lost in reading the card;

Darling!
No doubt you've read of Daddy's latest disgrace.
I'm with Mummy in the South of France. Heavenly.
We've taken a villa. Would love to see you. Any chance? Come!

Magda's name is scrawled with almost the usual flourish. I study her name closely. The flourish is perhaps a bit weaker, perhaps a bit tired. I read the card again and turn it over to look at the expanse of blue sky and endless golden sands. Brilliant and empty.

'There's no date on it and no address,' I tell Sister Peters and, for some unexplainable reason, I start to cry. 'There's no date and no address,' I say, 'how can I go and see Magda?' I go on crying because I am not able to stop.

Sister Peters, her hands dropping flour, comes round the kitchen table. 'You've got Helena in the pushchair,' she says, 'out there in the porch, go for one of your little walks, dear.' She puts an arm across my shoulders without letting her floured fingers touch my jersey.

'Put an extra wrap round Helena,' she says, 'and have a little walk. There's a good girl. Just you take a little walk.'

If when I walk alongside the big gardens, casual with trodden-down flowers, broken bushes and scattered tricycles and dolls' prams, thinking of them as sacred places to which husbands return every evening, sacred in that closeness and trust which I long for and which I believe to be in every marriage, I console myself, even more now as I walk, in imagining that such a place, a large old house full of children and their untidy bedrooms, all surrounded by a neglected but safe and contented garden, will one day belong to me.

The particular garden, to which I am always drawn and which, particularly in summer, suggests all that I wish for, has today a snowman in the middle of the trampled snow. The lights are on and the long uncurtained windows offer a glimpse of the magic of the life within; the desirable warmth and harmony of a family, and the idea of having been especially chosen to make this family.

I walk too far with Helena in the pushchair, my mind being occupied with thoughts and the going over repeatedly, in these thoughts, the overheard conversation between Sister Peters and Mr Peters.

'She's cried this afternoon, Hoob, like no one I've ever known, out loud, like a child, couldn't stop, like crying I've never ever heard.' Sister Peters telling Mr Peters, thinking I've already gone while I am still on the kitchen stairs with an extra little scarf for Helena. 'She'll have to find some other life Hoob,' Sister Peters' voice crossing the space from the stove to half way up the small staircase. 'She'll never ever meet anyone here. And the child, she's...'

'There's nothing to worry about,' Mr Peters is adamant. 'They're better off here than anywhere just now. And that little girl she's a little princess with us...She's a duchess...'

'No, she isn't,' Sister Peters interrupts him. 'She's left for hours strapped in the pushchair. She cries for ages because Vera's busy. She's pale to transparent with those blue shadows under her eyes. Vera's obsessed with the routine, the work she does and the child hardly gets a look. I'm worried Hoob really I am. The child could have TB or something.'

The stairs creak as I try not to move. Mr Peters flips the newspaper and clears his throat noisily.

'And listen to this Dolly, the couple alleged,' he reads, 'that they ate a hot Sunday roast in bed where intimacy took place before the murder...oops...where intimacy took place before the *double* murder...' He looks up as I creak on the bottom tread of the kitchen stairs. 'Hey!' he says, as I step into the kitchen, 'thought you'd gone for a walk.'

'Eavesdropper!' Sister Peters shakes a finger at me. 'Eavesdroppers never hear good of themselves.'

As I walk I reflect that it is possible to know from a changing quality, a different sound or resonance in voice and a greater energy in speaking that people's real thoughts are different from those actually uttered. When my mother says that Helena is pretty and dainty her voice betrays the thought she has which is, in reality, that Helena is neglected and starved.

This resonance and energy and the changes in quality are particularly noticeable to me when I overhear conversations. So that when Sister Russell and Dr McCabe talk about 'clearly defined ideas in abundance', and 'creating an unbelievable harmony in imagery', they might well be discussing a book or a play, but the intimate lowering and closeness of their voices during a delivery which is, after all, itself an immense thing, the emergence of a whole new person, shows me that there is something else of importance in their lives, something extra to their serious and necessary work, something extra even to their reading, something extra which I do not have.

I hardly notice the fast fading light of the afternoon and walk too far. And, when I turn back, the pushchair is facing a biting wind. I have to drag the pushchair in the wet snow which is now beginning to freeze again into thick uneven ice on the pavement. For a time this intense cold and Helena's small pinched cold face are my only concerns. I try to wrap the inadequate scarf round her face and I hurry as fast as I can home to the Hilda Street Wentworth. I shall be too late, I realize, to do the upstairs afternoon washing basins and the afternoon teas. My flying tears are only partly caused by the cold wind.

Sister Peters has saved a hot toasted fruit bun for Helena and one for me. She pushes extra butter in them while I take off our outdoor clothes. One of the mothers has left earlier than expected she explains. Instead of staying the full month she has gone home a fortnight early. Not only is there one person less upstairs, two if you count the baby, but there are a whole fortnight's rations which she did not want to bother with.

'The sugar,' I say, 'a whole fortnight's sugar.'

'Yes,' Sister Peters says, 'you'll be able to save it out for your growing sugar weight. Not now!' she says. 'For heaven's sake, child, have your tea first.'

Because we are one less unexpectedly there is extra hot water and Sister Peters says to me to have a hot bath before I go to bed.

Having a bath and going to bed is one of the things I look forward to. Sometimes when I am getting up in the morning I think of bed time and how I will try to be as early as possible to bed. Bed time and clean clothes and clean sheets are all part of what I have come to look upon as the little celebrations especially when Helena is all dressed in clean clothes too.

When I was a child I liked cold sheets. Sister Peters, at first, does not understand what I mean when I tell her this.

'Oh,' she says, after a bit, 'you mean linen sheets, they would feel cold.' I tell her I suppose that must be it.

'No one has linen sheets now, or only rich people,' she says. And then she remembers some worn old sheets she has, put away somewhere. So we get these out and machine them sides to middle. I like doing this.

Helena, in her cot, has patched sheets and I have the old linen sheets, seamed down the middle and am reminded every night now of the seamed sheets of my childhood. It is a sort of comforting thing. In a way I imagine myself as half way between a child and a married woman. Because, I hope so much to be married one day.

⭐

THE BIBLICAL DIGEST

'Matthew Daniel Samuel Ruth Sarah and now Elijah, a veritable Biblical Digest, don't you think?' Sister Russell and Dr McCabe are taking off their gowns after delivery. The Hilda Street Wentworth is full once more.

Lady Poynter tells me after the birth of her fifth son, Elijah, that Sir Harold will kill her when she goes home with yet another stocky, short-legged bullet of a boy.

'Just like his father,' she moans when I bring the new baby, washed and fragrant in new baby clothes, to her bedside. 'Here I am mother of another boy!' she raises herself on one elbow. 'Ripped to ribbons yet again for *this*!' she says. 'You'll simply have to let me adopt Helena since *you* won't come to Poynter Hall, you stubborn girl!' She lies back on her pillow turning her face away from the soft little bundle. 'We've enough heirs for the Works,' she says. 'I daren't take home another. You *must* let Helena come home with me. She's a dear little thing. Sir H will dote on her. He doesn't want another son with stubby fingers and a scrubbing brush for a head, he wants a – a little girl, a daughter to sit on his knee and play with his watch chain. He wants a pretty little girl with long, fine, fair hair and long legs, the long legs of chivalrous aristocracy, my dear, like yourself, my dear, and your little girl. Helena, you see my dear, would, later on, sit so gracefully on a horse. Her hair would be the envy of all the other girls and she would be our pride and joy.'

I try to put the baby in bed beside Lady Poynter but she pulls the sheet up close to her chin.

'Sir H would give her everything,' she says, 'he'd have her *be* anything she chooses, he's all for education for girls as well as boys. She could be a lady doctor or a concert pianist – whatever she would want. A princess if she likes. Helena has your aesthetic lips, my dear, a delicate refined little mouth, whereas the boys all have buckets, much as I adore them, instead of mouths. Exquisite fingers you have and Helena too, my dear. Please *please* consider my request. At Poynter Hall, she could be anything and have anything – down at Poynter Hall...'

'Don't cry, Lady Poynter,' I say, 'please don't cry.' Quickly I tuck the new Poynter baby into his cradle and I tell Lady P she really must try to lie quietly and sleep as I have to clear up the Cabbage Patch before lunch.

'Sister Peters likes the walls washed,' I say in a soothing voice. 'You know how much she values cleanliness.' The truth is I am listening to Sister Russell and Dr McCabe who are, in their well-bred voices, having a conversation which interests me. They are just along the passage resting by the deep window sill with their cups of tea, where I stood once, pausing in the intervals between pains during my own labour to watch a woman hanging out washing, as if that was all that mattered at that moment, a few gardens away.

Russell and McCabe, though reserved, seem to know each other quite well. Perhaps they have both been reading the same book or have been, possibly, to a play together. They are talking about the looking back on the supposition that it is possible to learn the pleasures of love without being obliged to become acquainted with the sorrows as well. It must be a book or a play as it is clear that neither of them are sorrowful with love. I wonder which book or which play. I wish I could know.

I take my pail of soapy water along the passage to empty it hoping to hear more but now they are on to the ineluctable changing of the season, the coming of the spring. Ineluctable is a word both of them would use. I have never heard it before and now, hearing it for the first time, it is as if, in spite of the bitterly cold wind and the shining wet blackness of the horse-chestnut trees on the other side of Hilda Street, the irrepressible new leaves are beginning to appear in little bursts of fresh green, shining with moisture as if unable to prevent their own appearance. Just as, in the same way, the green spears of first one crocus and then another are showing in the dark earth in some of the gardens.

When I hear Sister Russell and Dr McCabe talking together I am reminded of staff nurse Ramsden and staff nurse Pusey-Hall. As now, I only ever heard then, snatches of what was being said. Sometimes I have an indescribable longing to have conversations like this with someone. There are times when I long for the company of another person, for the excitement of a deepening of understanding and the making of a lasting friend. I want to find in someone else the things which match with me. Mostly, most of the time, other people do not matter all that much but I could, if I had the chance, set great store upon one friend trusting that friend completely and needing him, or her, so much for what I think of as happiness – that is, a contrast in feeling from sadness and a freedom from anxiety, a state which I imagine then becomes happiness. The person I could become attached to in what they would have described at the hospital, Ferguson and Lois that is, as a neurotic way, could become tremendously special to me; a person of music and of poetry and of skills – not a neurosis – a person whose fingers are nimble, either in embroidery or on the keys of the piano or in the deft changing of a complicated surgical dressing. Such a person was embodied in staff nurse Ramsden and I feel that Sister Russell and Dr McCabe have these same qualities but these qualities are not there for me, not actually there in them for me.

All the same I resolve, up and down the stairs, in and out of the rooms, the Rose Garden and the Meadow, the Gooseberry Bush and the Cabbage Patch, to emulate Sister Russell and Dr McCabe and what I remember of Ramsden. It is a long time since I read a book for one thing. And then there is another thing, my hair. My hair is awful. It's depressing me. I'm heartily sick of this Olympia roll, this long heavy hair brushed for ages every day and rolled up on a boot lace which I have to tie round my head with exactly the right tightness. Because I am in a hurry I often push my hair into a net. It's out of the way while I am working

but when I see myself as I go by the long mirror on the landing
I have to look the other way. Hair bundled up and sagging in a
hair net is ugly, it is worse, much worse than a head scarf. How
can I read a book or expect an intellectual conversation when
I simply do not know what to do with my hair. I hate my hair.

One of the differences between Mr Peters and Sister Peters is that
Mr Peters says an aitch with an H. Haitch he says when spelling
Hilda Street on the phone. He likes Haitch P sauce. Sister Peters
remembers to put it out for him. She does not like it herself but
puts it in her rabbit stews and her other casserole dinners together
with a big spoonful of camp coffee, an essence, she says, which
helps to create the spectacular rich dark gravy. She says the special
ingredients of the sauce, the dates, the molasses, the rye flour,
the raisins, the tamarinds, and the other things must have been
really hard to get during the war; but the sauce, she says, never
lost its piquant flavour. Not her special choice of flavour, she says,
but a favourite of the mothers and of course Mr Peters.

'I'll go along with that,' Mr Peters always says whenever Sister
Peters holds forth on the HP Sauce.

Mr Peters has HP Sauce with everything. He is already having
his lunch when I come down to fetch the trays for the mothers.
'That Poynter Place, Hall, whatever it is,' he is saying to Sister
Peters, 'is certainly being stacked up with livestock. Sir H and
Lady P must be Roman Catholics or something, you know,
assuring themselves of places in heaven. One brat after another!'

'I don't think so,' Sister Peters says, 'they are seriously trying
to get a daughter.' She arranges a plate judiciously putting on a
bit more carrot and lifting off a fragment of meat. She explains
that the wealthy, with good brass in their pockets, and the very
poor have the big families. The boys, she says, will be useful in
the iron and steel. Born with the iron works in their mouths. I
can just see Sir H expanding. 'All the same,' she goes on, 'he wants

a girl. You must,' she says to me, 'consider their renewed offer to adopt Helena. Lady P is adamant about this. Listen! Why not let them have Helena for a few days to see how she gets on?'

When I pick up the first tray my hands shake so much I have to put it down. I am shaking all over.

'Hurry up do!' Sister Peters has the hot plate ready. 'Hurry, dear, do,' she says, 'it's hot lunches today and I don't want them served cold. It's a very good opportunity for Helena,' she adds. 'You must think about it seriously.' Her eyes fill with tears. 'I wouldn't want for her to go away,' she says, 'but we do have to think of her future – and yours.'

I take the first tray and as I start up the kitchen stairs I hear Mr Peters saying that Sister Peters should keep in mind that the next time the old cow calves she may well drop a filly.

'You've got your animals and their verbs mixed,' Sister Peters tells him.

'You know full well what I mean,' Mr Peters says. 'When Sir Sauce gets his own little girl *you know* what'll happen to the adopted one...'

'Sir Sauce? Sir Sauce? I don't get it.'

'Sir H.P.,' Mr Peters, with his mouth too full is laughing. 'Sir Harold Poynter Sauce.' He almost chokes. 'Haitch P.'

'That's a below stairs sort of joke.' Sister Peters' voice is cold and hard. 'Really, Hoob!'

'And that's where our little girl will be,' Mr Peters says, 'she'll be *below stairs* when Princess Poynter makes her entrance.'

'Hurry, Vera! Hurry up do!' Sister Peters calls up the stairs. 'Eavesdropping never does anyone any good. I've told you before. Eavesdroppers never hear good...'

'I know,' I shout back and I go on upstairs, my own heavy steps making too much noise on the uncarpeted treads for me to hear the next bit of their talking.

★

TRENT'S VISIT

'She's you!'

'D'you think so? I suppose she is...'

'She's you all right. Well, how's things?' Trent, in black from head to foot, is standing in the kitchen just inside the back door. No one was about so she stepped inside, she explains, she's come to see me and is it a bad time to come she wants to know. Oh no, very good I tell her, we're slack at present, I say. All six mothers are up, walking about, carrying their babies out of doors to sit on garden chairs on Mr Peters' little lawn out there. We have a cold lunch today I tell Trent. All very easy, the Peters are going out. See, I tell her, the trays are ready, plates all served and arranged with cold cuts and green salad, cold sideboards, Sister Peters calls them, corned beef mainly and some sort of meat loaf she makes with left-over roast, usually a leg of something or other cooked for hours in a big old tin we have. I am surprised and a bit embarrassed to see Trent so I talk too much. At least that is how it seems. After a bit I stop talking and look at Trent. She is looking at me. She says the trays look very nice, very appetizing and the idea of a blue cornflower on each one is sweet. You have to feed private patients, especially nursing mothers, well I tell her. The flowers are all blue, I go on, because we've a run of boys, this often happens, all boys in the Hilda Street Wentworth or all girls. Funny, but that's how it is.

'It's been a long time,' Trent says. 'She's you,' she says again, looking at Helena more closely. 'I've never seen such a likeness, never ever. Peek-a-Boo!' she says to Helena who covers her face and peers at Trent through her thin little fingers.

'Ask your friend to have some lunch with you,' Sister Peters, who is dressed for going out, says. Trent says thank you she would just love that. She draws a kitchen chair near to Helena's little high chair and sits down. Sister Peters, in her hat and coat, helps me to take the six trays to the mothers who have asked if they can eat in the garden while the sun's out.

'It'll save you the stairs for once,' Sister Peters says. 'Shall you manage the clearing up all right?' she asks me and gives herself a look of approval in the little piece of mirror we have over the sink.

'Of course,' I tell her. 'You'd better hurry,' I say, 'Mr Peters has been waiting Ages.'

'I know. I know,' Sister Peters says and she's off.

'She must be three if she's a day.' Trent nods her head towards Helena.

'That's right, nearly three and a half.'

'Time flies,' Trent says.

'It certainly does.'

'You haven't changed Wright,' Trent says.

'Neither have you Trent,' I say. 'Not a bit.'

'Though we've both been through a thing or two,' Trent says. 'We've seen the world a bit, you and me.'

'I suppose so.'

'Your hair!' Trent says. 'It's still the same.'

'Oh my hair!' I say. 'Can't do a thing with it.'

'Have it cut,' Trent says, 'that's what they're doing now. Razor cut it's called, the urchin cut. It'd suit you a treat. Short hair. Everyone's going for it.'

'D'you really think so? I haven't had a hair cut for years.' Nervously I push at my hair, pushing it into the net.

'This meat,' Trent says, 'this meat's lovely. Really beautiful, this meat.'

'Have some more.' I offer the plate with the extras on it. Trent puts both hands, fingers outstretched over her plate to show she's had enough. I am not sure why Trent has come here. Quickly I gather up the bits of food Helena has thrown all round her chair and when I make the patients' tea I pour a cup for Trent. She drinks gratefully.

'Don't top it up,' she says, 'you'll spoil it. Good tea!'

'Yes good tea.' I rush with the cups of tea to the mothers and bring in the trays as quickly as I can, two at a time.

'Don't rush because of me,' Trent says. 'I don't have to hurry away. How d'you like my Black?' she asks. She stands up and turns round slowly. She picks up her hat and her handbag.

'It all looks nice and new and smart,' I say, knowing my mother, had she the chance, would dismiss the clothes as cheap and not at all elegant, one of her favourite words. Trent seems pleased with her new things. Her shoes too are new and black.

She's in mourning she tells me, widowed, she says. Married three months and then all of a sudden, she says, a widow. She isn't nursing now, she tells me, not any more. She's selling ladies' dresses and accessories.

'Accessories?' I am wiping Helena, who is protesting, with a grey-looking face cloth. In front of Trent I am ashamed of the dirty colour of the cloth.

'Yes accessories,' Trent says. I can see that she has noticed the cloth. 'Yes,' she says, 'you know, ornaments, jewellery, imitation pearls, imitation opals, imitation gold – things to go on black or with red or blue or grey or green, all kinds of accessories, necklaces, pendants, brooches, those sorts of things. And I help customers to choose perfumes and hat trimmings and collars and little scarves and whether to have spotted net or voile or chiffon...' I stare with admiration at Trent. How does she know all this? I never think about these things, about fashions. It's as if she has come here from another world. A place of pleasure and brightness and of choosing for oneself, a place where people have lots of clothes for different occasions. And not only clothes, they have accessories, all kinds of pretty things, kept in charming little scented boxes in special compartments in their dressing tables.

'Allow me.' Trent teeters on high heels towards an imaginary customer. 'Allow me, modom, allow me to show modom how to tie the teeny leetle knot in the teeny leetle scarf... to place the bow just heah on modom's...' Trent, in her special voice, demonstrates. We laugh. Tears come into my eyes with my laughing. I don't seem to have laughed for years, I tell her. We laugh some more.

'You can laugh yourself silly like this,' I say and I tell her I'm sorry she is a widow. Trent says she thinks it might be worse to be married for life to the wrong person than to be widowed. Did I know, she wants to know, that one of the girls hanged herself in her mother-in-law's kitchen? 'No one you know,' she says. 'She came after you left, got herself pregnant, married secretly, though we all knew of course, got turned out, nowhere to go except her mother-in-law. You can picture it! No idea of the background. See? I mean, the men all look the same in pyjamas or hospital blues, a man could be anything. The mother-in-law found her hanging dead, pair of stockings round her neck. There's no way of knowing,' Trent says, 'what you're marrying into if you marry pyjamas.'

Trent, who used to amuse us with her one man, vocal and tap, band and who danced me, one night, all along the bombed passage, the forbidden locked-up residents' corridor, where the doctors had their rooms on the fourth floor of the hospital, picks Helena out of her little high chair and waltzes, whirling round and round on the red tiles of the Peters' kitchen, singing; 'A wun a tew a tree a wun a tew a tree a wun ah Danube so blue pom pom pom pom my heart is so trew pom pom pom pom,' holding Helena up so that she is laughing and laughing.

'Remember your gramophone?' Trent collapses on her chair. 'Stuffed up with a towel and shut in the wardrobe? I really missed the music after you left,' she says.

'Did you?' I'm remembering all at once the Tango Bolero and Lois dancing naked in a strip of moonlight when we took down the black-out curtain once during a hot night. I remember too how she hid herself in a heap of bedclothes when the Night Sister came up to our room to complain about the noise. Later Lois came out naked still, straight into my arms.

'I really missed you when you left,' Trent says, 'you and the music and the poems. Remember? The Emperor? And The Serenade for Strings, I loved that.' She puts Helena back into her chair and takes the plates one by one when I have done swirling them round in the big tin bowl of soapy water. My washing up seems more messy than usual.

Trent's black coat has wide shoulder pads and a belt of the same material as the coat which ties in front. My own coat, when I think about it, is my school coat which has not worn out. My coat is shabby, I have never liked it. I don't like Trent's coat either.

'The hem line,' Trent says suddenly. 'There's a new hem line, it's called the New Look,' she says. 'Lots of material, a new mid-calf length, they call it Ballerina, bright colours, lace all over the place and broderie anglaise, square necks and high waists, should suit you a treat, Wright. A square neck, not too low and a bodice of broderie anglaise. It's you Wright.'

'Me!'

'Yes, you. Don't you ever think about a dress? Don't you ever go out to look at dress shops or anything? I'll bet you never go to a show or to the pictures. I'm right aren't I? You never go out. You used to like a film or a concert when you had the chance.'

'I have plenty to do here,' I can feel my mouth thin in a prim line, the way I don't really like my mouth. Trent is making me nervous and restless. I'm picking up knives and forks and then putting them down in the same place I pick them up from. I'm wishing I knew what to say. She's right I don't go anywhere and there's no music at the Hilda Street Wentworth. We have the news on the wireless and the football match and that's about it.

'You've certainly been left holding the baby.' Trent gives a little laugh, not unkindly. 'She's too quiet,' she says.

'What d'you mean?'

'Your little girl, Helena, she's too quiet, too subdued. She needs to bash around with others her own age. She needs to go places with other children.' Trent looks across at Helena who is sitting quietly in her little chair turning the pages of a picture book. Her thin little white fingers carefully lifting the pages one after the other.

157

'I do take her out,' I say. I'm wiping the trays before setting them for the next meal. 'We go for walks to the Botanical Gardens and sometimes we go to the ordinary park. We can't go this afternoon because the Peters are out.' I feel awkward wiping the trays.

Trent nods her head. She wants to know what these Peters people are really like. I tell her they're nice, the Peters are both very nice. Trent wants to know what money they pay. 'Excuse me asking,' she says in her politest way. I tell Trent that the Peters have lost some money at the races. I tell her that they go to the races. Horses and sometimes dogs.

'Say no more.' Trent hangs up the sodden cloth. She tells me I need to get out and about. 'You'll rot here, Wright,' she says, 'without clothes, without money and without friends. It's true, the patients are friendly and nice, I'll grant you that, but they're here today and gone tomorrow.' Trent tells me she knows that childbirth is important and that the care of the lying-in mother is very necessary. 'Important and necessary as they are, Wright,' she says, 'it all fades, every bit of it. Women don't live with their childbirth, they forget it. These mothers aren't your friends at all. They're nice enough but they'd have fits if you and Helena turned up, visiting, on their doorsteps. You'll never see them again and though they give you presents they aren't interested in you at all and, Wright, believe me, in the life you're living you'll never meet anyone.'

'I don't want to "meet anyone", Trent. Really I don't.'

'Everyone wants and needs a true friend, Wright, and you're no exception.' She goes on to explain that being happy is only possible if you're with someone you can really trust. A person you can have a good laugh with or a good cry and who likes what you like and hates what you hate is a good friend, she says. 'I'm in the same boat as you with customers,' she says, 'that makes two of us. The customers seem like friends when they're trying on clothes and asking, with complete faith in me, for my opinion. But when they're truly pleased with a corsage I've made, you know, something in real velvet, looking like the petals of an exotic flower, pinned on the bust properly with the pin not showing, off they go smiling and admiring themselves in every mirror they pass and I'm forgotten straight away. We're two of a kind all right. We really are two of a kind. You and me.'

'Oh God!' Trent says after a pause. 'Oh Goddy God!'

'Shall I make us some more tea?' I lift Helena from her chair and she fetches her little dust pan and brush and sets to work sweeping the kitchen tiles.

'She's you,' Trent says, 'take a look at that, will you. She's you all right.'

'Shall I make us some more tea?' I fill the kettle.

'Have you got it to spare?' Trent wants to know. I tell her we had a whole tea chest of tea from one of the patients whose grandfather is in the trade. I tell her I'll make a little parcel for her to take home with her.

'Remember our bike rides?' I say. 'Remember what a fool I was always lending Ferguson money?' I'm trying to make Trent laugh. 'She was always borrowing from me,' I say. Trent doesn't laugh.

'Ferguson,' she says, frowning, 'that one! How was it she used to go, *Can you lend me money for breakfast if Queenan and Trent pay and you'll pay them and I'll pay you back later*, how could you, Wright, have gone on the way you did. That's how Ferguson was. Always saying she'll pay back and she never. She never!'

'We were at school together...' I start to say.

'That's no reason for her to bleed you,' Trent gets up and brushes her black skirt with her hands.

'Have another cup?' I'm trying to keep Trent, to stop her from leaving. She disturbs but at the same time I'm holding on to her company. I am surprised about this and unable to help myself.

'Ferguson,' Trent says, 'that one! I suppose she's never sent you a penny. And she must have known.'

'No,' I say. 'She owes me. I don't expect she knows.'

'God knows what she owes you. She could have got your address from your mother. You'll never hear from her I'll bet. D'you hear from Lois?' she wants to know. I tell her that I never wrote to Lois. That I don't even know where she is.

'She's a tough one that Lois,' Trent says, 'a tough little lady but

159

all the same she needed you to fasten on to. I used to watch you, the two of you, you trying to read and listen to music and her pretending to be doing both but just waiting her chance to get some thing out of you.' Trent puts on her hat in front of the bit of mirror over the sink. 'I could always read you like a book, Wright.'

'I know,' I say.

'I'd rather read you than her any day. I wonder who she's with and what she's doing. I've never written to any of them.' Trent admires her hat, in the mirror, turning her head from one side to the other.

'Neither have I.' I hold up the tea pot. 'There's more tea.' Trent sits down once more and pushes her cup towards me.

'Lovely tea,' she sighs. 'Lovely tea this. Black market tea eh? Remember Sister Bean?' I tell her yes I do remember Sister Bean. Trent changes her voice; '*Abbott Abrahams Ackerman Allwood* ...' She manages to sound exactly like Sister Bean. '*Arrington and Attwood. Nurses Baker Barrington Beam Beamish Beckett Birch Bowman D Bowman E Broadhurst Brown Burchall* ... How could we forget?' Trent resumes her ordinary voice and tells me that on the day after I left, when Sister Bean called the nurses' register, no one answered for me. 'She called you twice,' Trent says. She tells me that on the next morning at the end of the register Sister Bean called her. She changes her voice.

'*Nurse Trent?*' Trent sounds exactly like Sister Bean.

'Yes Sister.'

'*Nurse Trent. Matron's Office nine a.m.*' Trent tells me that she goes along to this nine a.m. Matron's office thing and Matron asks her straight out does she know where Nurse Wright is and Trent says no she doesn't know but perhaps Nurse Wright's mother would know and Matron says yes that is a possibility. Then Matron asks Trent if she would like to tell anything, in confidence of course, she might know about Nurse Wright. For example if Nurse Wright is in some sort of trouble. She cannot, she tells Trent, let one of her nurses go into some difficulty or trouble without offering help of some sort. Trent doesn't know what to say and then blurts out that she thinks Nurse Wright might be going to have a baby. 'Matron,' Trent tells me, 'doesn't bat an eyelid. She just sits at her desk with that great calm she always has.' Trent goes on to say that Matron tells her that it is a pity about a baby at this stage; later on would have been more appropriate because, Matron says, because she is sure Nurse Wright would have been in line for the Gold Medal.

And then, Trent tells me, Matron simply said she would be grateful if she, Trent, would come straight to her if she heard anything.

'So there you are, Wright,' Trent says, 'that gives you a picture of how Matron really is and what you might have been! Such a quiet little thing you are.' Trent turns to Helena who has come to stand close to Trent's chair. 'I'll have to be getting along now,' Trent says to me. I nod and turn away, my eyes suddenly full of tears.

'You'll have to get away to some place,' Trent says, 'where people read and talk and where there's music – I mean, Wright, have you read any good books lately?' We both have to laugh at this. Then Trent tells me seriously, 'Seriously Wright,' she says, 'you'll have to get Helena to other children. She needs company. I've never in my life seen such a quiet and, pardon my saying this, such a quaint three-year-old. I suppose you forget to speak to her. And here she is tucked away in a corner of this old-fashioned and, pardon me again, none too clean kitchen while you work yourself to death. I just know you, Wright! But you've got to think of her.'

'Surely it's not that bad,' I try to smile at Trent. 'Oh, the tea.' I jump up quickly to make the little package. 'You will come again, won't you?' I have to ask Trent. But she shrugs.

'Don't know,' she says. 'I'm off to London in a couple of days.' And she tells me that she's been offered an appointment in the London shop. 'I don't know if I'll ever be back here,' she says.

'Let's write then, shall we? Please do let's write.'

'Yes, we'll write,' Trent says. She's pulling on her black gloves, smoothing the fingers, one by one. 'Wright,' she says, 'you must pick up your life after letting that rotten man and his wife ruin it, because ruin it they did. You must get back into what you are meant to do, Wright, I mean this. I really do mean this, Wright.'

'Trent. I know you do, Trent.'

I mean, I can't write to Trent and ask her who she married and what did he die of. Was it an illness, an accident, a suicide or was he murdered? How can one person ask these questions of another person? Does Trent have any in-laws? I can't ask her this either. What are the in-laws like, I would like to know; and is there a sister-in-law she can be fond of. She did not say anything at all about any of this.

I have an address for her in London. As soon as she left, because I missed her so much I thought I would start a letter to her. I thought I would start a letter straight away to try to keep hold of her but I have no idea what to write. I am not able to imagine her life at all and how it will be in London. I feel I want to be near her and writing to her would bring her close but I have nothing to say.

The afternoon is going by slowly. I seem to have forgotten the things I would ordinarily be doing to keep ahead with the work. The mothers all brought their own tea cups to the kitchen. Back upstairs they are washing themselves and changing their babies in readiness to sit together, up there, in 'the Rose Garden', to feed their babies. I can hear them talking and laughing together admiring and praising, being modest and proud at the same time.

Mothers during lying in seem to like to describe their husbands and their clothes in great detail. One of them hides in the bathroom till her husband has gone to sleep because she gets worn out with his passion. Another describes a little close-fitting hat she has, entirely made of the most beautiful feathers from the tails of Indian bantam roosters. This particular group of mothers has formed a little clique as schoolgirls do. They do not seem to need me though I have been very close to all of them in turn being the first, mostly to address the new mother, the new mother of the first born, as mother for the first time in her life. This is always a pleasure for me to be the one to say 'mother' to someone who is mother for the first time and who, in those few minutes when I bring the baby, washed and fragrant and warm, to the bedside and into her arms, suddenly realizes who she now is. I have done this for all the six mothers here at present and because of this have special feelings towards them but I have to understand this afternoon, after Trent's visit, that these feelings do not exist the other way round.

Mostly the mothers in the Hilda Street Wentworth ignore Helena. If they do notice her it is when she has a cold and they are fearful like Daddy or Mummy Doctor might be that someone with a cold is sure to pass it on. It's possible that Lady Poynter might have been an exception.

This afternoon I do feel left out. I wish I could have gone for a little walk to the bus stop with Trent or even to the station to see her off. Helena would have liked that. Sister Russell is 'on call' in case of some emergency but my going to the station because I feel like it is hardly reason enough to telephone for her to come.

Trent was here in the kitchen with me and the next minute she was gone. That is how it seems now.

Trent's visit brings back all sorts of things from an earlier time. Strangely not from the weeks and days leading up to the evening of the day when I packed and left. Seeing Trent again I am reminded more of my arrival, with Ferguson, at the hospital, the smell of the cold enamel tea pots in the nurses' dining room, the signing for keys to our rooms and then being shown how to make up the white caps, damping the stiff tapes with a wet toothbrush so that they would draw through the starch making the neat pleats at the back. Ferguson's first question, on arrival, was to ask when we would have a day off. The question was recorded on a note pad in Matron's office but no answer was given.

And then, up in our rooms, there were the black-out curtains, hanging permanently but looped up during the day letting the sad sunlight of the late afternoon lie in pale shafts across the bare floor boards. My school trunk, already in my room unroped and unlocked, waiting to be unpacked was a betrayal. The wildflowers gathered from the fields near school, pressed and labelled in exercise books, spilled across the floor as I searched for the special buttons for the uniform. All round me were these reminders of other times, the saxafrage, campion, vetch, violet, buttercup, King cup, cowslip, coltsfoot, wood anemone, shepherd's purse, lady's slipper, Jack in the pulpit, bryony and the pretty celandine.

. . . I saw Lois first not in uniform but in a tartan dress. The material was shabby as if she did not have many clothes and always wore this dress. And once, quite soon after our first meeting, when I sat behind her during a lecture I saw the soft little curl at the back of her neck and the sideways droop of her head when she wrote some notes. This remembered Lois is not the same Lois I came to know later. The first time of seeing a place or a person can hardly ever be recaptured. This is the way of all friendship. The deeper and more intimate the more painful the discovery. Can I write that to Trent?

I can't write in a letter to Trent that we are both lonely. She has just told me that. Helena *is* a quiet child. I *know* she is quiet. I am not alone because I have her but I know how really lonely it is to be alone with your child. I look at Helena who is standing waiting with a ball. Something about my look upsets her and she starts to cry. When she cries her voice is hoarse as if she spends her life crying. I see her mouth go square and the tears seem to splash out of her eyes. She drops the ball and wrings her hands. I know I ought to gather her up and hold her on my lap and read to her and then go out into the garden to play ball with her. I sit at the table as if I am unable to move. I watch her crying. She stands by the kitchen door crying and crying and still I sit at the table, too miserable to move. Gradually the crying changes to a whimpering. She is no longer looking across at me.

Life, having come suddenly to a standstill because of a single remark which, cutting deep beneath the skin causing an unbelievable unexpected hurt, has to go on, has to go on with an equal change of pace, equal that is to the abruptness of the standstill. I, who never once in my thoughts felt need of harshness towards

Dr Metcalf and Magda, have now to soften for myself somehow the abrasive judgement with which I am left.

As I continue to watch Helena it seems as if she is wringing a whole world of sorrow through her small fingers without knowing at all the reason.

★

GAMIN

'Suits you,' Sister Peters says.

'D'you think so? Really?'

'Yes,' she says, 'I wouldn't say so if I didn't think so.'

I keep putting my hand up to feel my hair, the freedom of my hair, to feel with my fingers the strangeness of the short hair all round my head. Every time I pass the landing mirror, at the top of the stairs, I take a quick look at this different person who is me.

'It's the urchin,' I tell Sister Peters.

'The whatter whatter?' She has both hands in the pastry bowl and I am peeling potatoes.

'The urchin,' I say, 'it's cut with a razor, a cut throat, not a safety, and the hairdresser's a man!'

'Good heavens!' Sister Peters says. 'I bet it cost a lot.'

'It did. The man, the hairdresser, called it gamin. He even sounded French.'

'He never!'

'Yes, he did. And my hair lying all round the chair. You know, on the floor, seemed not to be mine, seemed as if it had belonged to someone else. For one thing it looked green.'

'I suppose that was the artificial light.'

'Yes, that would be it.'

'Anyhow it suits you, it really does.'

'Really?'

'Yes, I've told you.'

I wear my linen dress, which is really my best, and I polish my school shoes and I answer an advertisement in a magazine. A better quality magazine one of the mothers upstairs has. I apply for a post, not a position, in a progressive boarding school.

I leave Helena with my mother for a whole day and go to see the school and the headmistress and the glass cabinets filled with ceramics and pottery and other art works done by students. Through half-open doors I see little beds bright with coloured blankets (the children bring their own), pianos in at least three different places, a harp in the headmistress's own room and, in the dining hall, hand-hewn refectory tables and benches. The staff sitting room is hung with paintings, and someone called Tanya is at work on a mural, mainly nudes for which she is apparently well known, in the hall. All these things beckon me into another world.

Josepha, I am told, is to be my assistant. She is from Switzerland. Though she speaks English she does not say anything when we shake hands. The headmistress is called Patch by everyone. Myles, the Deputy Principal, is out somewhere with the dogs. And Frederick, another member of the school staff, is writing poetry and not to be disturbed.

I am shown the kitchens and the slow-combustion stove. Patch walks with me a little in the grounds of the school and asks me how soon I can come.

'Almost at once,' I tell her. 'Splendid,' she says, 'splendid.'

On the way down to the main road I slip in the mud oozing from a large manhole at the top of the field path which is a short cut. I suppose the drains of the school are there. Drains have to be somewhere. I wait at the edge of the corn fields for the bus to London and my train.

The next day at the Hilda Street Wentworth I feel I must leave for the school as soon as possible. I start at once to stuff my life back into my school trunk. And, all the time, I run my fingers through the freedom of my short hair. The urchin cut.

The Peters do not try to persuade me to stay. They tell me they really like my hair. When I describe the school to them they listen and nod with approval.

'I'll be buried in the country,' I tell them, 'and Helena will run wild with other children of her own age.' I like the phrases 'buried in the country' and 'run wild'. I imagine Helena laughing, rolling in the grass and rosy with the fresh air. The phrases, the little phrases, suggest an entirely new life. I use the phrases repeatedly to Sister Peters and to Mr Peters, to the lying-in mothers upstairs, to Sister Russell and Dr McCabe and, at home when I fetch Helena, to my own mother who says to me to leave Helena with her and to try the school on my own first to see what it is like. 'She can run wild here,' she says, 'in the garden.' And she says that she will take Helena to a dancing class in town. 'How much was your hair cut?' my mother wants to know. She rummages in her handbag. 'You could have had a nice perm,' she says. 'My Mrs Crossley would have done a nice perm for you.' My mother goes to this hairdresser once a week for a shampoo and set. Sometimes she has a henna rinse as well.

'I like my hair like this,' I tell my mother and I take the pound note she holds out to me.

'Vera. Leave Helena here with us,' my mother says.

'But it's for her that I'm going to the school. I'm doing this for her.' I tell my mother that it's a good school. 'Progressive,' I say. 'I'm to be Matron there. All the children have their own face flannels. They all have their own little hooks in the bathroom.'

I am afraid that something will happen to prevent my going, that someone will stop me from keeping Helena with me. I tell my mother again about the bathroom hooks. These hooks are the kind of thing she would like and approve of but she doesn't seem to hear. She keeps on saying I should not be taking Helena away. In the end I shout at her and she cries and I promise to come once more to visit her before I leave for the school. My father puts his boots on and comes with us to the station to see us off.

The visit from Trent was in the spring. It is a day in early summer, the middle of May when I have to leave the Hilda Street Wentworth to go once more to see my mother. I am wishing I could go straight to the school. Helena is four years old. My mother wants her to come for her four-year-old birthday.

We are in the hall. Sister Peters gives me a post-office savings book which she has been keeping for Helena.

'It's not much,' she says. 'I just don't know where money goes in this house!' She started the book she tells me with the money the Wellingtons insisted on paying me after I sent back their cheque all scribbled over. They came, both the Wellingtons together, apparently to try to persuade me to go back to them.

'You were in bed very early that night,' Sister Peters said. 'We chatted a bit and then they said they owed you some money and would I give it to you. That was all there was to it.' The bank book has ten pounds in it.

In Helena's hat there is a folded five pound note which I, thinking it is a bit of paper, almost throw away. It is from Mr Peters. He has written his name with an indelible pencil on the back. He says that people do this with Bank of England five pound notes, and that I should put my name on it or else go straight to the bank.

I cry then and tell them I can't take their money and Sister Peters says that's the least of it.

'Four years,' she says, 'is four years.' And how is she going to manage? How is she, she wants to know, can someone just let her know, how she is going to face each day without having Helena run up to her the way she always does? To say nothing of the Help she is going to have to do without. She had not meant to break down the way she has, she says, but there it is, she says, four years is four years. We are both crying, howling I suppose it is and, when the phone rings we don't hear it and Dr McCabe who has, she says, just inserted a duckbilled speculum upstairs, has had to come running down to the hall leaving, she accuses us, the patient up there in the left lateral stuck with the duckbill...

'Imagine that!' Sister Peters says. 'Just imagine, duckbill!'

'I can,' I say. 'Duckbill.' We listen to Dr McCabe's seriously gentle voice as she speaks on the phone.

'Someone's on the way in,' Mr Peters says. 'Out of turn, early.

Someone's early. Could be,' he says, 'our very own Lady P, maybe she's on her way now for a girl.'

'Or another boy,' Sister Peters says, 'sure to be a boy.'

'Could be you're getting out just in time,' Mr Peters says to me. 'And another thing,' he says, 'take no notice of this, I mean take no notice of what I'm saying, if you don't want to. What I'm saying is – leave that trunk of yours with your mother, at your mother's place. Just take a case to that school where you're going.'

'Whyever?' I laugh. Mr Peters laughs too, but not his usual big laugh with his head back, it is a little laugh in his throat as if he's a bit nervous.

'Oh Hoob!' Sister Peters says, 'don't be daft.'

'I know I'm daft,' Mr Peters says, 'but it's been my experience as it's best to be able to carry, at times, by hand. To be able to carry by hand is better than to have to rely on being sent on. Hand luggage see? Instead of luggage in advance or sent after by Goods.'

'Yes Vera,' Sister Peters says. 'Hoob's got a point there.'

'Thank you,' I tell Mr Peters, 'thank you.'

FAIRFIELDS

MY FATHER'S VISIT

Perhaps one of the greatest difficulties is the piecing together of people and events. This is often a blending together of the present with the past. One remembered thing leads to another. Some match with an exquisite naturalness and others have first to be hunted and caught and then fitted.

'*No man putteth a piece of new cloth unto an old garment, for that which is put in to fill it up taketh from the garment, and the rent is made worse.* St Matthew, chapter nine verse sixteen.' My father is telling me that not only is there a present and a past, there are several aspects of the present and several layers of the past. My father, during one of our little walks in the rain, asks me if the children in the school have enough to eat. He thinks Helena is a little pale. Does she have enough sleep he asks me. Immediately I reassure him praising the diet of raw cabbage and lettuce and, at the same time, trying to convince myself. I tell him, laughing, that at the school we have the awful problem of preventing the mothers and fathers of the children from arriving at the school to visit, both, on the same day. The mothers and fathers, I tell him, can't bear each other. My father stands still, the rain running off his oilskin in little rivers. He seems, as he listens, to be studying the wet ground. We walk on and I have to understand, as if from his silence, that there is no father to come and see Helena. And, when I tell my father that most of the children come from what are called broken homes, that is they have no home to go to, it is suddenly clear, though my father says nothing of this, that my position with Helena is no better.

'Fix a time,' my father said as soon as he arrived. 'Fix a time,' meaning the time when his visit should end. This is something he has always insisted upon, that the end of a visit should be decided at the beginning. He has always wanted to know in advance the date and time of departure. He is staying for one week. He tells me, he has always avoided, whenever possible, a damp bed. During our walks he never tries to persuade me to leave, to return with him when the time comes.

When I am busy, my father walks alone or in the vegetable gardens with Frederick, the one we call Frederick the Great, and discusses agricultural methods with him. Tanya tells me later when I come in from walking back with him to his hotel down on the main road, that Frederick has told her that he thinks my father is an old fool but harmless. Tanya is in the middle of one of her Frederick rows. She has been up to his solitary room over the stables to seduce him, she tells me, without success. Apparently they have both been telling each other that they are no good at their subjects, poetry (Frederick) and painting, dancing, singing and the piano (Tanya). Tanya wants me to hate Frederick too so that she can enjoy her own hating more. All he can talk about, she says, is his mother. Imagine if you can, she says, imagine him with his underpants down round his ankles standing there shivering and crying. 'What if Mother could see me now.'

All he can talk about, Tanya says, is his mother.

My father has brought with him a small bag of things which, in my haste to escape from my mother's accusation, her anger and her tears, I left behind. In the bag are some small toys including a little wooden hedgehog and a tiny doll in a pink basket. Helena is pleased to have them. He brings too one of my mother's cakes made with insufficient ingredients because of persisting post war shortages of sugar, butter and raisins. She uses up their rations, he explains, making cakes for people in the street at home. He has with him, as well, all Gertrude's letters written to me when I was at the hospital, some before I knew the Metcalfs, but more after I stopped visiting her because, more and more, I was visiting the Metcalfs. The letters are just as I left them in a small brown paper bag.

'Your mother has been having a great clearing up,' my father explains. He tells me his desk is now out in the shed and I try to imagine the varnished yellow roll-top open out there in the damp. My father's treasures in the place where, every year, the rats get at his seed potatoes.

It is perhaps my father's unexpected arrival which makes me understand that Fairfields is unbearable. And it is after his visit that I write to Ramsden asking for her help, though I do not realize this at the time. That is, I do not realize it while I am walking in the wet withered grass of autumn, with my father, during his short visit. Perhaps it is, too, because of the things he brings with him.

Dear Ramsden, I write late in the evening after he leaves, *Dear Ramsden, I have no way at all of getting away from this place. Please Ramsden can you come? Please?*

I have no idea where staff nurse Ramsden is. It is several years since she wrote saying that she was still nursing and inviting me to stay in her little flat. I have no idea how to address her now. She may not be nursing still. Instead of working quietly alone, preparing syringes and needles for penicillin, in the sterilizing room, she might be on a concert platform, somewhere, coming to the end of a complicated piano sonata, turning to smile at an audience who are unable to stop their applause. Perhaps Ramsden is travelling from one concert platform to the next.

Another thing brought by my father is the little book of poems written and copied by Ramsden. The cardboard cover is decorated with edelweiss and gentian, a circle of neat pen and ink flowers. The night she gave me the poems we were in the subterranean corridor of the hospital, each going in opposite directions. She, with indescribable tenderness in her eyes, told me not to read the poems just then as there was not time.

It was Ramsden who said once, in that quiet way she had, that love was infinite. That it was possible, if a person loved, to believe in the spiritual understanding of truths which were not fully understood intellectually. She said that the person you loved was not an end in itself, was not something you came to the end of but was the beginning of discoveries which could be made because of loving someone. I have to understand now when it is too late that Gertrude, though she did not use the same language as Ramsden, was, in her own way, saying the same thing.

I do not remember seeing my father in shoes. He always wore boots. Ordinary black boots with long laces which he wound round the ankles before tying them. He walked firmly in the boots. At night sparks flew across the cobbles. He explained then that this was because of the metal tips. Heels and toes, he said. The metal, he said, prevented them from wearing out too quickly. At home, in his chair beside the hearth, he took off his boots and studied the soles before placing them carefully beside his chair. This intense silent examination was never explained.

'I'll put my boots on. Wait, I'll get my boots,' my father would say at the last minute. 'I'll come to the station with you.' My father was always meeting a train or going to the station to see someone off.

It is cold and wet, the week my father comes to Fairfields to visit Helena and me. He seems quiet and sad and is, of course, out of place. Helena, who does not know him really, is shy. We walk together in the long wet grass in the rain, Helena trying to hide under my coat.

It has been clear to me from my first few days in the school that nothing has been added from students' work to the exhibits in the front hall for at least thirty years, so I do not spend time showing these to my father.

I concentrate on the gardens and grounds of the old house which, in spite of my unhappiness, I try to think of as special. I have had to learn during the summer that the cascades of roses and the beech trees, with their smooth trunks and nutty fragrance, and the meadows, deep with pink-tipped summer grasses sprinkled with the delicate blue and yellow of harebells and buttercups, cannot alter a mistake and that it is not possible to be lifted from sorrow by pretty surroundings. Sadness is enhanced by the sweet breath of summer fields and the sound of the cuckoo calling.

In this place all that I wished for, this being buried in the country and Helena running wild and happy with other children, is not what I thought it would be.

My father takes off his wet boots in the school playroom and examines them before putting them beside his chair. I fetch some of the older girls to talk to him. He wriggles his toes in his socks to amuse Helena. She seems frightened of his stockinged feet. He is surprised when Helena screams and screams and tries to hide from him. I feel irritated with Helena for being stupid when he is being gentle and kind. I tell her that her grandpa has come a long way to visit but her crying drowns my voice. She goes on crying. I leave her and warm fresh socks for my father.

My father is staying in a small hotel on the main road not far from our field path. He says the room as well as the bed might be damp. When we walk we talk uneasily because of this. The field path is steep and slippery with mud, the bottom part through the cornfields is easier.

I have seen the corn growing from its first frail stalks to its green softness and on to its waving golden ripeness, red splashed with poppies. Now the corn on both sides of the field path has been cut and the sturdy stubble, my father thinks, will survive the cold.

Patch invites my father to have meals with the staff during his visit. She makes a few remarks to which my father replies with a sincerity which seems to expose Patch's position as vulnerable with a doubtful suitability to be headmistress of the school even though it is her own. This is something he would never do on purpose. He offers his replies from unshakeable convictions, attitudes and standards. He sits at the refectory table, on a bench, and eats the brown bread and raw cabbage. He sits next to Olive Morris who tries to talk brightly to him when he admires her four children who are in the school. He has already seen her children gathered at the partly open door of the music room watching the dancing class in which, in Myles' words, staff offspring are not to be included. Tanya was conducting the class, pounding the piano and counting aloud for the dance. Tanya, because my father was present, had quickly drawn Helena into the class. Helena, previously uninvited, was unaccustomed but held up her little skirt, her fingers grasping the hem too tightly on either side. She skipped bravely to and fro, a little dance of her own, which had nothing of the rhythm and the movement required by the music. I had to turn away from the eager strained expression on Helena's white face. Without wanting to I had to see her small knuckles whiten.

At table, Olive Morris is trying to explain to my father, without actually giving the reason, why her four children did not dance during the morning. Because Olive Morris's husband was taken away to prison, in front of all of us, she is ignored in the school. Financially ignored, as well. Because she has four children here with her she is worked to death. I have not had a chance to tell my father this. As I watch Olive courageously talking in front of Patch I have to remember that I have only been paid once during the months I have been in the school and that was not a full payment, it was just 'something on account'.

Myles says nothing during the meal. When my father admires the two enormous dogs which accompany her, like hunting companions, she continues to be silent except for the smallest murmur one person can give another when obliged to acknowledge a compliment.

'Tanya,' I say quickly, catching up with her as we are leaving the dining room, and while my father lingers to reply to Olive. 'Tanya, perhaps you could, for a little while avoid, for your mural, some of the subjects, I mean, er...'

'But of course Darling!' Tanya screams, 'I'm painting fruit and sunsets at present and I promise, as far as my sexual habits are concerned, and those of the headmistress and her illustrious paramour,' she jerks her head towards Myles who is by the long windows, 'my lips are forever sealed.'

Josepha (as it turns out, I am *her* assistant) is too busy to notice my father, though when he speaks to her slowly and carefully in German she smiles and answers him. She gives a little laugh and looks pleased for a moment and then hurries off to the pantry, where she always spends a lot of time banging the girls' dresses with a scorching hot iron.

Tanya's piano playing is terrible, everyone says so but, until this morning when Helena was allowed in the class, I have tried to hear her play as often as I could. There is no wireless here. At the Hilda Street Wentworth there was a wireless. It was on for the news and for the football pools and then switched off. Sometimes on my walks, then, I would pass a house and, hearing music from a partly open window, I would pause to listen.

I am hungry for music. I thought before I came to Fairfields that there would be music here. The harp in Patch's room has no real strings. Most days when Tanya is playing the piano for the dancing class I hang on to every crashing false note and, to be near, clean the windows in the hall.

'All that cleaning,' Tanya says to me, when she comes out,' all that cleaning, you're just guilt ridden, trying to get the guilt out.'

I feel I have to finish the windows though, when I think about it, no one has asked me to clean anything. No one tells me to do anything. Josepha seems pleased if I am slow. She races ahead bathing the children or dressing them before I know what is to be done. Her only communication is her scowl.

Tanya says all kinds of things just when she feels like saying them. She does not say them in front of my father. I am in a curious state of almost telling him the things Tanya has already told me, as if I should tell him, but carefully, paraphrasing everything. It isn't as if he would not understand. He is shy and reticent, Tanya notices this, she says he seems to consider every word before he speaks. He is not used, she says, to people like her who rip off all their clothes if they feel like it and make remarks without weighing the consequences.

Josepha, Tanya told me one night, is at her zenith of sexuality when scrubbing floors and walls. 'Gives her as good as an orgasm,' she says. And, did I know, she went on that night, that Josepha makes Rudi sleep on the floor with only an old army blanket over him. 'On the bare boards, mind you, while she's up on the bed all heaped up with blankets and beautiful Swiss cotton sheets. 'You should see the sheets,' Tanya said. 'Embroidered, pure white on pure white and well laundered, not our filthy old wash house here, but a proper laundry. Spends a fortune on laundry that one. Boy! Has that gurl got problems!' Tanya's attempt at an American accent makes us both smile. I said that I thought Josepha and Rudi were married. Tanya explained that Josepha's family won't allow the marriage. 'Every time she gets a letter from her mother she scrapes another layer of paint off the wall. She's here,' Tanya said, 'because she can't have Rudi any other way. She can have him here and no word said. Not to her face anyway.' Josepha and Rudi have moved rooms several times, Tanya explained. 'Chasing an orgasm,' Tanya said. 'Patch, the mean old bugger, is pleased, though she'd be the last to say so, because they're doing up the rooms, bit by bit, that new distemper in your room is because Josepha thought bright yellow would be the colour to make her come. They were in there less than a week. Didn't give themselves a chance did they.'

Sister Bean always said that if a patient lay with his hands up behind his head it meant he was not going to sleep. It is the position, she always said, adopted by a person who does not expect to fall asleep.

It is when I find I am lying like this during the night that I get up quietly and carefully so that I do not wake Helena who has a small bed in my room. I tie my cardigan round the light and look up the word orgasm in my *Pocket Oxford Dictionary*. The unfamiliar word is used often here at Fairfields. Orgasm. 'Paroxysm of desire or rage or other passion (Greek orgaō swell).'

I am seeing Fairfields and the people here as if my father's visit has put them through a sieve. In my father's presence I see them differently. Perhaps a girl, living at home with her mother and father, when she is married, begins to see her husband through her mother's eyes and then experiences her mother's distaste as if it is her own. Certainly a fault, like scattering bread crumbs on the carpet during meals, could be magnified in this way. Other faults, more intimate, could become distorted making married life impossible.

My father, in his innocent visit, is removing all hope of a desirable new way of living. I think of him in the cold bed at the hotel down on the main road and hope that he is asleep.

Gertrude's letters have a strange power. When I look at the folded sheets of rough paper covered with her sloping black handwriting I know that, while reading them over again, I can lose sight of immediate surroundings and be back once more in her small living room, where the window, with its low sill, looks out on to the slope of grass going straight up towards the top of her field, a place where the sky seems to rest low and close on the horizon. I can't re-read, now in the night at Fairfields, these letters, because of the incredible loneliness and sense of desolation which comes over me when I have to remember that Gertrude is no longer alive. These feelings will not be comforted not even by knowing that my kind father will be walking up to the school, from his hotel, first thing in the morning.

If I think now about Gertrude I seem to see her looking westward towards the setting sun, the grass of the field to the side of her sloping up in shadow, a deep, darker green heralding night fall. I remember too the little round hill and the spinney and the road climbing up, in summer, through the cow parsley and the

179

purple willow herb. And, in winter, the road narrow with the snow drifted up into the hedgerows. I can think about Gertrude until I am held in the magic palm of memory and I can feel sure that her place, Gertrude's Place, is only round the corner from where I am. That I have only to step outside and walk the smallest distance, turn a corner, and I shall be at the foot of the path, trodden through the long grass, leading to her door and on to the poultry speckled field with Gertrude, herself, sitting at her open door, as she so often sat, a partly plucked fowl across her apron and her face turned towards me, smiling. It is only then, in this point of remembering, that I can disregard the great distance in time and place and event and, in this forgetting, take the few steps which are needed and, putting out my hand to reach her hand, my whole self to receive the blessing of the welcome she never failed to give.

It is the cardigan scorching round the electric light shade which reminds me where I am. The ugly smell of scorching wool. I pull it down and turn off the light. From across the passage I can hear, muffled through the closed doors, the endless monotonous conversation in another language as Josepha and Rudi try to come to some sort of reconciliation. From further away there is the sound of a bath being filled. I have come to know that Tanya uses up the hot water during the night after one of her failed suicides.

It is like being on the edge of a precipice of falling crumbling sand, the precipice of the bad dream during a time of illness and high fever. Fairfields is not at all the place I thought it would be. I can't go home with my father however much I might want to. I always want to leave as soon as I am there. I can't stay at Fairfields either.

I will go with my father to the station when the time comes for him to leave. After he has gone I will re-read Gertrude's letters and I will write to staff nurse Ramsden and ask her to help me. But first the station with my father...

★

DISORDER AND EARLY SORROW

My father often arrived when it was raining. There are times now when I seem to hear his voice calling for a towel. He disliked having a wet head. Sometimes he kept the towel over his head in order, he said, to avoid a draught. Being in a draught was something he disliked too – perhaps dislike is too strong a word, perhaps it is better to say he avoided draughts, both for himself and other people. When he came in calling for a towel he always asked, as well, for a newspaper for his wet boots. Often it seemed that his ancient overcoat hung dripping in the kitchen without any possibility of being dry again.

My father's picnic at school is not easy partly because of the war and partly because of the rain. It rains all that day in autumn when he comes one Sunday, unheralded, to school. It is a surprise for me to see him standing amazed beside his motor bike and sidecar in the street outside the school. His amazement is over a threepenny bit on the pillion seat of the motor bike. He explains that he stopped for petrol about four miles from the school at a village. He says that the threepenny bit was the change. His ride, he says, must have been very smooth. He shakes his head marvelling at the smoothness. He takes up the tiny coin to examine it and then puts it down once more on the cushion of the pillion. He says to ask my friends out to a picnic. 'Get permission,' he says, 'we'll have a picnic.'

'But it's raining,' I say.

'It won't be much,' he glances at the sky. This has always been his attitude towards rain, the fact that it will not be much and what there is will do good.

181

'It's doing good,' he says looking with approval at the dripping beeches and at the puddles in the village street.

I invite Helen Ferguson and Amy, and I include Bulge who is back at school after her appendix holiday. I have to repay the present her mother gave me when I was ill I tell Helen Ferguson when she asks, 'Why on earth do you have to invite Muriel?' For a moment I can't think who Muriel is because of always calling her Bulge to myself. She does bulge I insist, to myself in my own thoughts, everywhere. Her tunic pleats, her stomach, her behind and even her eyes, everything about Bulge bulges. In my secret game of comparisons Bulge is far worse than I am in every respect. I almost explain this quickly to Helen Ferguson but my father is saying two can ride in the sidecar and two can walk and he will drive so far and turn and come back to pick up the two walking ones while the dropped two will walk on. 'A sort of relay,' he says.

'You see,' I say to Helen Ferguson quickly, 'her mother brought me *Treacle Wins Through* when I was ill that time. It's a boarding-school story, a lovely book – well, not all that good really. I must force myself to include her.'

'Well then,' Helen Ferguson says, 'don't speak to her then. Let her come but no one speaks to her. Right?'

'Right,' I say, not explaining what I now know about Bulge, that her father died being a missionary, and that Bulge has told me that people find fault with missionaries, blaming them for everything that has gone wrong, without pointing out the good things they do. Even Albert Schweitzer, Bulge has told me, people complain about him in spite of his hospital in the primeval forest. I let myself think for a moment of Bulge's mother and her gentleman friend who is so kind and polite to Bulge and even to me. And I do not say how thrilling and wonderful the *Treacle* story is and how pleased I am to have it.

Helen and Amy ride first and I walk in the rain with Bulge. Bulge starts off talking a bit. She tells me about a doll she had once and how she left this doll in the long grass by a bench in the park and then, remembering the doll in the night, she cried.

And when she went, with her mother, the next day to look for it, it was gone. Bulge gives a shy little laugh as if to say she was silly to have cried like that over a doll. When she laughs she turns towards me and I see her cheeks bulge round while she laughs. I want to ask if she found her doll later, and what other dolls did she have, and what were their little clothes like. But, of course, not speaking I turn towards the hedges, as we walk, as if looking for natural history things. I look into the hedges closely as if knowing where tiny birds' nests would be. I make my close watching of the hedges seem as if it is some kind of hedgerow research, as if I am noting how many alders are in the hedge and how often an elm rises from the skirts of hawthorn and elderberry.

Bulge walks in silence then. Our feet splash on the wet road. It is partly because of Bulge telling about her doll and partly, I think, because of hearing my father's voice, after not hearing it for a long time, that I can't help thinking about Tulip. My arms are suddenly empty. This is one of the worst things about being at school.

I have a great longing to be at home holding Tulip, changing her clothes and rocking her in my arms and hearing my father's voice, downstairs, talking to my mother, soothing her at intervals in her misunderstandings.

I keep going to the pram to put my hand on the broken head. It's under a cloth. Every time I put my hand on it I can feel the three broken pieces move. They grate on each other badly.

Tulip, I said, don't, do not, sit there. You will fall backwards in the hearth and you know perfectly well what will happen. Of course she doesn't listen and she does fall and her head breaks in three places. She looks at me with her worried eyes. Tulip, I say, I did warn you. I'll put you in the shawl like this, all round your head, and I'll wheel you about in the pram. I'll leave you in the sun by the apple tree and I'll sit in the tree and watch over you. I'll spit on anyone who comes.

No one comes. I'm thinking about Tulip's solid little feet. I mean, she came without toes. I loved her little feet straight away. You have sweet little feet I said to her. Straight away, I said this. Marigold came with Tulip. Sometimes Marigold and Tulip whisper. We are a large family and desperately poor. Fatima, Fatty for short, is my baby in long clothes. Margaret and Patsy have hair which can be brushed and combed. Lovely long, soft, silky hair with ribbons. Margaret is fair and Patsy is a brunette. Margaret looks quite nice really with her new short bob. Her hair is in an envelope marked Margaret's First Haircut and the date.

What do you mean, first hair cut? Jap asks. How will she ever have a second hair cut? he asks. Jap is Japanese and is called Jap.

When her hair grows again, I say. He is older than the others. I am surprised at his silly question and tell him so. I tell him that I'm busy, that I have to fold the clothes. I go to the pram again and feel Tulip's head. In spite of the shawl and having the pram to herself she is no better. I can feel that the pieces of head are still not joined up.

Jap, I ask him, how many flowers did you sell today?

One daffodil and one snowdrop and that's only, he says. He sinks down in an exhausted little heap. Why Jap, I say, you're wet through. I undress him quickly and put him to bed next to Patsy. She was out in the rain all night and her clothes have to be put to dry too. I can hear Patsy, in bed, telling Jap that she is going to earn money for us by being a prostitute. She feels, she says, that she must save the family somehow. I don't catch Jap's answer. Perhaps he is begging her not to take this terrible step.

The next morning, unable to stop my tears, I place Patsy on the street corner. First she persuades me to cut the neck of her dress really low. It looks daring and her pink chest shows. She insists on lipstick too. She has borrowed Margaret's hair ribbons and her button shoes and little white socks. Her own are still wet. She stands there all day with her little handbag firmly on her round arm. From the apple tree I can see her leaning against the lamp-post. And I can see her babyish legs wide apart to help keep her balance. I can see her rounded cheeks and the expression in her eyes. She has always had rather startled eyes. I cry silently to myself because of her determination and courage. A few people pass but no one stops to take up her offer. Jap says he'll sell his flowers near her to attract customers. I put him and his little wicker basket of paper flowers in the gutter close by and then I hide by the gate to watch. The street is very quiet. No one comes by.

I check Tulip. There is no change. If only her head could be whole again under the shawl! Perhaps a few drops of scent sprinkled like holy water...

Did you earn anything? I ask Patsy later but she is too tired to reply. As soon as she is undressed and put to bed she closes her eyes.

Jap, I ask him, how much money did she make? I jerk my head towards Patsy who is lying very still in bed.

None, Jap says. Your father came by on his bicycle just as I was sure a client was approaching. Your father got off his bicycle. He dismounted. Remember how he throws his leg backwards over the saddle? What is Patsy? It is Patsy, isn't it? What is Patsy doing out here? your father wanted to know. I told him, she is a prostitute. Was it her own idea? he wanted to know. Yes, I told him, it was her own idea. Your father, Jap says then, said he would give Patsy a ride home. He also, Jap adds, offered me a ride too.

Tulip is still wrapped in her shawl. I am nursing her. Fatima, my baby in long clothes, is soft all over except for her head. Fatima, I say, not in the hearth, do not sit in the hearth. Fatima has fallen backwards and broken her head. She folds up well in the music case and will go to the hospital. I am nursing Tulip. Perhaps if I rock her and sing to her her head will heal tomorrow...

Bulge is saying she can hear the motor bike coming back. Her voice in the quietness of the gentle steady rain is a shock. I almost explain to her about Tulip.

It does not stop raining. We have our picnic in the rain. My father shares out the tinned sardines and the bilberries and explains that he meant to buy some bread. The dark-brown ploughed fields slope up on all sides towards the low sky. My father, in his slow careful way of speaking, talks to Bulge. He asks her questions about our science experiments, about the results obtained when burning magnesium in air, and he is pleased with her replies.

I am not able to really understand this but my father seems to actually like Bulge.

The hungry hedges lean over the dismal road.

HELENA'S TEARS

The Peters do not write letters. I mean I've seen Mr Peters lick the point of his pencil to note down the name of a horse or an address where something is for sale, cheap. Neither Sister Peters nor Mr Peters would think of writing a letter.

To begin with, at Fairfields, I write to them almost every night telling them about the school. It's because I miss them, not having them to talk to. I make the most of the wholemeal bread and the lettuce in my letters, and I describe the avenue of beech trees and the stateliness of the old house. I don't write about the children and how they quarrel and fight in the sandpit instead of making sand castles. And I don't tell them how tired I am, that on some afternoons I lie in the long grass trying to rest without falling asleep. I would like to tell the Peters things because I find I do not really understand why the children, who have a lovely field where they can pick flowers and play, never do play. They fight all the time over one little broken spade. I can't tell the Peters that Helena tries all the time to hide in my skirt, that she cries if she can't see me. And I can't tell them that I have never been paid, that there is no such thing as Matron of the school. And if I try to put into words that I want to return to the Hilda Street Wentworth a terrible sense of hopelessness comes over me. If I write that Patch walks about the school with a fresh loaf under her arm, picking off the crust and eating it, singing sinister remarks in a contralto voice, which I have discovered is the prelude to trouble, it all becomes more unbearable. To write these things, to dwell on them means that I would relive them and in each reliving find them worse. I long for the safety and the happiness of the Hilda Street Wentworth. After my first few letters I do not write to the Peters any more. By the time my father comes on his visit I have no idea how either of the Peters are and whether the Hilda Street Wentworth is still as it was when I left. In my mind I am still dwelling in the picture stopped, in a sense, as it was while I was there, cheerful and busy, urging patients during delivery, running deep hot water for the first baths the new mothers are permitted to take and hurriedly eating big meals in the Peters' kitchen, laughing with Sister Peters about things like the home-made stirrups and the duckbilled speculum.

Some of the children have an infection and I have to get up in the night to clean the lavatory.

The upstairs lavatory of the Hilda Street Wentworth is old and decorated, like the heavy china chamberpots and bed-pans, with roses and green leaves and embroidered with a whole world of cracks and shadows, the rivers and foliage of a strange country mapped under water. The Fairfields lavatory has the same stained-glass door as that of the Hilda Street Wentworth. I reflect that, as winter comes, the upstairs and the outside lavatories at Fairfields will need candles inside inverted flower pots to prevent the pipes from freezing. In the night, when I think of the winter and how cold and miserable it will be here at Fairfields, I can't imagine how I shall be able to stay here. During the long night when I think, too, of Olive Morris and her four children and their dreary future in the school, I can see that my own future, and Helena's, will not be any better.

The world is so big, my father says when I go with Helena to see him off at the station. But even, so he tells me, we all, when we look up, are seeing the same moon. We must remember, he says, to look at his moon.

I stand on the platform until his train is out of sight and am, for once, in the place, that of seeing off a train, in which he usually is.

Helena holds my hand and, as we turn to leave the station, I see that tears are overflowing from her eyes. Instead of whimpering or howling aloud as a child does, she is crying quietly to herself as a grown-up person might cry. The tears are welling up and running over her cheeks as if they will never stop. When she looks up at me I see my own sorrow looking back at me. I see now, all in one moment, that in her reticence, her stupid shyness, she really wanted to be near her grandfather. She must have needed his presence and liked it. She must have liked to hear his voice and she must have been pleased to have his kind hand holding hers. I know from memories returning and returning during the nights when I could not sleep that it is the sound of his voice which recalls and comforts. It is not hard for me to long for the sound of his voice and for other voices which are no longer heard.

'Come along,' I say to Helena. 'I'll buy you a cake.'

In the station buffet there are cakes under a glass bell jar. They are yellow.

We wait for the bus back to the cornfields and Helena tries to eat the cake. The dry crumbs stick to her cheeks.

JOURNEY

*It's only you I'm concerned about. I am most concerned when
I see your Happiness in life threatened. I want you entirely
surrounded by love. I want every cloud lifted from your life.
Things are not ever as easy as just wanting. Wanting all that
for you has not given it. I only now regret that I am sure I
forfitted your confidence and drove you off in a vain endeavour
and was 3 to 6 months too late. I'm thinking you won't
understand what I've just written. It's only another way of
saying I expect you regretted ever confiding in me – I want you
to know you will always be very welcome ... I am loving you
and thinking about you every hour. My best love to you
always ...*

Gertrude's letters are written in strong black handwriting on
the paper she used for the fowls, for wrapping up the dressed
fowls which she sold privately to people who would pay the price
she asked. 'That old red fox has had a wing offer one of 'em tell
mother,' she would say about a badly maimed boiler. 'Tell her
as I'm sorry about the wicked fox.' Gertrude neatened the
damaged fowls with her dressmaking scissors. She often supposed
the fox to be a vixen with cubs. But, in her opinion, this did not
excuse the fox's habit of raiding and killing beyond the need for
food. Some women, she said, were vixenish same as foxes.

After my father's visit to Fairfields, the night after seeing him off on his train, I open the small brown paper bag and re-read Gertrude's letters. I read all through her wisdom and her kindness, her persuasion and her love. And while I am doing this, for a small space of time in the long unhappy night, it is as if she is still alive and waiting for me to come to her Place. And then I write my letter to Ramsden;

Dear Ramsden I have no way at all of getting away from this place. Please Ramsden can you come? Please?

But it is not possible to still be at Fairfields should my letter reach staff nurse Ramsden and should a reply come to me from her.

'Fortnitt? Fortnitt?' Patch says during her sinister pacings between tables, in one door and out of another. 'Fortnitt? Deah? But you must go today, deah. There's a bus at the end of the field path at three o'clock. Do leave today, deah. What's all this? A Fortnitt?' She's tearing crusts off a loaf she has under one arm, she's tearing off the bread crust and stuffing it in her mouth. As she walks she is watched by the children who have only their lettuce leaves in front of them. They watch with hungry eyes.

I try to explain that I am thinking I should give two weeks' notice before I leave. A fortnight...

'Fortnitt! Fortnitt!' Patch sings in the contralto we all dread. 'By all means do go today. There's a bus...By all means...' She exchanges a raising of the eyebrows with Miss Myles who is, just then, with her dogs, passing the open door.

The girl whose bed Helena and I have at the women's night shelter in London, this girl who is having a propelling pencil removed from her bladder, the woman in charge tells me, hasn't a coat. 'She does not have a coat,' she says. She has been watching while I try to force my winter coat, the one which has accompanied me since school, into the hopelessly bulging case.

Why not, the woman suggests, leave the coat for this girl who has nothing she can call her own, not even her baby. 'Lorst her baby pore thing. The things these girls 'll do to theirselves! The things they'll try! It'll sort of show your gratichood,' she says, 'for having the use of her bed so to speak.' The woman takes my coat and folds it over the end of the bed.

'But I'll need my coat later,' I start to say, 'I'll be needing it quite soon.' But she has made up her mind about the coat and who shall, in the future, have it. After all the girl is in hospital and hasn't got anything...

There are several advertisements in the magazine, *The Lady* I think it is, the outside cover is torn off. While I drink the cup of tea and eat the slice of bread and margarine supplied at the night shelter for breakfast, I read quickly down the positions advertised. Skipping the flower arrangings and the dressmakings I come to one where a live-in housekeeper is required, 'one child no objection'. It says to apply in writing. The address is Glasgow. It means a long journey. A journey which will use up all my money. There is no time to write a letter.

Fairfields, which was only yesterday, seems a long time ago. Waiting all those hours at the final stop for the Green Line bus from Hertford was the silliest thing I have ever done. The long evening moved slowly into the night of soft dusty warmth. A few people walked by on the pavement where the slabs were still warm with the trapped sun. All those people had places they were going to. How could I have expected Ramsden to come? I waited not knowing whether she had ever received my letter. In the letter I told her everything that had happened, about Helena, about my leaving home, about my loneliness. I sent my letter to the last address I had from Ramsden several years ago, the letter in which she said she was still nursing and that she had her own little flat where I would be welcome. I told her in my letter that I would wait for her at the terminus of the Green Line.

When I think of Ramsden I remember her shy kind eyes and my own eyes fill with tears. I have to understand that she might be anywhere at this present time. Unreachable, perhaps playing the piano on concert platforms in towns up and down the country. A curious feeling of having been rescued comes over me when I think of the policeman who, after passing me several times in the street, brought me and the case and Helena, who was asleep on the case, to this women's shelter. I would not have known to come here myself.

Helena has eaten her breakfast slice. It is time to leave.

'You can have the book if you want it,' the woman in charge of the night shelter says as she collects the two small towels she lent me.

'The book?'

'Yes, the book. You can have it.'

'Oh yes, the magazine, thank you.' I almost tell her I don't want it, that I have read it but realize, in time, that she is giving me a present. I tell her again, 'Thank you.'

It is time to go. For some reason it requires an effort to leave this place. It is a place I would never have come to and now I have to make myself leave. Perhaps it is the idea of safety, the shelter is very much a shelter when compared to the streets and the pavements. I must leave. My mind is made up. I have the address. I must take a chance.

When I think about Gertrude I remember how she tried to save me from what she thought of as a pitfall. When I think about her I have to remind myself that she is no longer there, within a short bicycle ride from my mother's house. Remembering this makes me feel alone and helpless in the compartment especially as the train is rushing now through landscape made familiar by the fields and hedgerows and the small patches of woodland similar to those surrounding my school and, a bit further on, as we race through the rapidly unfolding countryside, similar to the place where Gertrude lived.

If, after thinking about Gertrude, I think about my father and how he would not have understood the truth behind Olive Morris's attempt to hide the truth and, at the same time, give an explanation as to why her children were not in the dancing class, it is because, like Gertrude, he would never imagine for one minute that any child would ever be left out, excluded on purpose, from something so pertinent to childhood as a dancing class. Similarly Gertrude, when she tried, as she thought, to save me, could never have imagined for one minute that the fashionable Metcalfs, Dr Metcalf and Magda, could not be persuaded to refrain from seeing me, to stop inviting me, to stop all that she thought was happening, through them, to me. She would willingly have braved what she called the grand house and the well off folk to rescue me without imagining for one minute what those well off folk, as she thought them to be, were really like. Gertrude had no idea of the lengths the people, who frequented Magda's parties, would go to in their elaborate jokes and methods of ridiculing someone. Their intentions were for amusement and not for hurting but, for someone like Gertrude, the hurt would be deep and lasting and never understood.

All at once I am remembering my father's pleasure in his school dinners. I went to his school once and watched, with my mother, as the ragged children went, in single file, up to my father who offered the thick slices of bread for them to eat, soaked with the gravy, so that it would not be left on the plates wasted. It is all I can do not to leave the train now at the all too well-known station where he has so often seen me off on a journey or come to meet me on arrival. The train, hissing and steaming, stays here for some time. I lean out looking eagerly up and down the long platform as if it could be possible that he, sensing my travellings, could be there now to run alongside as the train starts to move again, slowly at first and then gathering speed resuming the journey, pushing, in his usual way, a magazine and a comic, a last minute final gesture, through the window. I look with longing at the familiar station slipping by. I have never thought before what it would be like to be so near the place I have always thought of as home and not go there. I think with longing of that first half hour in the house with my mother and her delight to have Helena with her. This delight which turns so quickly to her disappointment and anger over me and then the way in which

193

this is followed by her ability to reduce me to an unwilling rage and to tears.

Because Helena is so sure we should be getting off the train she starts crying; a terrible howling, as I pull her down on the seat beside me. She cries till she is sick and I have to try to clean her with the inadequate drips of water which have to be coaxed from the faulty tap in the lavatory.

Later when she sleeps, rocking against me with the motion of the climbing and then speeding train, I feel a great tenderness for her and I cover her small relaxed fingers with my hand. I reflect on chance. When I left the night shelter I took two chances. The big one, to make this journey and a quick small chance which was to lift, as I went by the end of the bed, my school winter coat and put it over my arm. In a sense I did give the coat when asked, or rather, told to. The night shelter woman happened to have her back to me as we passed along the narrow hall and out down the steps into the street.

In the hoped for peacefulness, enhanced by the presence of the ugly coat, rescued and curled loosely in the luggage rack, I try to rest while Helena sleeps, but the darkening afternoon threatens a storm. Driving rain and heavy banks of cloud accompany the journey towards an incredible loneliness and the mistake I might be making in travelling at such speed into the unknown.

CABIN FEVER

My father used to say that learning something was not really of any use unless it was fitted to some other thing which had been learned. Perhaps a better way of saying this is to say that facts should be linked and everything should then be applied to where it belongs in human life. This is true about fiction, he said then, fiction places people where they belong in society. There is no such thing he said as a dated novel. The novel set in a particular time gives a picture of that time with all the details of life as it was lived then. In any case he said human beings have not changed except outwardly in fashion where clothes and food are concerned and in the equipment they have learned to use. Love and hate and revenge, ambition, jealousy and grief are all as they have always been.

But back to facts. To know the population of a town or a country is not enough. Other things have to be included, how and where the people live, what they wear and what they eat, what their illnesses are, where their drinking water comes from, what they grow, what their houses are like, what their work is, what their hopes and ambitions are and what they fear most in their lives; all these things are only a beginning.

My Father's Moon

Over and above all this my father would always remind me that if I looked at the moon, wherever I was, I was seeing the same moon that he was looking at. 'And because of this,' he said, 'you must know that I am not very far away. You must never feel lonely,' he said. He said the moon would never be extinguished. Sometimes, he said, it was not possible to see the moon, but it was always there. He said he liked to think of it as his.

At the Georges

'How can you say that! How can you say a thing like that!'

'What d'you mean – like that? Like what?'

'Saying that on the phone. How can you say that? And another thing, don't take that tone with your own mother. What will...'

'...people think? There's no one here to listen at present. What did I say then? What's the trouble?'

'How can you say "it's his wife speaking".'

'Well, I can hardly say, "This is his mistress here", to the plumber, can I.'

'You're not his wife. You're not married to him. How can you do this to your own mother!'

'I'm not doing anything to you.'

'And another thing, you can't call her Rachel.'

'Whyever not? It's a pretty name. I like it.'

'No one calls a baby Rachel these days. No girl can have this name. Rachel was the Queen of the prostitutes.'

'Don't be silly. That's not true, it's silly, a silly made up...'

'Im Kloster, they always said...In the convent they said...'

'You're not in the convent now. And *if* she's a girl she's Rachel. It's a Hebrew name and it means "ewe" and is a symbol of innocence and gentleness. It's a pretty name.'

'Anyway you're not his wife. He probably will never marry you. Whatever will people think?'

'At present everyone thinks we are married so there's nothing

197

to worry about is there.'

'And another thing, you know what men are like. You'll be turned out of the house on to the streets with two children. The house isn't even *partly* in your name.'

'We're going to put the house in our joint names. We're going to get married too. It's not that easy. We'll have to go somewhere else and have a special licence and be married in the Registry Office...'

'What about your family and witnesses?'

'Oh for Heaven's Sake, blow family! This is just something that has to be done, and as privately as possible. We'll get a couple of witnesses off the street.'

'Oh. How can you do this to me, your own mother! You're an adventuress! How could I have had a daughter like this.'

At this point my eyes fill with tears as I imagine how my mother will start to cry with the deep disappointment she has with me. I shall feel sorry for her and try to comfort her. It is remembering the way her nose goes red when she is upset, I can't bear remembering this. Also she's sure to have in her lap a partly unwrapped parcel of the new little pink clothes she has made and brought for my new baby, for Rachel. She will have made the long journey and be tired. I persist. 'Look,' I say and my own voice, echoing aloud, alone, surprises me. 'Look, you'll feel better later. You'll like him. You'll like everything. I promise you, he's going to marry me. We want to be married. We're going to have an au pair girl and I'm going to study to be a doctor like you always wanted me to. Everything's going to be all right. Look, if you like I'll study music too...'

My mother, when she comes, is sure to be uneasy and unhappy. It will be her first visit to this enormous house. Helena will be shy and not give her the welcome she hopes for and she will be meeting the Georges for the first time because, of course, they have never seen each other.

'I don't expect the sister is at all pleased,' my mother starts again. 'How old is she? Seventy-five, you said. *Seventy-five.* When she knows, *knowing* might well kill her. She might well have a stroke. You'll spend your life nursing her. And what about him? *Fifty-eight? He's older than I am.* Vera, how could you! *He's older than your father.* Vera, how can you! You'll spend the rest of your life nursing these two people *and* being an unmarried mother...'

These conversations of the future, like past conversations relived, circle round and round, voiceless, leading nowhere. While I am preparing vegetables, dicing carrots, turnips and parsnips for a bland soup with pearl barley, I can see clearly my mother's tears on her soft cheeks; and her lap strewn with tiny garments, a small hand-knitted vest tied with ribbons, little knitted boots, some pink and some blue, to be on the safe side, something she calls a matinee jacket, white, because it might upset a baby boy to lie in his cradle dressed in pink, even if the pink is of the most delicate and dusty sort.

My mother has never really believed that Helena's father is not still around.

'Why can't the father, the father of your – what I mean is why can't he do something?'

'I've told you he's dead.'

'How can you say that, he was on the phone – I could tell by your voice, that's who it was.'

'He's dead. I've told you.'

Round and round in my head the words leaving no room for other thoughts.

'I simply can't understand you. How could you with your education and your background breed like a rabbit – '

'You're always saying that, for years you've said it. I've told you, rabbits have six, I only one.'

'How can you speak to me, your mother, like that.'

'Oh shut up and remember this. I'm never coming back home. Never!'

The conversations, without my wanting them, return and return.

There are other things on my mind too. One of the troubles about doing work which requires very little calculating thought is that it leaves the mind free to suffer in its own inimitable way.

While I am washing the stone flags in the kitchen or the mosaic of richly coloured tiles in the porch between the stained glass of the front door and the outside storm doors which are unlocked and folded back on each side every morning, I try to think clearly and work out in a private internal discussion the best ways in which to follow a hoped for plan of action based on certain facts and promises.

Some of these things are hypothetical because, to start with, promises made by other people are not always honoured and I am not altogether sure of certain facts.

'How could you have been so stupid, Vera,' my mother's critical voice echoing, possibly echoing my own unrealized thought. 'How could you, Vera, have been so stupid getting pregnant as soon as you arrive, practically the minute you arrive! The brother can easily declare his innocence and the sister will believe him and both will be certain you were already pregnant before you came to them.' I must try to silence my mother's unwanted voice.

Early on, as soon as I arrived here, it was clear that I had to understand that my need for survival was great and if something fell into my lap, an illness for example, there was a moral profit to be gained by making use of this in spite of a desperate request for silence on the subject. During that night my argument, which was once more an internal one, was that I must, as in the past, make the best use of my knowledge, take what comes my way and make use of that. It seemed then that I could have the moral profit of acting in such a way that I would help someone and simultaneously benefit my own life and Helena's hugely.

'How can you propose to spend your life with someone you don't know at all *and* who is so much older. Sixty, Vera, how can you!' My mother's voice, breaking with indignation, in my head as it has always done all through the years. 'This man, Vera, is older than Daddy. You'll spend your life, your whole life, nursing, and nursing a relative is not the same as nursing in hospital. Not at all.'

My mother has not yet come here for a visit. She will be coming. She will be coming, not just in my imagination, but in reality. Not even the prospect of being unwelcome will stop her. She will come because she thinks she must come. She will try to take Helena home with her. She will come, uneasily.

Knowing the Georges as I am beginning to know them I don't think she will be unwelcome. For myself I don't seem able, in my mind, to get rid of my mother's thoughts, her voice or her tears. And there is no welcome, at present, for her in me.

Another conclusion I have come to is that it is almost impossible to get married once you are living in the same house and sleeping in the same bed with someone, even if the bed part is a secret. It is impossible, in certain circumstances, to announce to friends, relatives, colleagues and shop assistants that a marriage is intended. There seems to be no way of dealing with this. The only reason why I have not given my mother words about this is because it will be beyond her thoughts. Up till now this particular difficulty has never occurred to me. My mother will have no idea about this problem.

'I'll slip into my negleege, pardon my deshabbee,' Sister Peters used to say on the occasions when she relieved me during the night when I had been up with a fretful baby.

'Go back to bed, Vera,' she would say. 'I'll walk the floor for a bit with his Highness. You get back to bed and get some sleep.'

When I hang out the washing here at the Georges I am reminded of the walled garden at the Hilda Street Wentworth. In the spring there, the pear blossom filled the sky, overflowing the boundary of the wall, cascading in streams of pure white like the dress and veil on a silent bride. There is a gnarled black tree in the Georges' garden. Perhaps it too is a pear tree waiting for a wedding dress.

Every day when I take in the washing, as the weather gets colder, it is damp still and smells of the soot-laden fog.

I would like to see Sister Peters and Mr Peters. Perhaps I can make some jam here. It would be like being at the Hilda Street Wentworth, not that I want to be back there. Not at all. Just to see them for an hour or so, that's what I would like.

'And another thing Vera, sixty-two is a dangerous age for a man.' My mother at my elbow again. If only she would leave me in peace. 'Men of that age,' she's persisting, 'men of that age like to be congratulated on having an affair with a younger woman. But people shake their heads, you'll see, over the girl and her uncertain future. Sixty-four, Vera, is an age when men make fools of themselves. I shouldn't be at all surprised if his sister thinks he's making a fool of himself mark my words, Vera, *She* will have her revenge. An elder sister takes care of a younger brother. You'll see, she'll have her revenge.'

I go upstairs, two at a time, in the empty house. Helena is outside sweeping the wet bricks of the wash house with a small broom we found out there.

'You're to come home with me Vera!' my mother follows even when I take the stairs three at a time. 'You're to come home with me. I've come all the way to fetch you. If you won't come, at least let me take Helena. What's all this going to do to her? Have you thought about that? You never do think! I regret every day of my life that I gave you that book.'

'What book? Whatever has a book to do with this?'

'That book about that sculptor woman, Elizabeth something or other, Elizabeth Ney, she had a baby in that book without being married. And now you'll be having a second baby and no husband. I should have thought your nursing training would have taught you...'

I'm pleased the house is empty this morning, I hurry on up to the bathroom, which is not the servant's bathroom. I go there all the same as quickly as I can. For some reason I feel dreadfully sick. I would so like to see Sister Peters just now even though I know she would remind me soon enough that the Nurses' Insurance Company make the four pounds maternity payment once only and it's not just because of being an unmarried mother.

'What about diseases, Vera?' I hear my mother still as I bring up all my breakfast, thankful to be in the bathroom and not on the stairs. 'Surely they taught you about diseases in your training, Vera.' I look at my reflection in the bathroom mirror and wipe the tears from my eyes.

'A man in his position can't suddenly change,' my mother's voice, at my elbow, once more. 'A man of his age, if he has never had children, is not used to babies and children. You'll see, Vera, it's one thing to have a housekeeper who has a child. He can smile at the child and drop coins in her shoes now and then, but you do see, Vera, don't you, you'll be in an impossible position. Oh Vera! think of Helena. How can you do this to her! And, another thing when he has a child of his own, this . . . this Rachel, he isn't going to want the older child. Helena will be unwanted. Oh Vera, let me take Helena home. Your Daddy and I can look after her. She's fond of us . . . Vera, you can't, you cannot let Helena be *unwanted*.' I wipe the basin after washing my face.

'And Vera,' my mother again, 'Vera, I'm certain the sister, his sister, is not likely to suffer fools gladly. She will quite rightly be annoyed at her brother making a fool of himself, making fools of both of them. How will she be able to go out socially with everyone knowing her brother, a professor at the university, has been – well, seduced is the only word I can think of? This poor innocent man! That a daughter of mine should be such a person to do what you have done. I can't believe it . . . '

After I am sick again I cry. My mother will be coming here later on for a visit. I won't listen any more to what she's saying in my head. That is, if I can manage not to. But the stupid, the really stupid thing is that I want my mother. I want my mother as she was, delicately scented, her hands hovering above an earache and her shadow, twice its real size, moving across the ceiling in the candle light.

I suppose there are times in a person's life when there is an unexpected need for the mother.

I wipe my face once more on someone else's towel in the Georges' bathroom.

Every time my mother, in my head, mentions Mr George's age he is two years older than he was. I mean he has aged six years in a few seconds. How can I know what his age really is?

FLOWERS

When I thank him for the flowers Mr George says the greatest pleasure from flowers is in the sending of them. He says the sender has tremendous pleasure because of enjoying the thought of sending them in the first place. And then there is the thinking, he says, the thinking about going to the shop to choose them. Deciding which flowers, in all the wealth of flowers, he says, deciding which flowers and what sort of an arrangement is an extra pleasure especially when the shop assistant seems very interested and pleased with his choice. He says too that he thinks it is an extra pleasure, extra because it is so unexpected, to write the name of the person, who is to receive the flowers, on the little card provided by the shop. The little cards are all pretty, he says, and this makes it hard to know which one to have. He says he has never sent flowers to anyone before.

I have never had flowers sent to me before. I am alone with Helena in the house when they are delivered. When I see my name on the small envelope I am taken aback but recover quickly.

'Don't,' I say to the delivery boy, 'do not lean your bike up against the paint work.' My heart is thumping. I take the flowers through to the wash house out the back and put them in a bucket.

SNOW

'I'd like to have a gas boiler and I'd like to be a doctor,' I tell Mr George when he asks me what I want most in the world. I tell him that his question does not strike me as being a naive question at all when he says he is sorry for asking such a naive question.

'It depends on when and where the question is asked and why,' he says, as if explaining things to himself. That is the kind of man he is. We have to lie very still, our bodies close, on the single bed. We have to whisper so that we are not overheard.

'Funny you having such a narrow bed,' I say.

'I've always had this bed,' he says. There is, of course, no reply to this.

'About the gas boiler,' he says, 'there's no reason at all why you should not have a gas boiler *and* be a doctor. A gas boiler!' He laughs a bit at that but does not laugh about my wanting to be a doctor.

Pale foggy fingers of light show in the sky outside Mr George's bedroom window. It is almost time for me to be getting up so I go as quickly and as quietly as possible up to my own bed in the attic. There are two attic bedrooms. The other one is occupied at present. A discovery which I make surprisingly quickly will lead, I am certain, to the other room being empty soon. Helena will go on having a little folding bed in my room as I shall not feel disposed to move her into that other room in the circumstances. Not at present, anyway.

It is interesting to me to have discovered something about myself. It interests me, on reflection, as I slide between the cold sheets (cold, thin sheets, linen, soft with age and frequent washing, just as I like sheets to be) of my own bed, that I seem to prefer being kissed on the neck rather than on the lips. Lips are all right but the neck is better, much much better.

'This may prove to be purely an intellectual exercise,' Mr George says to me the first time we are in his bed together. 'I hope you will not be disappointed,' he says. I tell him I want him too much to be disappointed and he tells me he wants me terribly much. I tell him I often think of his pullover, the soft red-coloured one, and that I love the way it wrinkles slightly at the back. He seems pleased and he tells me he loves me and I feel with pleasure the force of his love. 'I love you too,' I tell him and I mean it.

It is so nearly time to be getting up I do not have long to enjoy my own sheets and my exquisite memories. So busy is my mind with the strange way in which things have turned out that I scarcely notice the hardship of getting up on a cold morning in autumn. It is cold enough to be winter already, as the Georges say, with the early snow, a light-falling snow storm and then the freezing fog for several days in a row.

I wash, splashing my face with ice-cold water from the attic jug imagining I am like a peasant girl in a Tolstoy story. I even clatter across the stone flags of the kitchen as I think Tolstoy's peasant girl would have done. I like to think of myself as nimble and unafraid, able to do all sorts of things which the Georges do not seem able to do, like going up through the landing skylight at the top of the main staircase to shovel snow off the flat roof. Between the attic gables there is a flat roof. The snow settles there and when it melts it seeps through in places causing mould on the ceilings. I wash my neck as well as my face with the icy water. It is something I have been taught to do.

Because of not having a house of my own I seem always to be living in the kind of house I would never be able to afford to live in in the ordinary way. Things are quite good in my life at present, very good in fact, at present, in terms of a spacious house, the kisses and the sheets. There is an obstacle to start with, a hindrance, but fortunately I have a kind of patience and foresight to see that something will happen which will enable me to take rewarding action.

There is a tide in the affairs of men which taken at its flood leads on to fortune...

Because of the way in which things happen for me I think of this quotation, something we had at school, but mostly I remember it because Magda, whenever she hailed a taxi, and took it out of turn, always recited it. 'Shakespeare, Dahling, when dear stupid Brutus is being tricked into an evil plot. It's called irony, Dahling, and you have to jump right in to the flooding river and take your chance, your opportunities. This taxi, Dahling, is gorgeously comfortable isn't it. Such a piece of luck getting it so easily. And all those people in the queue. Just look! I wonder why their mouths have all dropped open like that.' Magda often hugged me in taxis.

Going up on the flat roof and out on to the fresh first fall of snow is the first thing I do here. Well, not really the first thing, it is a sort of first thing. It's like this, after the first fall of snow I go up there. Up through the roof trap knowing that the Georges see me as light and young and strong. The Georges, on that morning, make me feel that's what I am like. I shovel off the snow that morning early. There is not a great deal but what there is I shovel it off, scraping gently and throwing it lightly over the parapet into the fog-pink sunrise. I love this snow. My cheeks burn in the cold air. My face continues pleasantly flushed all day and, in the evening, Mr George notices.

Strictly speaking the first thing is my arrival. Really first is my arrival, not expected by anyone.

★

ARRIVAL

Really first is my arrival, not expected by anyone. No one knowing about my long journey, not knowing about my destination. To travel without being expected to arrive is something new for me. When I arrive, naturally I am not expected. It is late in the remains of the half light evening of summer moving into autumn. I am cold and wet through because of a sudden downpour. Helena is asleep on my arm and flopping over my shoulder. My other arm is nearly out of its socket with dragging my case the length of the street from the tram stop on the corner.

'I've come,' I tell them when they come, lamplit, from the dark hall, leaning together to the front porch in answer to the doorbell. They, the Georges, both tall, bending over with concern, asking me, 'What did you say? What is it you're saying?'

'I've come from London,' I tell them. 'I've come about the position,' I manage to say, 'child no objection. Live in.'

In the subdued murmuring of the two soft voices, now near and now far away, I understand that they are suited, that the advertisement was placed months ago. It must have been an old magazine. I have to understand. They have someone. I sink down under Helena's weight on the steps and lean against the outside door. Above me their voices are gentle, like voices in a dream. They are sorry, they say, echoing each other, but they are suited. Suited, that is the word they use. They have someone. I cry then telling them I have used up all my money. Helena wakes up and cries. One of them lifts Helena up away from me. One of them is saying to close the storm doors and lock up.

'Lock up, now.' The words from one to the other are hardly heard.

They tell me they are called George, these people. They hover, uncertain, in the kitchen. They make some hot milk in a small saucepan and pour it over bread broken up in two basins. Helena has never eaten bread and milk before and I am nervous that she will be rude to the old lady and refuse to eat. But Helena spoons up the new dish quickly and I do the same. There is hot water, they tell me, if we would like a bath and a bed which we can share.

Helena is very hot all night. Helena is feverish. Unable to keep awake I feel her through my sleep, her hot thin body next to mine, sinking in the feather bed. And I hear her coughing, a little dry double cough. Two coughs, cough cough, and a pause. I should get up to attend to her but can't wake up enough. She coughs, hot beside me, all night.

In the morning the sparrows are all round the edges of the grey light of the roof windows. The little black shapes of these birds are busily edging each other off the edges of the windows. The sloping ceiling of the attic room reflects the light of the coming day. Helena, awake, is lying looking up at the birds. She looks refreshed. The cough is not hers. Someone else is coughing. The dry double cough is coming from the other side of the wall, from another little bedroom up here under the gables.

I remember immediately, the people, the Georges, the two kind elderly people, already have their maid. They have her now for several weeks. She suits them. She is in the other room.

The little feet of the sparrows skid across the skylight. Like Helena I lie watching the sparrows and listening to their chirping. The attic room appeals to me. There is a strip of thin worn carpet across the plain boards, some simple wooden furniture and a washstand with a jug and basin. Maid's furniture. The wish to stay in this room is overpowering. I long to be the maid who comes up here to the top of the house to rest her aching feet, to sleep the innocent sleep maids sleep when their work is done. How simple life could be for a maid, especially in a solid house like this. This is what I want. And then I hear once more that small restrained dry double cough through the wall. One maid is enough. The Georges will only want one maid.

They are brother and sister George, Miss George explains. She tells me repeatedly how sorry they are that they are suited. The housekeeper has two days off to go and visit her family. Would I like to stay two or three days? Miss George asks me. She suggests I try and find a place and in the meantime I am welcome to stay. 'Stay awhile,' she says, 'till you get things sorted out. Doris,' she says, 'has gone, she's gone for the early train. She always goes before breakfast.'

'Thank you,' I tell Miss George that I am very grateful, I tell her, 'thank you.'

So I don't see Doris, the real housekeeper, straight away. The only thing I know about her is the sound of her cough.

'Now a *red* one and now a *blue* one.' Miss George is bending over Helena at the kitchen table. She is showing Helena how to colour some cut-out paper flowers. Miss George does not scribble with the crayon. She does not scribble round and round pressing hard, tearing the paper with the coloured pencils. Miss George holds the crayon lightly in her long fingers and shades in the colour in delicate strokes all slanting in the same direction. Helena looks on and is pleased. She tries to copy Miss George's precision. Helena's pale hand is small beside Miss George's hand which is brown flecked and elderly.

The first few days with the Georges go by very quickly. Miss George shows me the house, the damp linen cupboards, the sideboards of china and silver and the rooms full of books. I take Helena out with me and queue for fish and leave a neatly written grocery order which will be delivered. Miss George says it is fortunate that the grocer and greengrocer have resumed delivery even though the boys arrive at awkward times and tip everything out on to the kitchen table so that earth from the potatoes goes through everything. Her voice is never raised and her complaining is mild. I imagine how Sister Peters would shout from the upstairs landing, in the middle of a birth even, if she thought a heap of vegetables was being dumped on the table downstairs.

I discover straight away when I dust Mr George's desk that he is Professor George. I try to make out his subject from various papers, a historian perhaps.

These Georges, they fascinate me. They make me feel I want to do things for them. And the little attic bedroom is a place I like to think about. I look at the floor boards up there and think how they will be warmed in summer. I want to be up in the attic sitting on the sun-warmed floor. I want to stay in this house.

There would be a moral profit in the possibility of getting rid of the present housekeeper. Moral because of the circumstances in which there would be a virtue in my telling certain things, a certain thing, that is, which I think I have discovered without even seeing her. I think I know something of the present housekeeper's predicament.

A message from Doris is telephoned by a relation. Hanging over the landing bannisters I can see and hear Miss George's concern. She tells me later that Doris has another cold and will be away for a few more days. Miss George says that Doris never seems quite well, that, in spite of good food and an hour or so in the fresh air every day, she continues pale and unwell.

'I insist on her walk,' Miss George says. She is not able to understand why Doris does not look better. I almost say then what I think about what Miss George goes on to call Doris's persistent cough. I listen and nod my head but do not say anything. Having made up my mind, in a sense, to be ruthless, to stop at nothing to keep the attic bedroom as mine, it is almost impossible not to speak, especially as Miss George adds that sometimes Doris is almost green in her paleness.

★

THE OWNERS OF GRIEF

'Vera,' Miss George says, 'Vera you have been here a week, it is your turn and Helena's to have a bath.'

'Thank you, Miss George,' I say, 'thank you.'

These Georges, they are refined. I am still here with them. Helena is asleep in the attic and Doris is back, coughing in her room. Doris and I, during the day, do not have much to say to each other. I see her looking at me sometimes and am prompted to remark that I've had no luck with the advertisements. And Doris agrees that it is hard to find a place. She's lucky, she says, to have found the Georges. She has four children she tells me. They are at her mother's. I try to imagine what it must be like making the journey, going home to four children, all girls, and a grandmother, on her days off. I try to imagine what it must be like to be separated from the children and I wonder if the grandmother is full of reproachings as soon as Doris arrives.

'One awful place'll have me,' I tell Doris. 'It's a man and three grown-up sons and the house is really small and nasty. It smells, and you should see the bathroom! And the room meant for me is no more than a cupboard.' Doris is sympathetic and says she wouldn't want to go there either and perhaps I should look around a bit more. She says Helena is tall for her age and is about the age of her second youngest. She says she hopes something else will turn up.

'If it doesn't I'll just have to go there,' I tell her.

These Georges, they like nice things. They have delicate taste and polished manners and when they speak to each other it is with subtle thought and language. Just now I am listening to some music, cello. And I'm thinking how nice the bath was. I feel free because Helena is asleep upstairs and Doris is up there too, coughing. Doris goes to bed very early. Because of her cough she does not get enough sleep. I am sitting on the stairs, at the bottom of the main staircase, listening to the cello from Mr George's study. Miss George went to bed some time ago.

I have been cheating the Georges. I have thrown away the advertisements, telling Miss George I was too late or that a child was unacceptable. The man with the three grown-up sons will be expecting me to come because I did not tell him outright that I was not coming. I have been working hard here. There is plenty to do as it is a very big house and Doris does not manage to do all that needs doing. All the same, two maids are not required.

My cheeks are flushed and hot after my bath. There was a light fall of snow, an early snow storm this morning.

'Snow in autumn,' Miss George says as she takes her place for breakfast. She shivers. Mr George asks me to fetch Miss George's shawl please. He smiles.

The sloping ceilings of the attic reflect the light of the snow-covered gables. As soon as I see this I get up and go downstairs. Mr George has the step ladder on the landing. Both the Georges are anxious about the settled snow on the flat roof.

Mr George is particularly pleasant to look at when he is wearing a dressing gown.

I have no difficulty, in the face of the Georges' admiration, in raising the roof trap and in climbing through to clear away the very small amount of snow. My cheeks are pleasantly red all day because of this.

This night starts well for me with my rosy face and the music of the cello. It is so long since I heard any music that my eyes fill with tears even though I do not know the particular piece. Mr George, coming out for more coal, asks me if I would like to come in by the fire. He explains it is Beethoven, a quartet. As I listen, the notes, one after the other, climbing, entering and combining, are all in my head. And afterwards, when it is over, I tell Mr George that I have been to a quartet from school but never since. Mr George is so nice, without meaning to, I go on talking and tell him about Ramsden, staff nurse Ramsden, and how I wanted once to tell her about the downward thrust of the cello and about the perfection in the way the other instruments come up to meet the cello. I tell him that I did not feel able to tell her that I thought someone had measured the movements of the notes controlling carefully the going down and the coming up in order to produce this exquisite mixture.

Mr George seems interested and pleased but I am not sure if this is not just kindness and good manners. He suggests I come nearer to the fire. I sit on the floor near the hearth and closer to him. Very gently he touches my cheek saying that the snow storm has made me look well. He lifts my hair away from my face and says that the red cheeks suit me.

All I seem to see is his russet-coloured pullover and his smile.

It is when he guides me upstairs in the sleeping household to his room where he helps me undress before taking me in his arms and then into his bed with him that he tells me he is susceptible to music and he hopes I will not be disappointed.

'I am susceptible,' he says, 'to music which seems to contain an everlasting youth. It seems to restore one's own youth.' And he hopes he has more than just this susceptibility to offer. He wants me terribly he says but I can escape to my own room if I do not want to stay in his.

I tell him then that I have no wish to escape.

'You are a remarkable young woman,' Mr George says afterwards when we are lying close to each other in his narrow bed and I have been telling him about the nightmare of Fairfields, about Tanya, about the Metcalfs, about Lois, Trent and Ferguson and about my father and his moon.

'You are a very remarkable young woman,' he says once more. 'My mentor!' he says. There is something in his way of holding me which is powerful and, at the same time, restrained. He explains that he responds to music and that he feels, now, he should not have directed this response towards me. I tell him I wanted him to, that I am susceptible to music too but would never have thought of the words to describe myself. When I tell him I want him one more time, he says I am wonderfully shameless, and when I ask him what there is to be ashamed of he seems pleased and says he'll never forget my question.

Somehow it is, just then, as if the remembered reddish colour of his pullover is blending with the glowing floor boards and the cherry-wood furniture of the attic bedroom, and I wonder why I should, during the sweet wild moments, consider this woollen garment and the attic chair, the woodwork of the wash stand and the floor boards.

How can I tell anyone of this, least of all my mother who would be reassured if a time comes when reassurance is needed.

The silly thing is that I miss Tanya, actually miss her. When I think about her, like now, I can see that there is something about her which makes her like Magda, or rather, which reminds me of Magda. Perhaps it is that they are both people of misfortune. They could be called owners of grief. When I think about that, I too am an owner of grief, but I am completely without the flamboyance which gives Magda and Tanya glamour. And of course money makes a great difference, the possession of money. Tanya and I are different from Magda. Tanya and I have no money.

How could I, just now, have considered that there could be anything reassuring in the fact that I am lying naked, held by Mr George's arm, as he sleeps beside me. I am actually stupid enough to imagine that my being loved by him will reassure my mother. If I should try to speak of it to her she would immediately reply using some phrase which would not match with her ordinary way of speaking but would be, perhaps, the only way in which she could express her fear and distate.

'You *are* a *fast worker*, Vera. How could you be so *cheap?* Cheap and wicked. And Vera, he's got *white hair*. How could you, a daughter of mine, do this...'

I would like to have my books. Often during sleepless nights I would take up one book after the other and look inside them at the fond inscriptions and read bits here and there. But my books are all at my mother's house in the trunk which I did not take to Fairfields. It would be a nonchalant thing to do to read in bed in the arms of a man who is both a stranger and a lover.

Some of my books are the lives of painters and writers and explorers. Somewhere in the book about Monet there is an account of the difficulties he had trying to paint the long tresses of river weeds streaming in the clear water. The water is so clear that the long green fingers of the weeds, moving just below the surface, can be seen easily but are impossible to paint. He says that once more he has taken up something which he finds impossible to do. In the end, he says, this is what he is always trying to do. This idea of trying, almost without meaning to, to do something impossible seems to fit closely to my own life.

There is consolation in reading about the lives of composers, sculptors, painters and of people like Albert Schweitzer. In reading it is possible to take a long view over the difficulties and the suffering and the sorrow in these other lives and then it is almost possible to do the same over one's own life.

I do not have long to enjoy my smooth sheets and the sweet thoughts of the night. As soon as I am in my own bed it is time to be getting up. Helena is still asleep buried in blankets.

I look up the word mentor in my little dictionary: *Inexperienced person's adviser.* When I look up susceptible I find: *Impressionable, easily moved* and *of amorous disposition.* I hardly notice the icy water in the attic jug. I wash and dress and go down quickly to the kitchen to boil the kettle for the Georges' early morning tea. They have a little tea pot each and have their tea served in their separate rooms.

★

MENTOR AND SUSCEPTIBLE

I am an inexperienced person's adviser and Mr George is of an amorous disposition. Mentor and susceptible. I am susceptible too. Though both are words I would never have thought of using I like them, and I am always ready for Mr George to chase and catch me, silently like a thief, on the stairs, in the pantry and behind the kitchen door for his quick secret kisses.

I am in bed early, really early, without supper. Oliver, that is Mr George, is out to a dinner in a restaurant. He has been invited by his students, by some of them. Oliver, Miss George pronounces his name, Ulliva. Ulliva, she says, is very much liked by his students, especially by the young women. They are called the post grads, Miss George explains. She says at Christmas, every year, they have a party here at the house. 'They do seem to enjoy themselves,' she says, 'they stay an awful long time, practically all night.' She is not annoyed by this, I mean, she just seems perplexed.

I can't sleep. I'm jealous, I think I'm hideously jealous. In the hall when I help him into his overcoat, just before Miss George comes to see him off, I turn my face away from his quick secret kiss.

'Vera . . .' He has only time to say 'Vera' in a low voice. Later, I tell Miss George I am going to bed as soon as Helena is in bed and, no, I do not want supper, thank you.

Also Doris is back. She is in her room coughing. Doris has been away with her second cold for eight days. I have been here for

almost a month. I do not want to leave. Doris is here a day early.
Tomorrow is Sunday and Sunday is officially her day off. Miss
George says, when Doris turns up, that she should have her day
off and that since I am here, if it is all right with me, I can work
the day.

'Of course it is all right,' I tell Miss George. How can I tell Miss
George that I want to stay, that I don't want to try and find another
place. I don't want to leave. I want this room under the gable.
I have come to think of the sparrows on the sky light, every
morning, as mine. I like to see Helena lying in bed, every morning,
watching the sparrows. I suppose she is old enough now to think
of them as hers too, and to remember them and their noise for
the rest of her life. I want Helena to have some nice memories
like this.

I suppose I was hoping this time that Doris would not come back.

When I think about not wanting to leave a place it reminds me
that when I handed back the two uncompromising huckaback
towels to the woman in charge of the women's night shelter in
London, I would have stayed there if she had suggested it. It is
a frightening thought. I suppose I might stay in a place like that
simply because I have no alternative. It would, this kind of thing
would, in the end, cause Helena to be without a real home, like
being at Fairfields for ever.

Patch, on almost my first evening there when I am bathing the
children, one after the other, in the top bathroom, wants me to
have a little pause, as she calls it, to lie on her big double bed,
where she is lying with her thick glass of whisky, and listen to
Wagner with her. It is when I take the first little group of children
down to her room, where they are allowed to play on the rug with
some building blocks after their baths, that she asks me. Staff
offspring, Myles' phrase, do not share this privilege, this special
favour. She asks me then what the music is and I tell her I think

it is the Siegfried Idyll. She says the music was not intended to be for love between two women but it could be. It could be deliciously so and she says she hopes I will accept her invitation. Can I be tempted she wants to know.

I can see now things might have turned out differently at Fairfields. Patch starts to tell me then how Wagner came to write the Siegfried Idyll and I tell her yes I have read about the staircase music and that I must get back to the top bathroom to the other children waiting up there.

'Just top up my glass then, deah, will you, before you go.' Completely unruffled, Patch holds her glass out to me and, while I pour, she strokes my wrist with one fleshy finger extended.

In this whole house, next to the attic bedroom, the best room, in my opinion, is the maid's sitting room. This room is between the kitchen, with its stone flagged floor, and the dining room, a room solemn with polished furniture, a sideboard laden with polished silver and an explosive gas fire. Miss George handles the gas tap calmly with an enviable courage, Mr George explains this on my first morning in the house. The maid's sitting room is all doors; as well as the kitchen and dining-room doors there is one into the main hall of the house and there is a small door, two steps up, to the back stairs which come up directly to the attics. These narrow uncarpeted stairs can be approached half way up by a little passage from the landing of the main front staircase.

The special thing about the maid's sitting room is its tranquillity, a curious effect of the light which comes from a combination of colours, the ancient yellow-ochre of the thick tasselled table cloth, the cherry brown of the chairs, the wood worn smooth over the years, and the reflections from a small conservatory immediately outside the window. The tall window, hung with transparent lace curtains, looks directly into the deep green of the glass house.

Whenever I pass one of the open doors it seems as if the room has some magic about it, as if it is deep under water and unattainable. There is a little wireless in there too which I'm sure Doris never uses. All this makes me want this room. Of course it is Doris's and I never go in there. She does not seem to have any possessions strewn about, no books, no sewing basket and, since she has no child with her, no toys.

I had hoped and hoped that Doris would not come back. I would so much like to stay.

Doris has stopped coughing at last. In the silence I should be able to sleep. I turn over and then I turn back. I can't help wishing for Mr George, he is always so cautiously sweet.

I should not be put out that Doris is back but I am. She is back a day earlier than Miss George expected. Tomorrow is Sunday, Doris's official day off and Miss George has told her she can have it off. I wish Miss George would tell Doris she can have every day off.

'When's that flat-footed floozie going home? She's been here a week tell her she can flat foot it home – tell her she can buzz off allez voos ong. Scram!'

When I stay with Lois at her mother's house on the outskirts of the ugly side of Oxford, the motor-works side, her twin brothers, 'Bob's yer uncle and Nick's yer Aunty', soon make it quite clear that I should not be there, almost as soon as I come to understand this myself. The deep regret that I am in this house with Lois and her mother and her grandmother and her brothers and not at home with my mother comes upon me as soon as I arrive.

'Will one of youse boys fetch Gran off the lav so Vera can go?' Lois's grandmother sits in the lavatory, which is immediately outside the back door, and conducts the conversations which are going on in the kitchen. Not even the half-expected initiation to certain mysteries each night can make me really ignore the un-washed sheets of the bed I'm expected to share with Lois.

'Cornflakes and toast for breakfast.' Lois's mother puts her head round the bedroom door before leaving for work. She asks Lois why she is not wearing her pyjama jacket and Lois says because she was too hot. The sound of the front door slamming behind Lois's mother is an experience bordering on happiness. But this and the hitherto unknown pleasure of being naked in bed beside Lois does not make up, in the end, for the boredom in a house which has no books and no music. I long for bookshelves and for the act of picking up something to read. It is like being cooped up in a small desert. In the mornings, while Lois is seeing to her grandmother, I clear up the dreary pile of plates and cups in the sink and feel I am caught in a wilderness from which there is no escape. Even when we are out in the small roads through the hills which surround Oxford, leaning our bicycles into the dripping hedges while we search for primroses, trying not to mind the rain, I am able only to think that soon we shall, because of the rain, be forced to go back there to watch this rain running down the kitchen window and to wait for the return of Lois's mother and the two brothers.

'Lois is my pride and joy,' Lois's mother tells me repeatedly as if I am spoiling Lois in some way when it is Lois herself, who unknown to her mother, is the more experienced. I leave a day earlier than arranged.

It is with an unforgettable relief that I put my bicycle in the goods van at the back of the train. The trains from Oxford crawl through endless meadows as if following the flooded rivers and the curving lines of mourning willows. These trains stop for long intervals at the wayside stations. The journey is slow and long enough for me to have a return of tenderness towards Lois and I am full of regret for not being nicer to her in that awful place she calls home with those awful people who are her family.

'Which is my towel?' I call out to Lois on the first evening. I can hardly bear to think of this during the journey.

'I have never been in a house before where everyone uses the same towel in the bathroom.' I am sorry now for shouting my distaste, for displaying my dismay and anger, especially as Lois is fond in bed introducing me to previously unimagined experiments and sweetness.

When we are back at the hospital once more we shall be back on a deeper level of friendship.

Looking out across the dismal wet fields I think of a present I can buy for Lois. Something pretty, she has so few things. I look forward to the restful cleanliness of my mother's bathroom and to going over to see Gertrude and to shopping for something very nice for Lois.

All this, of course, is before I know the Metcalfs and before the great change which comes over Lois.

'What is the area of discussion? Eleanor?' Mr George pauses in the kitchen doorway.

'The weather, Ulliva, the weather that is all.' Miss George is standing by the scrubbed table where I am sitting on a chair weeping. I began to cry while I was scrubbing the table. Miss George has been asking me why I am crying. 'Can you tell me?' she asks. I am hidden from Mr George by Miss George. She waves him away. How can I tell Miss George that I can't face leaving to go as housekeeper to that squalid little house where there is the man and his three grown-up sons, that I don't like the way he looked at me, that there's nowhere in that house for me to be except in the living room with them or the scullery where there's no fire, that it's awful there? I can't stop crying and I can't speak.

'There there,' Miss George says, 'don't cry. You mustn't cry like that, my dear. There! Try not to cry so.' Miss George shyly pats my shoulder.

The worst thing about not being asleep is that I'll be a wreck in the morning. It's the morning already. The sky's getting light. I watched the sky getting light that first night I was with Mr George. That house where I went when I answered the advertisement reminds me of the time I went to stay with Lois. It's the remembering that makes all the unhappiness come back. And, I've simply got to find a place. I'll not be able to stay on here.

223

Mentor and susceptible, I watch the sky turning pale, drained of colour, in the circle of the gable window.

Helena turns over muttering in her sleep. There is someone on the stairs. Perhaps Doris has been down already. Perhaps I've overslept. It's Mr George. He comes at once to my bedside.

'Eleanor says you went to bed without supper. You didn't have supper.'

I breathe in Mr George's evening. He is still in his overcoat, his scarf loose and the coat unbuttoned. He is handsome in evening dress. I breathe him in some more, the restaurant, the food, the students, the fragrance of cigars and of exotic wines and, holding all this together, the cold air, the breath of frost, still clinging to him. He must have come upstairs to me as soon as he came home.

'Eleanor says you are very upset,' he says, 'she left a note for me.'

These Georges. They always leave notes for each other, pencil on paper on the kitchen table, sometimes with funny spelling and little sketches.

I tell him he must not come up here. Helena will wake up. 'You can't come up here,' I tell him.

'Please come down then,' he says. He says he's afraid it's all his fault. He wants me to come down to talk. 'Please do come down.'

I tell him I can't and that he has not upset me. It is something else. Just then Doris starts to cough. Cough cough, the double cough, the pause, and then the double cough cough. She is out of breath very quickly.

'Come downstairs, please, just for a minute.' Mr George touches my face and hair very gently and bends down to kiss me. Doris coughs and coughs. I have never heard her cough quite like this before. I take hold of Mr George's hand and tell him he must go down at once. 'Doris's cough,' I say, explaining.

'All right,' he says, 'later then.' He kisses me again, his breath is the breath of a stranger and, at the same time, familiar and desirable.

'Help me please,' Doris calls as the attic stairs creak under Mr George's careful tread. 'Please!' Doris calls in her coughing fit. I get up at once and go as quickly as I can into Doris's room.

✸

RITUAL

Miss George, straight after breakfast, wonders what we should all have for dinner. She stands, in an overall, at the kitchen table slicing the remains of the roast in order to determine whether there will be enough to go round. I am suddenly struck by the thought that, in all sorts of places, responsible people carve meat for other people. Sister Peters with her own sharp knife will be doing exactly what Miss George is doing, even to the time of day and the wearing of an overall. Cold sideboards, Sister Peters would make this announcement, usually on a Monday. Patch, at Fairfields, on the few occasions when there was meat – like the time Olive Morris's husband, before he was hauled away by the police, gave presents of dairy-fed poultry to the school (for which Patch received the bills) – she carved, placing judiciously a wing or a leg or a slice of breast on each plate. I never saw meat carved at the hospital or at school. It appeared on oval plates having been cut up out of sight. All the same, someone in an overall, wielding a sharp knife, would have carved it.

Before changing over to minced beef, the small ration during the war, my mother, at home, carved while my father asked a Blessing;

God bless this food that now we take
To do us good for Jesus' sake. Amen.

I suppose I am thinking about carving this morning because Miss

George is in my way in the kitchen with the meat, the oval plate and the sharpened knife. She is in my way, in her own kitchen, because I need to go through and out to the wash house with something I do not want her to see. In a sense I want to protect Miss George. You see, it's like this. Miss George's special skill is sewing and embroidery. Embroidery in particular. 'My girls...' she often starts a conversation relating something from years ago about her girls in the succession of needlework classes. 'Some of my girls' work.' She has shown me the cabinet in her room, a display of some of the daintiest and prettiest things I have ever seen. 'All hand embroidered,' she tells me when she takes out the cloths and the little garments. It is years since she retired, that is why I want to protect her.

These Georges. There is something innocent about them. I must go through the kitchen quickly with the bundle of crumpled blood-stained sheets and pillow cases. I have them rolled in a sort of ball I need to get them out to the wash house without causing Miss George distress.

'What about a green aitch,' Miss George pauses, the knife hovering, she leans towards Helena who is sitting at the scrubbed table. 'And now,' Miss George is saying, 'what colour will you choose for the e, and shall we make a little flower in the e? like this!' She puts her knife down and takes up a crayon. I hurry by them and, safely in the wash house, I turn the cold tap on hard and push the sheets down in the shallow sink to wash away the bright red blood clots and stains. The water reddens quickly. At once I realize I'll need evidence. Quickly I turn off the tap and let the blood patterned sheets float and bulge above the water. I shall have to tell the Georges. I'll tell Mr George first and then he can talk to Miss George. These Georges, they are very delicate with each other.

I know I should not but I feel relieved and even happy when I am back in the kitchen watching Miss George as she teaches Helena to write her own name.

'Vera,' Miss George says, pointing at the oval plate with the tip of her sharp knife, 'will this be enough d'you think? With some beetroot and potatoes?'

'Oh yes, Miss George,' I say, 'more than enough.'

Miss George is taking Helena with her this morning when she goes to church. Helena, pleased and happy in new long socks and with her little coat brushed and pressed, is going to Sunday School.

'Vera,' Miss George says, 'we have left Mr George resting after his night of pleasure for long enough, please take him some tea at eleven or thereabouts.'

'Yes, Miss George,' I say.

'And Vera,' Miss George says, 'I noticed, yesterday, some withered flowers in the wash house. Perhaps you should throw them away?'

'Yes of course Miss George.' The dead flowers are in a bucket out there, the white chrysanthemums and the bronze, and the expensive, out-of-season roses and carnations next to the sink now full of blood-stained sheets. 'Oh yes Miss George,' I say, 'I'll see to the flowers.'

If Miss George, in the mornings in her overall reminds me of Sister Peters, in the afternoons, at about half-past three, she reminds me of my mother. This is because most afternoons Miss George, tying a small apron round her waist, comes into the kitchen for the little ceremony of cutting the bread and butter for the four o'clock afternoon tea. Most days Mr George is home, after his short walk from the university, for afternoon tea which they have together in his study. My mother in her Aryan period, just before the war, a time of Heidi hairstyles, beaded dresses and twice weekly visits to the new Odeon cinema always, in a small apron, cut bread and butter for afternoon tea. The ladies then, visiting each other, kept each other company during this ritual.

How can I tell Miss George just before she leaves with Helena for the walk to church that I am afraid I might be pregnant and that Doris is asleep upstairs after the most terrifying haemorrhage I have ever seen.

As I take the stairs, three at a time, balancing the round tray with Mr George's tea pot, cup and saucer and milk jug nicely set on a clean table napkin, it seems to me that it's no wonder when the ladies meet in the afternoon, round the special little table cloths, that they talk endlessly about servants and their problems.

✭

THE LOG LIFT

The proximity of a sympathetic nurse is often the only treatment Sister Bean said once. The thing I remember most about haemoptysis, this frightening rush of blood, is Sister Bean kneeling, during the night by the patient's bed and the way in which she drew the man's head on to her arm, into the crook of her elbow really. She was so close to him, she leaned right over him, her arm under his head, close, not frightened of tuberculosis at all. And, all the time, she kept telling him that everything would be all right. She did this while I was clearing away the blood, wiping away the clots and slipping off the sheet and the pillow cases to put on fresh ones. She held him close and prayed, and afterwards she repeated the prayer saying that I should remember it in case I ever needed to say it.

Doris has a jug and basin like the one in my room. I soak her towel in the icy water and wash away the blood as quickly as it comes. She can't speak except with her imploring frightened eyes. I nod my head to her and tell her that it's nearly finished and that she'll be better directly. I pretend to feel her pulse and count it and I tell her the pulse is strong. When Helena appears, half asleep, in the doorway I tell her sharply to get back in bed and play with her doll. 'I'm coming in a minute,' I tell her.

'Everything's going to be all right,' I tell Doris.

'Don't tell *them*, will you,' Doris says as soon as she can speak.

'No, of course not,' I say. As quickly as I can I pull her night-gown off and I pull her sheets and pillow cases away rolling them into a sort of horrible bundle. The warmth of the clots through the rolled-up sheet makes me feel as if I've pulled part of her body away. I am shaking dreadfully. I fetch some clean water from my room and my spare nightgown. Doris lets me dress her in the gown and lies back exhausted. I tell her I'll get her some tea but she begs me to stay by her.

'Don't go down just yet,' she says. She says she'll be better in a few minutes and I say yes she will be better.

'Tell me about your children.' I sit on the edge of her bed. 'Tell me about your children,' I say. She is cold, she says, so I wrap her round with a blanket from my bed.

'Don't tell *them* about it, will you,' she says once more. She starts to tell me something about one of her children but she is unable to keep awake. I watch her fall asleep. She sleeps like a child, with her arms up on the pillow on either side of her head.

'Keep my place for me,' Doris looks at me. There is no reproach in her look. 'You will keep my place for me, won't you,' she says. 'I'll lose my place, you see,' she tries to explain to the two ambulance men. They carry her rolled in a blanket in what they call the log lift, the attic stairs being too sharply angled for their stretcher.

'I'll keep your place,' I promise Doris. I tell her that she'll be better soon, that going to hospital is the best thing.

'I'm afraid,' Doris looks back at me.

'Don't be frightened,' I say, 'everything's going to be all right.' I follow the log lift down the attic stairs, along the passage and down the main staircase to the front hall. I have pushed Doris's few possessions into her shabby case. It is dismal, the case, and very light.

I can't stop crying.

'It's because of her small luggage,' I cry in the hall after the ambulance has gone. Mr George, still in his dressing gown, puts his arm around me and guides me gently to the stairs. We go up together.

✻

THIRTY SHILLINGS AND KEEP

In the mornings after I have been sick I cry. I feel terrible and I keep hearing my mother's voice complaining, on and on, somewhere inside my head.

'There must be something not quite nice about him, Vera. If a man, however handsome and refined he might be, hasn't married by the time he's sixty, Vera, there must be something about him that's not nice...' I create replies telling my mother that Mr George isn't sixty. 'He's only fifty-eight,' I tell her. And, without wanting to, I make up an answer for her; 'Near enough, Vera, as makes no difference,' in the kind of phrases she would never use.

In the mornings, straight after being sick, I lie down for a little while, the house being restfully empty. Mr George always leaves early and Miss George goes for a walk. She has started taking Helena out for this walk. Often I lie down on Mr George's bed, before I make it, and I think of him, about how good looking he is, and kind, and how I like looking at him when he's asleep. When I tell him this, one time, he says he isn't asleep he's waiting for me to wake up because he likes watching me wake up. One morning he leaves a book on his bed for me, not a new book, but it is for me. Inside he has written my name and a quotation;

You have first taught me,
You have opened my eyes
To the unending value of life

The book is a collection of poems. He has pencilled little initials, mine, by certain poems. Some lines in another poem are underlined;

...when thy mind
shall be a mansion for all lovely forms
Thy memory be as a dwelling-place
For all sweet sounds and harmonies;

In his small neat handwriting Mr George has written *Eleanor* by this part of the poem, in ink, now faded, and I have to understand, when I read more of the poem, how much they have always cared for each other.

'He's fifteen years younger than his sister,' my mother chips in, 'fifteen years, and his mother dying when he was a baby! She, the sister, she will have been a mother to him. Brought him up like a mother, I would say. And he probably worships the ground she walks on.'

'Yes, that's right,' I tell my mother. My voice in the empty house startles me.

'Mothers often dislike their son's women friends.' It is as if I am, through my mother's voice, heard only somewhere inside my head, voicing my own uneasiness. And then I tell myself I am not uneasy. I have only to think of the way Mr George holds me and kisses me to know that he loves me.

'And another thing,' my mother goes on and on, 'how can a man, an educated man, ask a woman to marry him without any knowledge of her background? I've always said, Vera, academic men are never *practical*. I mean, has it occurred to this man yet that he might be the father of a child?' My creations in speech, haunting me throughout the morning's work of cleaning and polishing, surpass all the previous ones.

Something greatly in my favour, and I do need something to be in my favour, is the way in which Miss George and Helena have taken to each other. Helena follows Miss George everywhere in the house. Miss George is making a second little dress for Helena, this time of Viyella, pale blue with pink smocking. She is teaching Helena the piano, the alphabet and something they call number.

Miss George is a very sympathetic sort of person.

231

'Whyever didn't you come straight to me and tell me before?' she says on the day when Doris has to be taken quickly to the hospital. Mr George, on that day, tells Miss George what has happened as soon as she comes in from church, before she has even had time to take off her hat and coat. Miss George says then that Helena had told her, on the walk to church, that her mother was washing Doris, in the night, with a wet towel, and that Doris was crying. Her eyes are dark with pity and she goes, in the afternoon, to visit Doris.

I want Mr George to tell Miss George how things are between us. Sometimes I allow myself a little dream of Miss George sitting in the window of the front room here, overlooking the street, nursing my baby. I imagine her rocking gently to and fro and singing in that way people do sing over a new baby. For some reason I am certain my baby will be a girl. I shall call her Rachel. It would be better if Mr George tells Miss George. He is clever and gentle and furthermore Mr George and Miss George know each other so well.

'Vera,' Miss George says to me in the evening when she is back from the hospital and I help her off with her coat. 'Vera, I take it you would like to come in to the position, that you would like to work here. Will thirty shillings and keep for you and Helena be all right?'

'Oh yes,' I say, 'yes, thank you, Miss George, that will be quite all right.'

I want to tell Mr George that I think Miss George knows. Every day I hope that he will speak to her. I want to tell him that I think Miss George knows everything, that she has known everything since the first time when I listened to the Beethoven quartet with him in his study. I think she knows on that first morning, after our first night, when I take her tea in to her.

That morning, I want to tell him, she was lying back on her pillows and, though she seemed to be asleep, there were tears all along her eye-lashes. When I think of these tears they were the largest, most glistening tear drops, the most tremulous of all tears – not shed but trembling as if about to be. I want to tell him that I think she was crying because of us. She did not open her eyes when I said, 'Your tea, Miss George.' She simply thanked me without looking at me. She must know already, I want to tell Mr George, and so it would be better to tell her straight away.

On the other hand, if Mr George knows about Miss George's tears, that morning, it might be impossible for him to speak now.

'I am worried about Miss George,' I say that first morning when Mr George gives me a fond little kiss in the hall early before he leaves for his lecture. 'What about Miss George?' I ask him then. He kisses me again quickly and tells me he is sure Eleanor will approve, I am to leave it to him he says. He tells me he is very happy and he says a soft little 'thank you' close to my ear and that he is looking forward to coming home.

It is during that day that the flowers arrive for me and I hide them in the wash house. Later on, when everyone is in bed, Mr George tells me of the great pleasure he had in sending the flowers.

If I do belong to Mr George, as he says I do, how will it be about the attic bedroom, the cherry-wood furniture and the floor boards? And how will I be able to go on sitting in the deep watery green of the maid's sitting room? That wished-for shaded green of the conservatory mixed with the ancient yellow-ochre of the table cloth, will that have to belong to someone else? Where will I be, if I do belong to Mr George as he says I do, where will I be in this house? At present I am all over the house, everywhere, both openly and in secret.

The days go by one after another. Some days I long to go out to meet Mr George when I know he will be walking home from the university. I long to walk in the wind and the rain with him, holding hands, and showing the world that we belong to each other. Until he tells Miss George, we are not able to do this. In my thoughts I walk with him every day. After all thoughts are safe, neighbours and colleagues cannot see into them. All the same, I really do want to be seen with him by everyone. I want to be seen going through a door with Mr George, one arm gently at my back, holding the door open for me.

Perhaps tomorrow Mr George will speak to Miss George.

'The area of discussion, Eleanor.' I can imagine Mr George leaning forward to open the dining-room door and holding it open to allow his sister to go through first, one hand protectingly at her back. 'The area of discussion today, Eleanor, my dear, is in a field which is new to us, something which we have not discussed before but which we must talk about now.' I imagine the door being closed and then only the subdued murmur of the two voices in harmony without any words which might be usefully overheard.

I want Mr George to tell Miss George. It is only such a small thing we have to tell. Perhaps it is the small things which are the hardest to tell. They are the things which make all the difference. It is because it will be so unexpected for her. What we need to tell her will be so unexpected.

The coming of a baby, the birth of a baby is inevitable. In this house we are all pointing, because of my new baby who cannot be put off, inevitably in a certain direction.

Meanwhile my trunk has come, the trunk I had at school, at the hospital, at Clifton Way, at the Hilda Street Wentworth, but not at Fairfields and not here till now. My mother has sent it by rail and the carrier, an obliging man, brought it up to the attic.

When I open it books and shoes and clothes spill out. Some of my pressed wildflowers have come unstuck and I put them back between the pages remembering the sweet, wet grass near the school where we searched for flowers. I seem to see clearly shining long fingers pulling stalks and holding bunches. Saxafrage, campion, vetch, ragged robin, star of Bethlehem, wild strawberry and sorrel. Quickly I tidy the flowers – violet, buttercup, King cup, cowslip, coltsfoot, wood anemone, shepherd's purse, lady's slipper, jack in the pulpit and bryony...

I am unpacking my life, for the time being, into this top room, at the top of this house.

CABIN FEVER

*All this goes on inside me, in the vast cloisters of
my memory. In it are the sky, the earth, and the sea,
ready at my summons, together with everything I have
ever perceived in them by my senses...In it I meet
myself as well I remember myself...*

Saint Augustine

THE STOREHOUSE
AND THE REMEDY

My father had a deeply felt belief that the life he was living was
simply a prologue to some other kind of life or existence. This
did not mean that he thought people returned to earth as rich
when they had been poor, or as animals, dogs or cats, or as plants
or trees. He said that what had to be endured in life, as we know
it, was not the only intention. I suppose he saw the changing of
the seasons and the inevitability of birth and death as a resur-
rection and a replenishing. That the four seasons following one
after the other, the waxing and waning of the moon, the heat of
the sun, the falling of rain, the ebb and flow of the tides were
all part of a pattern was an indication to him of a power greater
than any human power. This belief, which he had, put a meaning
on what he called the earthly life. It was not an explanation he

said. This storehouse of experience was a mystery. In spite of not knowing, human individuals went along living their lives baffled when they questioned. But mostly, he said, people questioned only on a superficial level if they questioned at all.

During the sleepless night when I read through my papers and lectures they do not, in the confined overheated space of the hotel room, have any meaning. I read aloud putting in pause marks and asides which could spring from the text. But this act of the will, which is a necessary part of preparation, does not enable me to add anything useful or fresh.

I am still here on the twenty-fourth floor. When I sit in front of my mirror I can see, in the mirror, someone on the twenty-fourth floor across the street. He is sitting upright at a table and is in his shirt sleeves. I have no idea who he is.

I am frightened. I have lost count of the days.

For a long time I keep my light on. Without the light the hot airless room becomes a tunnel lined with earth. It is treacherous with a system of exposed hot-water pipes. The room is a cave where a dog might turn round and round ensuring his safety before lying down to sleep. I have been round this room over and over again. There is no escape, no bolt hole from the lair. The only way out is into the long dimly lit passage which seems to lead nowhere. There is too the feeling that I am alone here on the twenty-fourth floor. Insanely high, swaying...

The abstracts, when I study them, are elaborate and pretentious. And the names in the conference programme, though they are well known to me, probably belong to strangers.

The cure for cabin fever is to recognize the symptoms. In order to overcome the inability to cross the thin ice of the conference rooms it is necessary to collect all the images and the experiences as if they were treasures in a small storehouse. The cabin fever is the same as the pause with which I am familiar. It is the same thing, this cabin fever, as sitting at a bus stop, back home – when I am not actually waiting for a bus, watching the Easter moon climb the dark blue evening. It is the same thing as watching a woman in a neighbouring garden calmly hanging wet clothes on a line during a time of complete self-absorbing drama. It can be regarded too as being the same thing as travelling by an earlier train, earlier than usual (also back home) on purpose to see again the woman who reminds me of staff nurse Ramsden. This cabin fever is like the intention to speak, it is the long drawn-out pause of intention.

I have never spoken to the woman on the train. It seems to be enough that I promise this for some future time. It is enough, for the present, to create Ramsden in my own image. It's like this, certain phrases of music recapture Ramsden clearly. It is as if we are walking together once more in the rain as it drips through the branches of the beech trees in autumn and I am listening to her telling me something...

I never walked anywhere with Ramsden except in my imagination. And the music now, which recalls her, is not the music we listened to together. The Schubert piano and cello is not the piano and cello music of those other times. Perhaps the ability of the cello to suggest the tender reasoning I heard in her voice is a part of the mysterious process of acknowledging something which is to be slowly unlocked at some time later on.

I am certain that a confrontation of recognition, a reunion, with exclamations and animated conversation, on a train would be like the hoped for ending to a particular kind of novel. I mean, how can anyone's life, in reality, at the present time, contain the fulfilment of expectation and the happy ending of a romantic fiction.

Betsy Drinkwater's yearly letter with its repetitions of household repairs and endless responsibilities towards onion beds and herbaceous borders has something inevitable about it like the changing of the seasons but without the sensation of a change in the air and without the different gifts which each season, in turn, promises. I am not able to see, in my mind, the writer of these letters, to match her life with the lives of the people I see daily in my consulting rooms, lives which do not, for various reasons, go beyond a daily experience of an incredible loneliness. I do not try to recognize her as she must be now. Betsy Drinkwater remains youthful for ever, the schoolgirl in an innocent uniform hurrying across the fields to school. When I am holding one of her letters in my hand it is as if I could never have had any idea of what was lying in wait for me.

I do not have letters to look forward to now. At one time letters brought that excitement which accompanies the deepening of friendship, the discovery of the self in relation to someone else. It seems strange that there was ever a time when I waited eagerly for letters. At present letters received and sent are mostly brief communications and reports about the human condition, about diets and about medication.

Occasionally a warm fragrance in the days approaching summer prompts me to suggest to someone, who is coming to keep an appointment, that they take the path through the pines from the station. It is both a short cut and a pleasant little walk. A remedy.